THEY WERE PREPARED FOR HAND-TO-HAND COMBAT

The man nearest Remo took up a familiar Sinanju attack stance. One balled hand floated like a feathery mallet before his blank white face.

For a moment, Remo was distracted by the poetry of movement that was Sinanju. It had been so long since he'd seen anyone other than Chiun or himself ply the art.

Remo ducked away from the sweeping hand. He felt the push of displaced air as the arm whipped above his chest. He popped back upright once the danger had passed.

The ghost-soldier's momentum could not be stopped. As he slipped on the snow, Remo could hear the sound of muscles and tendons snapping as the force of his unspent blow was used in a way the man had not intended.

The pain was short-lived.

A pirouette that ended in a crunching loafer heel to the back of the man's head sent the ghost-soldier to sparkling eternity.

Created by Murphy & Sapir

THE Destroyer™

BY EMINENT DOMAIN

A GOLD EAGLE BOOK FROM

WORLDWIDE.

TORONTO • NEW YORK • LONDON
AMSTERDAM • PARIS • SYDNEY • HAMBURG
STOCKHOLM • ATHENS • TOKYO • MILAN
MADRID • WARSAW • BUDAPEST • AUCKLAND

First edition July 2001

ISBN 0-373-63239-8

Special thanks and acknowledgment to James Mullaney
for his contribution to this work.

BY EMINENT DOMAIN

Printed in U.S.A.

For Pete and Eileen Dedeian, Mary Hardy and Ann McInerney.

Also, for Heather Locken,
who puts up with way more than she should,
up to and including bad or nonexistent excuses for tardiness.

And for the Glorious House of Sinanju,
e-mail: housinan@aol.com

Sometimes, if he scrunched up his eyes tight enough and concentrated really, really hard, he could almost taste the warm apple pie. Other times it was roast pork, hot from the oven and spitting delicious, mouth-watering fat. This day, the last day of the rest of Brian Turski's young life, it was freshly baked chocolate-chip cookies.

In his mind's eye, they were baked to perfection. Not cooked so much that they were brittle. Just soft enough that when they were broken in two, the chocolate formed drooping, gooey threads between the two halves.

He took a deep breath, savoring the remembered aroma.

The smell that flooded his nostrils was that of diesel exhaust and commingled human body odors. And the cold.

Here, cold was a living thing—assaulting all the senses at once. You could see it, taste it, smell it. On a still night, when the snow fell, you could hear it. Each flake hit like frozen thunder. Mostly, though, you could feel it. Seeping through boots and gloves. Leeching deep into bone.

It was the cold Brian had to deal with every day. His wife's cooking—including her trademark chocolate-chip cookies—was a million miles away.

Brian opened his eyes. He was in the back of a truck. Fifteen other men were arranged on two benches around him. They were bouncing along a rutted rural road.

"Your wife's cooking again, huh?" grunted the man beside him. Like Brian, he was tall and thin, his strong arms hidden beneath his heavy parka.

Brian nodded glumly.

"Why do you torture yourself?" his seatmate asked.

More than once, each one of the men in that truck had asked himself the same question. The answer they invariably gave was that it put food on the table and a roof over the heads of their families. For eight months each year, they trudged out into rural Alaska during the long, dark months of winter for the same reason the surgeon went to the hospital or the baker went to the bakery. It was their job.

"If you live in Alaska more than two years, your feet will be frozen in it." So went the old saying. For Brian Turski, frozen feet were just part of a bitter reality.

Insulated boots stomped the floor for warmth as the big truck drove along the rough access road. Another dry winter had yielded little snow in this part of the Last Frontier. Patches of white dotted the land. When the tired old truck finally rolled to a squeaking stop, brittle scrub grass crunched beneath the tire treads.

Cold steel doors popped open on a featureless plain. A stiff breeze—like icy fingers—curled inside the vehicle. As he stood, Brian pulled his hood over his long, matted hair, knotting it beneath his whiskers with freezing fingers.

There was only one native Alaskan in the group. He had the broad, flat face of an Aleut, with eyes that were weather-battered slits cut deep in dark flesh.

The Aleut was first out of the back. Brian followed, with the others filing rapidly out behind.

The wan light of perpetual dusk painted the landscape in an otherworldly gray. The men ignored the sallow sky.

On the sleeves of their matching parkas, each man wore the APSC insignia of the Alyeska Pipeline Service Company. The same logo adorned both sides of their truck.

Daylight was already at a premium. Their foreman—a burly, urgent man whose once delicate skin had been ravaged by years of exposure to the hostile climate—rounded to the back of the truck from the cab.

"Chopper spotted the break over that rise," Joe Abady said, pointing with his chin as he tugged on his Thinsulate gloves. "We've got maybe a couple of hours if the generators hold. You all know what to do. Let's do it fast."

A second truck had trailed the first. The men hurried over to it. Tools and ladders were hauled out onto frozen ground. Plastic canisters were dropped beside them. The sharp smell of gasoline sliced the cold air.

Two men struggled to haul the generators from far back in the truck.

"Can't we drive around?" one panted as they lowered the second generator to the road.

"Access is too far down," the foreman explained gruffly. "We're doing this the old-fashioned way."

Brian Turski and three of the others hefted up the bulky portable generators. The rest of the men gathered the tools and the gas. They left the welding tanks to Joe Abady.

The foreman hooked a pair of leather straps around his shoulders and shrugged the big tanks onto his broad back.

With Abady in the lead, the group of twenty men struck off across the tundra.

Twenty yards off the path, the plain turned to hill. Brian Turski's breath was labored as he struggled under the weight of the generator. The hill had seemed gradual from the road but quickly grew steeper with each labored step.

"I'm not hauling this back," Brian panted.

"You wanna carry these?" Abady asked. The strain of the welding tanks stretched his leathery face.

"What I want is homemade apple pie," Brian said. His heart was straining in his chest. His lungs felt as if they'd been rubbed raw with sandpaper. "Or chocolate-chip cookies."

The words burned his hoarse throat.

Sweating and cursing, the men crested the hill. As soon as they reached the summit, they saw the problem.

The floor of the long, narrow valley below was stained black. Towering above the ground was a massive pipe that stretched in either direction. And in the side of that pipe, an angry hole was like the open mouth of Hell itself.

Moans rose all around.

"Swell," one man complained at the sight of the spilled crude oil. "We're gonna need a vacuum truck up here."

"Already on its way down from Wiseman," Abady said, not breaking stride. "Let's move it, ladies."

Hitching up his tanks, the foreman began to pick his careful way down the far side of the hill to the wounded section of the massive Trans-Alaska Pipeline.

TEN MINUTES LATER, crude oil swamped Brian Turski's boots as he eyed the gash in the pipe.

"That's not from stress," he said to Joe Abady.

"They only saw the spill from the air," the foreman replied with a frown. "Not this."

"Looks like someone took an ax to it," Brian said.

Still frowning, Abady glanced down the broad ravine. Some of the men followed his line of sight.

The pipeline slithered off like a great fat snake in either direction. To the north it was a straight run into the nothingness of the Alaskan wilderness. To the south it twisted around a bend in the ravine and was gone.

The forty-eight-inch pipe was built on raised pipeline support members that looked like field posts for

Titans. Here and there below the pipeline were dark, uncertain patches and bits of brittle scrub. A few broad streaks of windswept snow hugged the ravine walls on either side.

"Just a rupture," Abady announced gruffly. "Probably froze, then popped. No one'd be stupid enough to come out here except us. Let's get to work."

With the drop in pressure that signified a rupture, the line had been shut down. Twelve pumping stations and two million gallons of crude oil sat idle until repairs could be made.

Stepping carefully through the thick pool of oil, Brian headed for one of the support members. As he walked he cast a casual glance down the ravine. And froze.

Something had moved.

It was subtle, ghostly, caught more with his peripheral vision than anything else. But though his eyes had almost ignored it, his brain wouldn't let them.

He squinted into the distance.

Nothing. No movement, no anything. Just the land and the sky and the pipeline that ran between them.

For Brian Turski, an eerie silence descended on the ravine. The grunts of the men behind him faded to silence.

After a moment he grew less certain. He was about to chalk it all up to his imagination when the air seemed to coalesce. A shape suddenly appeared from the drab landscape where a moment before there had been nothing.

Brian didn't have time to give voice to his shock.

The instant the figure appeared, there came a flash of brilliant orange.

The bullet struck Brian Turski in the right side of the chest, spinning him. His feet went out from underneath him, and he went sprawling into the pool of black oil. Crude flooded into his gaping mouth.

Another shot, followed by another.

Brian pulled his face up, spitting thick oil. The pain in his chest was blinding.

Joe Abady was sliding to a stop next to him, a nickel-size hole in his forehead.

Men screamed and ran. Another flopped on his side in the oil pool, blood streaming from his open mouth.

More gunshots crackled off across the desolate Alaskan wilderness. And all around, bodies fell.

A few men tried to clamber back up the hill. Bullets found backs. The pipeline workers slipped and rolled back down to the valley floor.

Back near the pipe, panicked and bleeding, Brian struggled to get up. His arms were too weak, and he dropped back to the ground.

The oil was thick on his clothes, filling his mouth and nose. Spitting, he flopped over onto his back. Using the heels of his boots and pressing one hand to his bleeding chest, he slid back against a metal support member.

The gunfire had stopped.

The dead lay all around him. Steam rose from gaping wounds and slack mouths.

To Brian Turski, they were already a distant thing. As if he were viewing the landscape through a fuzzy telescope. His legs were growing numb. Already there was no feeling in his right arm. He let it flop to the ground.

Something rose before him.

It was as if the tundra had come to life. The figure was streaked with whites and browns.

Others appeared behind it. Phantoms of earth and snow.

No. Not ghosts.

Crude oil caked one eye. Squinting with the good one, Brian Turski peered at the figure.

His dying lips formed a surprised O.

It was just a man. The blurry figure carried a smoking automatic rifle. The other white-and-brown shapes became men, too. They fanned out around the area, kicking over bodies with the toes of their boots.

Sitting in the shadow of their leader, Brian took his last deep breath.

This time, he didn't smell the cold or the crude or the hint of blood carried on the frigid air. He smelled chocolate-chip cookies. Hot out of the oven. With the gooey brown chips that burned his numb fingertips.

A growl.

The man above Brian was speaking. The pipeline worker didn't understand the language.

Tasting chocolate, Brian looked up.

An angry rifle barrel stared down at him.

It didn't matter. Death could come and claim him if it wanted. Brian had finally gotten his wish. His belly warm and full, he gently closed his eyes.

He was already dead before the bullet popped his head open like a paint-filled water balloon.

As his body slumped into the pool of black slush, the shadows slipped away. One after another the stealthy figures disappeared, swallowed up by the Alaskan wasteland until all that was left behind were the bodies of the dead and the endless, desolate wind.

Although Brian Turski hadn't understood the words that were the last to reach his living ears, the language was not new to the Last Frontier. If he had understood them, they would only have confused him in his final moments of life.

For the actual words spoken by Brian Turski's killer—loosely translated—were a notice of eviction.

2

His name was Remo and he stared out at the world of the living through a dead man's eyes.

There was a time when Remo would have fought the notion that he was dead. For a long time he had insisted that his dying was nothing more than a ruse. After all, he breathed and walked and ate and loved just like the next nondead man.

But with the passage of time came a realization— like a hole finally worn through rock by a single, remorseless water drip. In spite of his early protestations, Remo one day realized that he was not like the next man after all.

Yes, he breathed. But it was not a process that involved gasping lungs straining to supply oxygen to a sluggish bloodstream. Remo breathed with his entire body. Every cell alive, alert and aware.

He walked, but it was without the effort of normal men. Remo's gait was a comfortable glide that flowed naturally. Entirely unlike the rest of the human race, which seemed always to move as if it were wading through wet concrete.

His diet was no longer loaded with fats and sugars—slow poisons all. The food he ate was specific and minimal. Just enough to fuel the perfect machine that was a body in tune with the forces of the universe.

The last thing—love—was something that definitely no longer had a home in the soul of Remo Williams as it did for other men. Not that he was incapable of the emotion. Far from it. It was just that his profession didn't exactly lend itself to the notion that he might one day link arms with the woman of his dreams and go tripping tra-la through a field of summer daisies.

Remo was an assassin. Trained by the Reigning Master of the House of Sinanju—the most deadly line of assassins ever to ply the trade. Feats seemingly superhuman were just a day at the office for the men from Sinanju.

In days gone by Masters of Sinanju dodged hurled spears and rocks. These days it was bullets. All the same.

Sheer walls were just things to climb. Fortresses were built from match sticks. Armies, merely toy soldiers.

The skills displayed by Sinanju Masters involved muscle and brain and bone. Breathing, conscious and unconscious thought.

Remo had long ago stopped trying to figure out exactly what made him different from other men. *Better* would have been the word his teacher used. Remo didn't think he was better. Just different. Of the world, yet apart from it.

And so Remo had one day realized that the man he had been was, in fact, dead after all.

Even though acceptance for him had been a long time coming, it had been far easier for the rest of the world to come to terms with the death of Remo Williams. Part of the reason for that was the grave on which he now sat.

The headstone was a simple no-frills number. Just a granite slab with a plain carved cross and his own name etched into the smooth, cold surface. The edges of the letters had begun to wear with age.

Remo had rarely found the need to visit what—to the world—was the final resting place of Remo Williams. There were only two other instances where he had stood above this grave and contemplated its significance.

Six feet below the spot where Remo now sat was a body. Little more than a few scattered teeth and bones by this point in time. Some faceless indigent who thirty years ago had unknowingly become Remo's stand-in so that Remo might be free to pursue his new calling.

America had been at a crossroads. Social and political upheaval were threatening to tear the nation apart. Down one path led anarchy. Down the other, a police state. In order that the republic could survive, a third option had to be tried, a new and treacherous trail blazed.

A new agency was created by a young President who would himself become an eventual victim of the incipient anarchy that plagued his nation. Called CURE, the organization would work outside the strait-jacket that was the United States Constitution in order to preserve the very document it subverted.

The existence of CURE was known to only four men at any given time. Remo was one of those four. And in order that the secret be preserved, all traces of his former existence had been eliminated, including his life itself.

Framed for a murder he did not commit, honest beat cop Remo Williams had been sentenced to die in an electric chair that didn't work. Only when he awoke in Folcroft Sanitarium in Rye, New York—the secret home to CURE—had Remo learned the truth of what his lifework would be.

After a rocky start, he had accepted his destiny fairly easily, all things considered. He had even agreed with the bulk of the rules governing his behavior as set forth by Upstairs. At least in principle.

It made sense that he should never again try to visit the nuns from St. Theresa's Orphanage, where he had been raised. Ditto his fellow cops from the old precinct. But one of the things he was absolutely never supposed to do was come to Newark's Wildwood Cemetery and sit on the frozen ground and stare at his own headstone.

Two out of three wasn't bad.

In his defense he had a lot on his mind these days. And although most people wouldn't have the opportunity to know it, sometimes your own grave was the best spot to sit and sort through life's real important stuff.

It was the third week of February, and already most

of the winter snow had been chased away. In another month it would be gone completely, wiped from the landscape by warming sun and drenching rain. The exposed ground was brown and cracked. Leaves from autumns past rotted to compost at the sturdy concrete base of the nearby wrought-iron fence.

The surface leaves were frozen stiff. Remo could smell beyond them, to the rich loam being born beneath. Deeper still, he could feel the worms twist in their winter slumber. High above the ground the soft scent of pines carried to his nostrils. His sensitive ears registered the flicking movements of the farthermost wind-tossed needles.

So was it to be trained in Sinanju. Even in the dead heart of winter, the world was still a vibrant living thing.

Although Remo was aware of all that was going on around him, he did not allow it to distract him from his thoughts.

He was trying to sort through something. Just what exactly, he had no idea. He thought it might have something to do with his last assignment.

A few days ago, Remo had been sent to California to pull the plug on an old Soviet superweapon that had somehow fallen into the hands of a group of radical peaceniks. That the first thing they had done upon acquiring such a device was blow the hell out of everything they aimed it at was an irony completely lost on these aging pacifists.

While on this assignment Remo had been stunned

to encounter an old flame, a beautiful Russian agent who had also been sent to defuse the situation.

Bumping into Anna Chutesov after more than ten years would not have been so shocking had Remo not thought her dead. She wasn't. And as was the case with most things in Remo's life these days, complications had ensued.

Sitting alone in Wildwood Cemetery, pale white moonlight shining down across his shoulders, the cold wind snaking around his lean frame like the tendrils of some invisible beast, Remo pictured Anna Chutesov.

The real Anna had looked pretty much the same as he remembered her, yet it was her younger face he now summoned.

She came to him in his mind's eye. Icy blue eyes, blond hair, strong cheekbones. An ageless beauty.

There was a time when he thought he loved her. Now she was just another face.

Nope. The something he was after didn't have anything to do with the Russian agent.

He placed her mental image carefully aside.

It was a frustrating process. There was something he felt he should know, something he should *do*. Yet the more he tried the more certain he was that he was just forcing it further and further away. But it was *important*.

The feeling that there was something big looming on the horizon had first come to him in California. It was a moment come and gone. Now it was like trying to remember a dream.

After leaving California two days ago, there had been a brief side trip to Russia in order to take care of some unfinished business. He had only returned to U.S. soil late the previous afternoon.

Once he'd landed in New York, Remo had sent his teacher back to Folcroft while he came out to the cemetery alone. To think.

Afternoon had long since bled into the postmidnight hours, yet Remo felt no closer to an answer.

Maybe it was nothing. His life hadn't exactly been a piece of cake lately. And according to a source he didn't really care to think about at the moment, it was only going to get worse. Maybe that's all this was. An unconscious concern for what might be.

After a few more minutes of trying to chase an inchoate thought around his brain, he finally threw up his hands.

"Ah, hell," Remo grumbled.

With a feeling of deep frustration he unscissored his legs and rose to his feet.

Even though he had sat in the same position for more than ten hours, there was no crack of bone or strain of tired muscle. With just a simple fluid motion he was up.

Dark eyes read the name etched on his headstone one last time before he turned abruptly away.

He had taken not a single step before he heard a sound.

The creaking of a gate. Hurried footfalls scuffed a gravel path. Hushed, nervous voices carried to his ears.

Remo's internal clock told him that it was 2:37 in the morning. Not a likely time for anyone to be paying a visit to the grave of a departed loved one.

Curiosity piqued, he took to the path. On silent feet he followed the sounds of the voices.

The path led through a knot of sighing pines and up a short incline. By the time Remo came to the top of the hill, a fresh sound had reached his ears. It was a grinding of stone on stone followed by a heavy muted thud.

Dodging moonlight, Remo came up beside a granite angel. The statue's wings were folded back, and the fingertips of its delicate hands brushed together in eternal prayer.

Ahead, more headstones dotted the landscape. Remo saw three figures slipping between the distant headstones.

Although it was dark, Remo's eyes took in enough ambient light to make it seem as bright as midday.

The three intruders were older boys. Probably no further along than sophomores in high school.

Breaking away from his companions, one of the boys crouched and vanished from sight. Remo heard a sharp rattling noise, followed by a faint hissing.

Remo recognized the sounds.

As he watched, the other two walked up to a big grave marker. Giggling nervously, they planted their shoulders against its rough side. Grunting at the effort, they shoved the stone off its base. It thumped heavily back to the cold ground. Panting happily, they moved on to the next grave.

The dark lines of Remo's angular face grew hard. Leaving his stone angel to her private supplications, he darted across the frozen ground.

Delicate crusts of ice had formed on the surface of the few patches of snow that yet clung to the ground. Where Remo came in contact with them, the soles of his loafers didn't even crack the crystalline veneer.

The boys failed to notice his approach. He halted a few yards from the trio of vandals, a shadow among shadows.

As he'd suspected, the crouching boy held a can of spray paint in his hand. He was in the process of painting a dripping swastika on the front of a big stone marker.

While the first boy worked, the other two laughed anxiously as they put their backs against another headstone.

Unseen by the trio of youths, Remo's face grew cold.

Increasingly this kind of desecration was becoming common. In years gone by it would have been big news if a cemetery was vandalized. Certainly statewide. Maybe even nationally. Now it barely rated a blurb on the local news.

Remo decided that it was high time someone spoke up for all the voiceless dead out there.

His expression more fixed than any name carved in granite, Remo slipped through the shadows toward the boys.

"Hurry up," one of the youths urged, laughing.

He already had his shoulder braced against the next

stone in line. His companion quickly joined him. As before, the two boys pushed in unison.

Although they put all their weight against it, this time something was different. This time when they shoved, the headstone seemed to shove back.

With a pair of startled grunts, the two boys toppled over onto their backs. The wind rushed from their lungs.

"What're you doing?" the kid with the spray can asked when he saw the others rolling on the ground. Not terribly imaginative, he was painting yet another swastika.

"Something pushed us," one of the others said, getting to his knees. There was a slight quaver in his voice.

With a frown the first boy stopped spraying. He looked to the headstone the others had been working on.

It was just an ordinary hunk of rock. All around was nothing but shadows and wind and swaying pines. They were the only living things at Wildwood Cemetery.

"Don't pussy out," the first youth growled at the others. He returned to his spraying.

The two kneeling boys glanced at each another.

"You must've pushed me," one accused.

"What the hell do you mean?" challenged the other, his nerve returning. "You pushed *me*."

They scurried back to the headstone.

The frozen ground at the base of the stone seemed suddenly to have gone all brittle. One of the boys felt the ground crack beneath his right foot. With a jolt, he sank ankle deep in the earth. When he tried to pull his foot out, it wouldn't budge. It was only then that the horror set in.

"C'mon, hurry up," his companion groused. He had his back braced against the stone.

The second youth refused to move. He just stood there, his foot stuck up to the ankle in a gopher hole.

When the boy at the grave marker glanced up, he found that every last drop of blood had drained from his friend's face. A look of fear like none he had ever before seen in his young life had flooded the boy's features.

The silent youth's lower lip stuttered in place. It was as if he were trying to speak but couldn't.

With an angry expression the second boy straightened. "What's the—" He sniffed the air. "Dammit, did you piss your pants?" he demanded.

Before his friend could manage to respond, the angry youth felt the earth grow brittle beneath him. His own foot abruptly cracked through the frozen surface. The first hint of concern had barely brushed his soft features when he felt something cold and unseen wrap around his ankle.

It felt like a hand.

His face grew ashen. He tried to scream but no sound came. And suddenly the world turned upside down and the two boys were flipping backward onto the frozen ground.

The boy with the spray can glanced over once more. "What the hell's wrong with you fag—"

The words died in his throat.

As the three boys watched, frozen with fear, the ground before the haunted headstone cracked and split apart. Clods of hard-packed dirt fell away. And with an unearthly silence that seemed to dull the beating of their very hearts, a dark figure rose slowly up into the chill night air.

The ghost was dressed all in black. His T-shirt and chinos were shadows that enveloped his lean frame. The face was like an accusing skull, with eyes set so deep in their sockets they seemed little more than empty hollows into an angry soul. A bare arm extended, finger unfurled. The specter pointed accusingly at the three terrified youths.

"Boo," said Remo Williams.

That single spoken syllable was the key that unlocked three frozen larynxes. In horrified unison the three boys let out a chorus of bloodcurdling screams.

Hearts thudding, synchronized by fear, they tried to run. The ghost appeared before them.

"Keep it down," Remo said. "You wanna wake the dead?" As he spoke he tapped a spot in the center of two foreheads. Two of the vandals promptly went as rigid as any stone angel.

The third boy suddenly felt the spray can pop from his fingers. So panicked was he, he hadn't even realized he was still holding it. His mouth was wide in shock. Remo took it as an invitation.

"Dead people have simple wishes," Remo instructed as he stuffed the spray can into the youth's mouth. "Really, all we want is to be left alone."

He jammed the can so far back that the little plastic button compressed against the soft tissue at the back of the boy's throat. With a muffled hiss, clouds of black paint began discharging from both of the boy's nostrils.

As the can hissed, Remo considered. "Maybe some flowers once in a while. A wreath at Christmas. That'd be nice. After all, corpses have feelings, too. But it's guys like you that take all the fun out of being dead. I mean, how would you like it if me and my friends zombied our way into your houses in the middle of the night and started knocking over your Nintendos and spray painting crap on your personal computers?"

"Fffssssss!" said the boy with the paint can in his mouth. With plumes of black paint coming from his nose, he looked like a snorting cartoon bull.

"That's right, you wouldn't," Remo nodded. "Well, we dead people aren't any different than you, except we waste less space."

The can fizzled empty. Remo pulled it out of the kid's mouth, tossing it in some bushes. Wet paint drizzled black from the boy's slack mouth.

"Now, here's what you're gonna do," Remo said. "When you leave the cemetery, you're going to flag down the first cop car you see and you're going to confess to what you did here tonight. Then you're going to pay for every last bit of damage. If your parents are like all the others these days, they're gonna try to blame your actions on your buddies, your schools or the NRA. You are not going to let them do that. You are going to stand up for what you did, and you are going to make it right. If not, the next time I grab one of you jerks by the ankle, I won't stop pulling until you've got the room next to mine in the Motel Hell. Got it?''

His darting finger tapped the foreheads of the two paralyzed youths. As one, the three boys nodded numbly. Three sets of knees knocked audibly.

''Good,'' Remo said. ''Now, if you'll excuse me, I've got to go knock over some furniture and rattle some chains at Dan Aykroyd's house. It's all pretty childish stuff really, but if it keeps him from making *Ghostbusters 3* it's worth it.''

With that he slipped into the shadows and was gone. It was as if the night had swallowed him whole.

For a moment the three boys just stood there. Eyes wide, burning from the cold. Their panting breath curls of white in the chill winter air.

All at once they seemed to reach some inner decision.

Wheeling around, they ran for all they were worth. Screaming in fear, they stumbled out of the cemetery gates and raced down the cracked sidewalk. Feet pounding, they quickly disappeared from sight.

Once they were gone, Remo slid out from behind a concealing knot of pines. He turned in satisfaction at the grave from which he'd appeared.

There was a man-size hole in the ground behind the headstone. Remo had only had to burrow a few inches below the surface to come up on the far side of the stone.

He knocked the clods of overturned earth back in

the hole, tapping them down with the sole of his loafer.

"It might not be what I was after, but it still felt good," he said in satisfaction. He turned from the grave.

Out of respect for the dead, he didn't start whistling until he reached the street.

3

The ancient Bell UH-1 Huey raced along the jagged length of the Trans-Alaska Pipeline. Swirls of snow flew up in its frenzied wake.

Eleven nervous men lined the rear of the helicopter. Although they all wore bulky headsets, the radios in most of them didn't work. The headphones were to dull the eardrum-rattling noise of the screaming rotor blades.

Anxious eyes stared out the scratched windows.

Below the belly of the racing Huey stretched the pipeline. It ran eight hundred miles down from the wastes of the north. Most people thought it followed a perfectly straight line from point A to point B. Not so. The huge pipe had been built in staggered sections to allow for certain elasticity during earthquake shocks. From the back of the Huey, it looked as if some giant vandal had taken great strides south, twisting the pipe as he went.

Right now, most of the men in the chopper would have preferred a giant. At least it would be something they could see from a distance. What they were actually after was unknown.

Something had happened somewhere down there in

the Alaskan wilds. Something that warranted pulling a group of trainees from their exercises.

One of the men pressed a gloved hand to his headset. He'd found that he could get it to work sometimes if he pushed the loose wire trailing into his right earpiece.

"Sir, do you know what this is all about?"

Most of the men couldn't hear the question. The ones who could strained to listen to the reply.

"Some kind of problem with some pipeline workers," Major Race H. Fordell replied over the scratchy headset. Their commanding officer was staring down at the pipeline.

"Couldn't the Guard check it out?"

The Major shook his head. "We were closest."

"Lucky us," another man mumbled.

Since his microphone was broken, the words were swallowed up by the howl of the rotor blades.

The First Civil Support Battalion had been conducting training exercises near the Chandalar River 150 miles north of Fairbanks when the call came. They were scrambled and soaring east in ten minutes.

The pilot was ordered to give it all he had. The vibrations were so great some feared the Huey might start rattling apart around their heads.

The men in the helicopter weren't true soldiers. Some in the Alaska State Defense Force had some service training, but many did not. Even though the ASDF was considered a military force—to be deployed during state emergencies—the civil servants of the ASDF really existed as backup to the Alaska National Guard.

In the back of the chopper, shaking hands wiped sweat from nervous brows.

A matching patch on each man's sleeve depicted a swimming wolf. Above was the legend 1st Bn, and below were the letters *ASDF*.

The Seawolves were based in Juneau. Only sheer dumb luck had plunked them down in the middle of nowhere this day. At the moment none of the men was feeling terribly lucky. A few of them jumped when the pilot's urgent voice crackled over the headphones.

"I think you'll want to see this, Major."

Major Fordell hopped from his seat and swept to the cockpit.

"What have we got?" Fordell asked tightly. He was already scanning the forward terrain.

"Down there, sir," the pilot said, pointing. "Dead ahead."

Squinting, Major Fordell spotted a cluster of trucks. They looked like toys. Bunched together, they sat cold and alone on the pipeline access road. A fat hose ran from the back of the last truck, vanishing over the hill that ran parallel to the road.

"Vacuum truck," Fordell said. "Those are the guys who radioed in." He pointed to the hill. "Let's see where they went."

Nodding, the pilot swept across the abandoned trucks and up the face of the hill. The instant they'd crested the top, the pilot felt his fingers tense on the stick.

"Sir," he whispered, his voice low with sudden shock.

Beside him, Major Race Fordell's mouth thinned. His unblinking eyes showed not a flicker of emotion.

In the valley below them the pipeline stretched like a metallic serpent. Underneath its massive support members, dozens of bodies lay scattered like abandoned dolls.

Hovering over the hill, the pilot cast a frightened eye at the Major. In the back of the Huey the men had taken sudden sick interest in the gruesome scene below.

"What happened, Major?" the young pilot asked.

Race Fordell's expression never wavered.

"That's what we're here to find out," he said flatly. "Take us down."

Nodding numbly, the pilot aimed the chopper for the valley floor. At Fordell's orders, he touched down just long enough for the eleven men in the back to spill out. Skids had barely pressed to frozen ground before the Huey was once more airborne. Buzzing like an angry insect, it soared off down the valley in the direction opposite the one from which it had come.

The hum of the rotor blades faded to silence.

Alone on the ground, the eleven ASDF men picked their careful way around the dead.

Stepping cautiously through the pool of crude oil, Major Fordell squatted near a pair of bodies.

Joe Abady was flat on his stomach, his chin resting

on the black ground. Almost as black as crude oil, blood had frozen to the hole in his forehead. Near the APSC foreman, Brian Turski lay on his side, his head gaping wide from a single, point-blank gunshot.

Wordlessly, Major Fordell stood.

There was no sign of anyone else in the area. They'd detected no other vehicles on the flight up. Snowfall had been too low this winter for snowmobiles. The chopper was searching now in the other direction. If the pilot could turn up nothing from a visual sweep, that left only two possibilities. The hostiles had either been airlifted out, or they were still in the area.

The ASDF men were looking everywhere, clustered tightly around Fordell, their rifle barrels fanned out.

"This was an ambush," the Major said with certainty. He kept his voice low. "We're looking for foxholes, burrows, trapdoors. Stay alert. Let's move."

Swallowing their fear, the men spread out across the narrow valley floor. Their eyes trained on the ground, they began moving south.

Major Fordell studied not just the ground. Every now and then his eyes flicked up to the pipeline. It hung above their heads, big and menacing.

A few hundred yards from the massacre they found nothing. Some of the men were allowing the first slip of relief to hiss from between their chapped lips. Major Fordell remained tense. As he walked along the frozen ground, his eyes and ears were alert to everything around him.

There was no doubt in his mind this had been an

ambush. The hole in the pipe back there was man-made, designed to lure the pipeline workers into a trap.

Could be whacked-out environmentalists trying to shut down the pipe. Hell, maybe it was agents of OPEC trying to screw with domestic oil production. No matter who it was, there was no way they were going to get past Major Race Fordell.

A flash of movement to his left drew the Major's attention. For an instant the air seemed to gel into a fuzzy solid. The instant it did, Major Fordell felt a rough tug at his hands.

His gun disappeared.

Just like that. Disappeared. Vanished as if sucked into a parallel dimension.

His fingers clenched empty air.

Panic flooded his hollow belly. Before he could even give voice to his shock, before he could alert his men, Fordell felt a blinding pain crack the side of his head.

He dropped to the seat of his pants, stunned. When he grabbed at the injured area, his gloved fingers returned slick with blood.

"Major, what happened?" a nearby ASDF soldier asked worriedly. His young voice suddenly dropped low. "Oh, God."

Nursing shock, Fordell looked up woodenly.

His gun had reappeared. It was clutched in the hands of a swirling figure. The barrel was aimed at Major Fordell.

The Major tried to blink the figure into focus. He

wasn't sure if it was head trauma or something else, but it seemed impossible to see the man clearly. Then all at once the intruder seemed to snap into reality.

The strange figure wore winter combat fatigues. A matching ski mask covered his face. His eyes were hidden behind a pair of black goggles. The gun aimed at Fordell's face never wavered.

Whoever he was, his intentions seemed clear enough. Race Fordell wasn't taking any chances.

"Shoot him!" the Major yelled.

His men ignored the order.

Still sitting on the ground and staring down the barrel of his own rifle, Major Fordell glanced at his men. What he saw made his heart freeze in his chest.

There were more of the commandos. All around. *Dozens* of them. They had somehow stepped out of the air to ambush Major Race Fordell and his ASDF weekend warriors.

"Oh, God," repeated the young soldier nearest Race. He was frozen in place. Three commandos stood like somber sentries before him, their guns leveled at his chest.

A twitch of movement came from the commando standing before him. Eyes darting, Race Fordell saw a gloved finger tighten over a trigger. *His* trigger. His own damn gun was about to kill him. Cold fury flooded his blood-streaked face.

"Shoot them, dammit!" Major Fordell ordered an instant before a bullet from his own gun ended his life.

As the Major fell, the rest of the commandos

opened fire. Guns crackled. One by one the ASDF men fell.

Panicking, some men threw down their weapons and flung up their hands. They were slaughtered where they stood.

The few Alaska State Defense Force men who tried to defend themselves found their targets impossible to track. They always seemed to be everywhere other than the path of the bullets.

The commandos disappeared and reappeared. Some abandoned guns for knives, materializing next to a terrified ASDF man just long enough to slit his throat.

When there was only one ASDF man left standing, the slaughter abruptly ceased.

The Alaska State Defense soldier had already thrown down his gun. He stood whimpering and defenseless, as the crowd of masked men formed a circle around him. He didn't even hear the hushed words from the commandos. Didn't see the crowd part. Didn't notice the lone man who strode into their midst.

The last arrival was dressed like the others, save one distinction. He wore no mask.

His features were delicate enough to be considered pretty. His eyes were powdery brown mixed with flecks of red. Although he was young, his close-cropped hair was prematurely white. He had the confident, graceful stride of a gymnast. With a perfect economy of motion, he stepped up to the last ASDF man.

The soldier was babbling incoherently. His eyes were unfocused as he stared blankly at the ground.

The white-haired commando paused before the man. He cast one pale eye around the circle of faceless soldiers.

All at once, his hand shot out. So fast did it move, most there could not even follow it.

The side of the white-haired man's flattened palm met the Adam's apple of the last soldier. There was a wet thwack as the ASDF man's head left his neck.

With a thud the head hit the ground. The body joined it a split second later.

The white-haired commando gave the decapitated body a single look of disdain. A sneer still on his delicate lips, he turned.

The others parted in quiet reverence.

As the lone commando walked away, a single word muttered by one of the masked men trailed behind him.

"Mactep," a man in the crowd said in awe.

And as if in response, the white-haired man vanished from sight.

4

Remo drove aimlessly the remainder of the night, arriving back in Rye a little after seven in the morning.

The lone guard at the security shed didn't even glance up as Remo steered his leased car through the main gates of Folcroft Sanitarium. He drove up the gravel drive and parked in the employee lot next to the rusty old station wagon of his boss, Harold W. Smith. He was heading for the side door of the ivy-covered brick building when he spotted something out of the corner of his eye.

Folcroft's rear lawn rolled down to the rimy shore of Long Island Sound. An old boat dock extended into the water. On the most distant plank stood a solitary figure.

The old man was so frail it seemed as if the gentlest breeze would send him spinning like a colorful pinwheel into the cold water. But despite the buffeting gusts that blew in from the Sound, the wizened figure remained fixed in place. His back to the shore, he stared out across the water.

Pausing in the parking lot, Remo studied the tiny figure on the dock for the briefest of moments.

"Do I want to open myself up to this or do I sneak inside?" he said under his breath.

Since he knew he'd been heard arriving—in spite of the seeming disinterest of the old man on the dock—he decided against ducking inside. On sure feet he glided down the gentle back hill and onto the dock. At the far end he paused next to the tiny figure.

"This a private party or is everyone invited?" Remo asked Chiun, his teacher and Reigning Master of Sinanju.

The elderly Korean continued to study the white-capped waves. "It is a free country," he replied, his singsong voice uninterested. "Stand wherever you like."

At only five feet tall, the old Asian's head barely reached Remo's shoulder. He wore a simple gold kimono that flapped like a wind sock around his bare ankles. His hands were tucked far inside his voluminous sleeves.

Two tufts of yellowing white hair clutched to a spot above each shell-like ear. His age-speckled head was otherwise bald. The skin was like tan rice paper left to dry on his ancient skull. Fine veins showed like a map of crisscrossing blue roads beneath the delicate surface.

The two men stood staring at the water for a few long minutes. Remo's thoughts were of his California trip and the lost thought his mind could not seem to retrieve.

Beside him, the Master of Sinanju sensed his pupil's frustration. He turned his birdlike head to Remo.

"You have had no luck remembering that which you have forgotten?" Chiun asked quietly.

Remo seemed surprised by the question. He looked down into his teacher's upturned face.

"How'd you know?" he asked.

"Please, Remo," Chiun clucked dismissively. "You always wear whatever you are thinking on that sandwich board you call a face. I have been tempted at times to stand you out beside the highway and rent it for advertising to that cowburger-frying clown. Now, what is it that troubles you?"

Remo bit his lip thoughtfully. "I'm not sure," he admitted. "You ever go in a room looking for something and then when you get there you forget what it is you were going in there for? That's what I feel like right now."

A bony hand appeared from the Master of Sinanju's kimono sleeve. With the tips of his long fingernails he stroked the thread of beard that extended from his pointed chin.

"Hmm," he mused softly. His youthful hazel eyes turned back to the water. He said nothing more.

"That's the best you can do?" Remo asked. "'Hmm'?"

"It is all I can do," Chiun said. "The path you are on must be walked alone."

Remo's face grew troubled. "What do you mean?" he asked cautiously. "Do you know what this is all about?"

Chiun appeared insulted by the question. "Of

course," he sniffed. "I am the Master of Sinanju. What is more, *you* know what it is about, as well."

The old man's tone was ominous. Remo had heard that same tone before. He whirled on his teacher.

"Oh, cripes, not again," Remo said, his face sagging. "Is this the start of some new ditfrimmy Sinanju ritual? 'Cause if it is, I'm throwing in the towel before it even starts."

"Too late," Chiun said. A stiff wind caught his thin wisps of hair. "It has already begun."

Remo shook his head. "I don't believe this," he muttered. "The worse thing is, every time one of these cockamamie things comes up, you tell me it's the last one and I *believe* you. I'm like Charlie Brown and you keep pulling away that goddamn football every time. So what do I have to do this time? Journey to the center of the Earth and battle the mole people? Go for a swim in the Big Dipper? What?"

"Nothing so difficult or so easy," Chiun replied. He held up a hand, halting further questions from his pupil. "And now is not the time."

"That's easy for you to say. You don't have some melting-ice-cube-of-a-thought slipping around your head."

Chiun's face softened. "Do not try so hard, my son. Put it aside. When it is time, it will come."

Beside the old man, Remo rolled his thick wrists in frustration. The advice his teacher was giving him seemed impossible to follow. His body, his spirit, *everything* seemed to be screaming something at him. He didn't know how to ignore it. Yet he trusted the

Master of Sinanju more than anyone else he'd ever known. If Chiun said to put it aside, the old Asian had to be certain it was the right thing to do.

With great effort of will, Remo forced the troubling thoughts from his mind.

The tension slipped slowly from his shoulders.

Chiun noted the change in his pupil's bearing with a nod of approval.

"Now, on to more-pressing matters," the tiny Korean said, his voice growing serious. "I assume by your hesitation before entering Fortress Folcroft that you have spoken to Smith?"

Remo frowned. "Not since I called him from London on our way back from Russia. Why, is something up?"

Chiun pursed his wrinkled lips. Troubled eyes gazed out upon the icy waters.

"That is for the Emperor to say, not his assassin."

Remo's brow furrowed. "Great. More intrigue. I'll go see him now. You coming with?" He was turning to go when he felt a bony hand press his wrist.

"You say you have not spoken to Smith since before you bundled me in a taxi like some nuisance fishwife and headed off to sulk alone?" Chiun asked quizzically.

"Yeah," Remo admitted cautiously.

"If you did not know why you should hesitate before entering Smith's palace, then why did you hesitate at all?" His hazel eyes had grown accusing.

Remo exhaled a heavy sigh. Though the air was

cold, his warm breath was invisible as it slipped from between his tightly parted lips.

"It's just—" He paused, gathering strength. "It's just you looked like you might be in a mood, that's all," he said. "You were standing all alone back here in that me-against-the-world pose. I figured it might be safer to tiptoe inside and hide under the bed." He held up his hands. "But it's okay. I assumed wrong. Mea culpa. Now, let's go see what Smitty wants."

This time when he turned to go, the hand that latched on to his wrist was less gentle.

"Mea culpa," the Master of Sinanju echoed. "How appropriate you should use that phrase, given your recent association with the hooligans of Rome."

Oh, God, why did I even open my mouth? Remo asked himself. Aloud, he said, "Good one, Little Father. Ouch. You zinged me but good. Come on, I'll race you inside."

"Why?" Chiun asked, his voice growing pitiful. "Is it garbage-collecting day? Are you in a hurry to throw my meager belongings into the refuse? I beg you in advance to please spare me the lash, Remo, for I am old and frail. It will take me some time to haul my trunks out to the curb."

"Okay, couple of things wrong with that. For one, you're as frail as an avalanche. On top of that, *I'm* the one who's always had to lug those trunks of yours around. Until a couple of weeks ago, I didn't even think you knew where the handles were."

Chiun held a weak hand to his heart. "As usual I suffer your abuse in silence."

Remo raised a skeptical brow. "For the amount of abuse you claim I dump on you, I'm surprised the Department of Social Services isn't kicking in the door and trying to stick you in a foster home."

The Master of Sinanju shook his head morosely. "I will not be taken in again by your false promises, Remo. When you said recently that others would give me a home to replace the one I lost, I, in my innocence, believed you. I know better than this now. Whoever these Fosters are, they will not put a roof over my aged head. And at the risk of being flogged for my insolence, I find it exceedingly cruel that you would test my trusting nature with the same lie twice."

On their recent trip to California, they had briefly visited a charity event that was being held to raise money for the homeless. The Master of Sinanju had decided that, since he was currently without a residence of his own, the first deed passed out should go to him. Things had not worked out the way he wanted them to, and he had returned to the East Coast empty-handed.

"I never told you anyone was giving you anything," Remo said firmly. "In fact, I'm the one who told you they *wouldn't* give you a house."

Chiun raised his button nose in the air. "That is not how I remember it," he said with certainty.

"Big surprise there," Remo said, rolling his eyes.

"I suppose you will next tell me that someone else is to blame," said Chiun. "You have been doing much of this passing of the puck lately. Ever since you and your Roman playmates set fire to Castle Sinanju.''

"Oh, boy, here it comes. I did not burn down our house," Remo insisted. "Those Mafia guys did it all by themselves. I've even got an airtight alibi, for chrissakes. I was out eating supper with you."

"Yes, dining while the Romans burned," Chiun droned. "However, that does not erase the fact that you have admitted your own foolishness led them there."

Remo had heard this one before. Unlike in the past, this time he had a response.

"I've copped to that one," Remo nodded. "But I've been doing some thinking about that night. If you hadn't tried tipping that waitress with counterfeit money, we might have gotten home in time to stop them."

Chiun's eyes saucered. His hands clenched to knots of ivory bone. The very air around him stilled. "Are you now saying it is somehow *my* fault?" he demanded coldly.

"No," Remo insisted quickly. "What I'm saying is it's the fault of whoever programmed the traffic lights that kept us from getting home faster. It's the chef's fault for being too slow in the kitchen. It's as much anyone else's fault as it is mine. I did *not* burn down our house. End of story."

As quickly as it came, the fight drained from Chiun. "Of course you are right. You are *always* right." His fragile shoulders rose and sank pitifully.

Remo had known the old con artist long enough to

recognize the pose he now struck. He had guessed it as soon as he'd spotted the Master of Sinanju from the parking lot. Chiun was angling for something.

"Why the shift to self-pity mode?" Remo asked warily.

"I am attempting to cope with my great loss," the wizened Asian said. Cold mist from the Sound kissed his leathery cheeks. "There are stages to such a thing, Remo. The first is fear, which neither you nor I experience. The next is denial." His voice dropped low. "You are steeped in that at the moment," he confided.

"I'm not denying anything," Remo sighed.

"Thank you for making my case," Chiun said. "As for the rest, they are unimportant. I have reached the final phase. Bitter acceptance." A pathetic sigh seeped from wrinkled lips, and his shoulders rose and fell once more.

Remo shook his head knowingly. "I know how this game is played," he said. "You haven't accepted diddly. You're up to the bargaining phase, and you know you can catch more flies with moping. So what do you want? And I'm warning you ahead of time, if it's a house you're after we're not getting an eyesore like the last one."

Although he had grown used to their home of ten years, he wouldn't have picked it himself. Chiun and their employer had gone behind his back to purchase Castle Sinanju.

This time Chiun's gloomy expression was genuine.

"Is there more than one Basilica Julia?" the Master of Sinanju lamented. "Where in the Forbidden City did the Chinese build another Palace of Heavenly Purity? Show me Egypt's second Temple of Karnak, that they would have another in the event disaster struck.'' He shook his head sadly. "There are no two gems alike, Remo. There was only one Castle Sinanju. My beloved home is gone forever.''

Remo shared the old man's loss.

"I miss it, too, Little Father,'' he said gently. "Believe me, I'm not doing cartwheels down the hallways now that we're stuck living in this loony bin again.''

He glanced at the back of the big building.

Folcroft was a throwback to another age. To the right of the rear loading dock, two stories up, a picture window of mirrored glass reflected tired sunlight.

"I'm sure Smitty isn't thrilled with us being here, either,'' Remo continued. "That's probably what he wants now. To send us packing. Speaking of which, he's probably having a spaz attack right now if he sees us out here like this. I better go see what he wants.''

Turning, he headed up the rickety old dock. Expression thoughtful, the Master of Sinanju kept pace. Not a single warped board so much as creaked beneath their combined weight. They hit the shore and began mounting the hill.

"It is possible after your audience with Smith that you will be the one who wishes to leave,'' Chiun said cryptically.

"Why?'' Remo asked. "He *is* kicking us out, isn't he?''

"Not at all. He has opened the gates of Fortress Folcroft wide for us,'' the old Korean said. "A decision fraught with risk given your questionable associates of late. There are other forces at work here."

"I bet," Remo said doubtfully. "Look, Chiun, I don't think Smith is too hepped on the idea of us getting another permanent home right now. We kind of made a scene on our way out of town with the last one. It even made the local news."

"We were not seen by any television cameras."

"Maybe not, but we were known around the neighborhood. People saw us off and on there for ten years. Then came the fire and us turning up missing afterward. Even though it's only local, I'm sure people are still talking."

"Any interest will soon wane."

"Probably," Remo said. "But you know how Smith is. He doesn't like us here any more than we like being here, but until the heat dies down he'll want us close enough to keep tabs on. If he is planning to kick us out, my guess is we've already got rooms in the seediest no-tell motel right here in Rye."

At the top of the hill now, they struck off across the short stretch of parking lot toward the building. Chiun's black sandals made not a sound as he padded thoughtfully beside his pupil.

"Necessity has forced us to find temporary lodging in this village," the Master of Sinanju said. "But Rye is Smith's home, not ours."

"No argument there," Remo said.

Beside him, Remo caught a flutter of golden silk. One of Chiun's hands appeared from his sleeve like a cobra from a snake charmer's basket. A shiny pamphlet was clutched in his tapered fingers.

"I am glad you agree," the old man said, his voice laced with cunning.

"Why?" Remo asked, stopping in his tracks. "What's that?"

A blissful smile cracked Chiun's walnut-colored skin.

"Our new home," he replied.

With a sinking feeling, Remo took the pamphlet. On the front, cheerful white letters read: Making Maine Your Own. Even as he was reading the words, Remo was shaking his head emphatically.

"No way," he said firmly. "I told you already, I'm thinking someplace hot. Florida. Hawaii maybe. Someplace with palm trees and sunburns and bikinis held in place by nothing but dental floss and wishful thinking."

"There are doubtless streetwalkers in Maine," the Master of Sinanju droned. "Besides, your soul cries not for scorching climes. It begs you to return to the mild temperatures of the land of your birth."

"That'd be Newark," Remo said, deadpan as he flipped through the pamphlet.

"Pah," Chiun snarled. "I speak not of the shell in which you walk and rut and speak ill of your betters. I refer to your blood. This place hearkens to your ancestral home of Sinanju."

When he glanced up, Remo's eyes were hooded. "And that's supposed to be a selling point, right?"

The pamphlet was gone, plucked from his fingers in a flash.

"Of course, O Visigothic one," Chiun said. "And since we cannot live in the true Sinanju, we must settle for the nearest available facsimile."

"That'd be the Rye city dump," Remo said blandly. "The rats can double for the people. Course, the rats won't try to stick a shiv in our backs and steal our teeth while we're sleeping."

The pamphlet vanished up the old man's sleeve.

"We will discuss this later," he said. He headed for the side door of the sanitarium.

"There's nothing to discuss," Remo insisted. "I'm not being bamboozled this time. I am not—repeat *not*—moving to Maine."

He yanked the door open. Chiun preceded him inside.

"It reminds me of home," the old man said wistfully.

"In what way?" Remo asked as they mounted the stairs. "The remoteness? The rocks? The freezing winters that last all summer? Help me out here. On second thought don't, because it doesn't matter. No Maine, no way, no how."

"Your lips say no, but your soul says yes." Chiun nodded wisely.

"Stop saying what my soul wants, dammit," Remo snapped in frustration. "*I* don't even know what my soul wants these days."

Chiun took special note of his pupil's troubled tone. Unseen by Remo, the old man's face darkened in sympathy. He grew silent as they exited the stairwell on the second floor.

Together, they walked down the hallway of Folcroft's administrative wing.

Smith's secretary looked up from her desk as they entered the outer room.

Eileen Mikulka smiled at Chiun. "Back again so soon?"

Remo shot his teacher a quizzical look, but the old man's eyes remained locked dead ahead.

"Dr. Smith said you should go right in," Mrs. Mikulka advised before returning her attention to the papers on her desk.

Wordlessly, Chiun preceded Remo through the inner-office door.

The room beyond was drab and functional. As they entered, a gaunt, white-haired man who sat behind a big desk across the room glanced to the door.

"Hey, Smitty," Remo said, bored. "I'm back. And in case you were wondering, capitalism hasn't made Russia stink any less, and I was afraid to use the bathroom at the airport for fear of getting contact syphilis."

"Ah, Remo," Harold Smith said, a hint of anxiety in his lemony voice. "I saw you out back."

"Three cheers and a tiger for you," Remo said. "You figured out how to use a window."

His senses were telling him something odd about the room. There was an extra heartbeat inside.

As Chiun padded calmly across the room to Smith's desk, Remo peeked behind the still open door.

He was surprised to find a young man in a business suit sitting on Smith's worn office sofa. The stranger smiled nervously up at Remo.

Remo shot a look at Smith. "Who's this goomer?" he asked, jerking a thumb at the man on the couch.

"Mind your manners," the Master of Sinanju warned in Korean. He had taken up an imperious sentry pose next to the CURE director's desk.

Remo raised an eyebrow at the old man's admonishment.

Smith cleared his throat. His chair squeaked as he sat up straighter.

"Remo, allow me to introduce Mark Howard," Smith said, gesturing across the room to the man near Remo. "Mark has assumed the position of assistant director of Folcroft."

The door was still open. Remo let it slip from his fingers. It closed with a soft click.

"Of Folcroft," Remo said flatly.

Smith leaned forward, shaking his head slowly. He tipped his face down, peering at Remo over the tops of his spotless rimless glasses.

"Of CURE, as well," the older man said gravely.

And as he stood near the door, the CURE director's shocking words echoed like dull thunder in the stunned brain of Remo Williams.

5

Beside Remo, Mark Howard climbed to his feet. The young man wiped nervous perspiration from his palm before offering Remo his hand.

"I look forward to working with you, Remo," Howard said, his youthful voice tinged with worried excitement.

Remo was coming rapidly back around. He looked, stunned, from Smith's serious face to the Master of Sinanju's mask of stone. He paused just long enough to glance at Howard's outstretched hand before looking back to Smith.

"What the hell is this all about?" Remo demanded.

"Remo!" Chiun scolded. He bowed apologetically to Howard. "Forgive my son's rudeness, Prince Mark. He was raised in a poorhouse where he had to fight the other urchins for crusts of bread. I advise you to do what the rest of us do and just ignore him."

"Ignore this," Remo said.

"Of course, sometimes it is easier to do than others," Chiun told Howard through tightly clenched teeth. His eyes shot daggers at Remo.

"You mean to tell me you knew about this and you didn't tell me?" Remo said to the Master of Sinanju.

"Master Chiun met Mark formally last night," Smith explained. "You would have, too, had you returned to Folcroft after your assignment was through."

"I had some thinking to do," Remo said. "It sure as hell didn't have anything to do with this." He stabbed a finger at Howard. "When did *that* happen to us?"

"Apparently, things were set in motion before the previous President left office," Smith explained.

Remo threw up his hands. "That's enough for me. This is wobble-bottom's revenge for not making him and his wife Mr. and Mrs. Kingfish of Siam for life, isn't it? Well, let's get this over with and kill him right now."

He took a step toward Howard. The young man stepped back worriedly, almost tripping over the arm of the sofa. He had to grab the back of the couch to keep his balance.

"Remo, stop it," Smith commanded.

The order wasn't necessary. As Mark struggled to regain his balance, Remo stopped dead. His deep-set eyes narrowed.

"I know you," Remo said slowly as he studied the young man's wide face.

"Yes," Smith said from across the room. "You met him several weeks ago during the Raffair business."

"We encountered Prince Mark at one of the lairs of your iniquitous Roman friends," Chiun supplied. He quickly offered Howard an apologetic bow. "It is to my eternal shame that I did not recognize your regal bearing straight away.''

Remo snapped his fingers. ''Miami,'' he said. ''You were the doofus who didn't know which end of the gun the bullets came out of.'' He wheeled on Smith. ''He's CIA, Smitty.''

''Formerly CIA, yes,'' Smith replied.

''There's no formerly CIA,'' Remo insisted. ''Not unless they started installing Brain-O-Matic 2000s in their agents when they issue them pink slips. They go in stupid, come out stupider.''

''I wasn't a field agent,'' Howard interrupted. There was a growing edge to his tone.

''Got that right,'' Remo scoffed. ''You should have seen this joker, Smitty. He actually made the rest of those Maxwell Smarts at Langley look like they'd know their spyglasses from their elbows.''

Sighing, Smith rubbed the bridge of his patrician nose with arthritic fingers. ''I didn't think this would be easy,'' he said wearily.

''He is stubborn, as well as rude, Prince Mark,'' Chiun explained. ''But in spite of his many—'' his eyes grew hooded as he stared directly at Remo ''—*many* character flaws, he has served his emperor faithfully for years.''

''Um, about that,'' Howard said, his voice vaguely troubled. ''Emperor, prince? Are these terms…?'' His voice trailed off.

Howard's implication was clear.

''This oughta be good,'' Remo said. He flopped

back on the couch, his arms spread wide across the back.

The CURE director fidgeted uncomfortably in his seat.

"They are not my idea, if that is your concern," Smith said, his gray face flushing with embarrassment. "Sinanju Masters are effusive in language and devoted to title. It eventually became easier to accept the honorific than to argue against its use."

"Perhaps, Emperor Smith, a clearer delineation is necessary now with the arrival of the prince regent," Chiun mused, stroking his beard pensively. "How would you feel about His Royal Highness, Smith the First?"

Smith's face sickened. "There is no need to change at this juncture," he said quickly.

"Yeah," Remo agreed. "Especially since the Campbell Soup Kid here won't be around very long."

"Remo," Smith said evenly, "like it or not, Mark has been installed here as assistant director of CURE. Given that simple fact, he will be here for the foreseeable future."

"Nope," Remo said, shaking his head. "Last CIA guy a President sent in to take over almost blew the whole shooting match *and* nearly got us all killed in the bargain. I say a corpse in time saves mine. You'll agree soon enough."

"That individual was NSA, not CIA," Smith reminded him. "And this situation is different. In that instance my taking ill caused the President to install a new CURE director. In this case the President simply wishes to have someone in place should something happen to me.''

"Dr. Smith?" Howard interrupted, concerned. "The President never told me he sent someone else in to run CURE."

"It was a previous President," Smith explained. "Years ago."

"May I ask what happened to him?" Howard questioned.

"That is not relevant," Smith said tersely.

"Got cooked to death in that very chair," Remo said, nodding across the room to where the CURE director sat.

"Remo," Smith warned thinly.

"What?" Remo said. "Weren't you gonna tell him what he's gotten himself into?" He leaned forward on the couch. "Guy before that got a pen stuck through his head," he offered conspiratorially.

"That is quite enough," Smith snapped.

"Hey, I'm just letting junior know he's not in Kansas anymore. This is the big leagues, Baby Huey."

Howard would not be baited. "I'm aware of what goes on around here, Remo," he said. But there was a troubled undertone to his words.

"Sure, you are," Remo droned. "Smitty," he continued, "why are we bothering to go through the motions like this? I mean, is all this even legal?"

"Pah," Chiun scoffed, dismissing Remo's words with a wave of one bony hand. "Legalities are for the peasantry. They do not apply to emperors or handsome princes." He smiled at Howard.

"That is not true, Master Chiun," Smith said gravely. "At CURE we are governed by a set of very strict guidelines." He leaned back in his cracked leather chair. "There is nothing in our charter that explicitly prohibits this," he said, steepling his fingers to his chin. "After all, I was appointed by a President forty years ago. That a later President would appoint a second in command at CURE does not violate our founding principles. And I had recently begun to consider the possibility that I might one day be replaced. I assumed that it would be after my death, but it makes more sense this way rather than bringing someone to the job cold."

"Why?" Remo asked blandly. "He's just gonna be leaving that way. Cold, stiff and with a really surprised look on his face."

Although Smith's lips pursed unhappily, it was Howard who broke in.

"I know this is hard for you, Remo," Mark said reasonably. "The three of you have worked as a team for a long time. I can see how you'd see me as an intrusion."

"Buddy, intrusion is way down the list," Remo said. "I mostly see you as a waste of space with just a smattering of pain-in-the-ass tossed in for good measure."

A dark thundercloud crossed the Master of Sinanju's leathery face. In a swirl of silken robes he swept around Smith's desk.

"You will excuse us, O Emperor, but your humble servants have taken up enough of your precious time.

We will leave you and your young princeling to the work of governance.''

"Yes," Smith agreed, his flint eyes trained on Remo. "Perhaps that would be wise."

Chiun gave a curt bow. "Move, lout," he barked, kicking Remo's feet.

With a deep sigh Remo pushed himself up from the couch. Before he'd even stood, a bony hand seized his bicep.

"Come, loudmouthed one."

"Yeah, yeah," Remo muttered.

Like a child being led to the woodshed, he allowed the old man to guide him to the door. Before they'd reached it, Remo paused abruptly. When he turned back there was a look of sincere concern on his hard face.

"Are you okay with all this, Smitty?" Remo asked quietly.

Across the room, the CURE director seemed lost behind his big desk, a wasted figure propped up from another age. Behind him, the one-way picture window overlooked the cold waters of Long Island Sound. A fitting backdrop to the thin, gray man. In that instant Smith had never looked so old.

"It will work out for the best, Remo," Smith promised, giving a tight nod. His bloodless lips were drawn into a grimace that could have been either a smile or indigestion.

"I agree with Dr. Smith," Mark Howard said. "I think we all just need a period of adjustment."

"Tell me how well you've adjusted when they're

tying on your toe tag,'' Remo said, annoyed. He winced as a long fingernail ground into his lower back.

"You have made enough friends today,'' Chiun whispered harshly. He popped the door and propelled his pupil into the outer office. The old man whirled rapidly on the others. "This is truly a momentous time, about which poets will be inspired to write odes and songsmiths will compose joyous anthems,'' Chiun sang. "May the wings of a thousand doves echo the celestial chorus that heralds this, the first day of your new great dynasty. All hail Emperor Smith and his heir, Prince Howard.''

With a formal bow to the two men in the office, he backed from the room, pulling the door shut behind him. The bolt had barely clicked in the frame before he was whirling to face Remo.

"What is wrong with you?'' the old man snapped in Korean.

"Me?'' Remo growled. "What's wrong with *you?*''

At her desk, Eileen Mikulka's wide face grew anxious. She couldn't understand the language the two men were arguing in, but whatever they were saying didn't sound good.

"It was your behavior that was inexcusable,'' Chiun accused, his hazel eyes burning. "And in front of Smith's lackey, no less. How do you expect to curry favor with him when your every word is an assault?''

"Hmm. Let me think about that one,'' Remo said,

tipping his head in mock thought. "Oh, yeah. I don't."

Spinning, he marched out into the corridor. The Master of Sinanju flounced after him.

"Are you so resistant to change?" Chiun asked, bouncing along at his elbow. "You cannot be blind to Smith's age."

"You're a lot older than him and you do okay."

"Even you are not so stupid, Remo," Chiun said. "Everything that is not Sinanju is less than Sinanju. Smith, while an adequate emperor, is just a man. We need to think about a contingency plan if the unthinkable happens."

"Unthinkable means you don't think about it."

"One of us must think once in a while," Chiun said. "May the gods have mercy on us if that someone is you."

They were at the fire exit. Remo stopped dead.

"Always the goddamn mercenary," he muttered.

Chiun's back stiffened.

"I do what I must to feed the people of Sinanju," he sniffed. "And they are fortunate that they have me to rely on. If it were up to you, we would be sending the babies home to the sea, their bellies swollen with hunger."

"I got news for you," Remo said. "It already is up to me. Half the gold that goes to those fat-faced free-loaders is *my* paycheck. Anytime now they're gonna be *all* my responsibility, so back off."

For an instant, Chiun seemed to expect more from Remo, but the younger man merely turned away.

Remo slapped the fire door open, ducking into the stairwell. Chiun slipped through behind him.

"The coffers of Mad Harold are deep," Chiun argued, his voice growing subdued. "Given his health, we cannot afford to squander every opportunity to dance attendance on his heir."

"Tell you what. You dance—I'll sit this one out."

"If you cannot be pleasant at least remain silent," Chiun said. "*I* will curry favor with him."

On the ground-floor landing Remo paused.

"You're amazing, you know that?" he laughed mirthlessly. "You're the one who's always beating me over the head with the scrolls of Sinanju. You're always going on about tradition this and the lesson-of-Master-that, but the minute your mood of the moment doesn't gibe with your so-called sacred history, you chuck five thousand years of Sinanju precepts into the fire in exchange for cold hard cash." He crossed his arms. "Or have you forgotten about Wo-Ti?"

The wrinkles of Chiun's face grew very flat.

"What of him?" he said dully.

"'No Master of Sinanju shall serve a succeeding emperor,'" Remo recited by rote. "Wo-Ti got that from getting stuck serving two pharaohs in a row."

The flesh around the old Korean's mouth tightened.

"I will not be given a lesson in Sinanju history by you," Chiun intoned, his voice steel.

"Why? Because I'm right and you're wrong? Wo-Ti's lesson has been passed down from Master to Master for centuries, but when the bank account gets threatened we just conveniently shove it to one side and slap on a set of blinders. Problem solved. But there *is* still a problem, Chiun, and you know it. What's more, *I* know it, because *you're* the one who hammered it into my skull.'' He exhaled hotly. ''Just forget it. I'm outta here,'' he snarled.

His final word delivered, Remo spun away from his teacher. He shoved the outside door open and strode angrily out into the morning light. When the door slammed shut, the walls of the stairwell shook from the force.

Alone on the landing, the Master of Sinanju remained fixed in place. His face unreadable, he studied the door through razor-slitted eyes.

In another, younger time Chiun might have been furious at such an outburst from his pupil. But things were different now. Remo's emotions were not his own. The younger Master of Sinanju had encountered too much difficulty of late. And there was the promise of more looming just over the horizon. Remo's anger was in part due to his frustration. His spirit understood that something momentous was coming, but his mind could not yet see it.

This was only part of why the old Korean could not be angry at Remo for having the temerity to quote the lesson of Wo-Ti to him, the Reigning Master.

Chiun could not rebuke his pupil for his insolence because in his heart he knew that Remo was right.

As Reigning Master, Chiun was custodian of the most sacred teachings of Sinanju. Yet in that moment Remo had proved himself the better guardian of the traditions of their ancient discipline.

In the wan light of the stairwell, Chiun's thin beard quivered. His hands were clenched impotently at his sides.

After a long moment he turned away from the door. Stone-faced, the old Asian padded down the stairs to the basement. To be alone with his troubled thoughts.

6

It was a room without sunlight. Cold and shadowy.

Four rows of weak yellow lights were caged by rusty steel grates. Many of the bulbs were burned out. The few that remained illuminated the water-damaged ceiling in uneven patches. The ceiling of the cavernous gymnasium was so high the lights hadn't been replaced. For years they'd been allowed to wink out, one after the other. A tiny galaxy of dull stars heading inexorably to extinction. To the utter, consuming dark of nothingness.

There had been windows at one time. But that was long ago. To see the sun now, imagination had to be employed to remove the bricks that had been stacked on the sills.

The perpetual night of this room was fitting. For the individual who sat alone on the dirty floor in that big, drafty space, there was no sun. For Anna Chutesov, there was only the darkness.

Somewhere in the distant bowels of the building, men worked. Anna could hear them from where she sat. Scratching like rats in the walls of the Institute.

The Institute. The greatest secret to be carried over from the ashes of the old Soviet Union.

For years it was not like this. Not only would strangers not be allowed to enter this, one of the most secure buildings in all of Moscow, but they would have been shot in the attempt.

All was different now.

Anna didn't bother to go check on the men who scurried from room to far-off room. There was nothing left to hide.

Well, that was not entirely true. But the most damning secrets left within the walls of the Institute were secure enough, hidden in two places. In the safe in her office and in the brain of Anna Chutesov herself.

And so the men worked and Anna sat.

She was a stunningly beautiful woman. Her high-cheekboned features, eyes of ice-blue and a fringe of honey-blond hair were the perfect camouflage for the mind within. Anna's looks could draw men like moths to a flame, but it was her intelligence that kept them coming back.

Right now, Anna's keen mind was trained on but one thought. How long had it been since the world had collapsed?

Was it three days? A week? She couldn't even be sure precisely when it occurred. Couldn't pinpoint a moment. She only knew that it had happened during her ill-fated trip to the United States.

For a time in the last great days of the Cold War, Anna Chutesov had been one of the Soviet Union's top agents and adviser to a succession of Soviet leaders. Though professionally she had always been at the top of her game, she retired from active field duty under a very personal cloud. On her last mission some thirteen years ago, Anna faked her own death and went underground. After her return from the West, she assumed a top-secret post back in Moscow. She became head of the mysterious Institute.

And there she worked in darkness, squirreled away from the prying eyes of a world that thought her dead.

But her years in seclusion didn't last. Despite her plans, circumstances forced her back into the field.

She recently journeyed to America to eliminate a former Russian general whose crazed actions threatened to expose one of the most dangerous and shameful secrets in her country's recent history. The mission was fraught with peril, and eventually brought Anna face-to-face with the very thing that had caused her to flee her former life.

While in California to track down General Boris Feyodov, Anna bumped into Remo Williams, an American agent with whom she had once had an intimate relationship.

Anna had always harbored a fear of seeing Remo after all these years. She assumed he would be unforgiving of, even hostile to, her deception. But to her surprise he was remarkably accepting. Especially given the fact that it was because of him she had feigned death so long ago.

Anna soon came to realize that Remo had changed in their years apart. It was a subtle thing that he himself probably didn't see, but he had a self-confidence that was absent before. He'd always been cocky. Aggravatingly so. But now he had the self-assuredness to back it up.

No, in her mission to stop Boris Feyodov, the worst thing wasn't seeing Remo again. The most terrible, frightening thing happened thousands of miles away— here, in Moscow. In the big concrete Institute building.

Upon her return, Anna found the building open wide. The chains that wrapped the main gates, which were meant to be locked in perpetuity, were cut.

Fortunately, the Institute had a reputation in the surrounding neighborhood of Kitai Gorod. It had sprung from the dying days of the Soviet empire when mobs demanding freedom had taken to the streets.

At that time all government buildings were coming under attack. Though the nature of what went on inside was unknown, the Institute would not be spared. But when angry crowds began to swarm the streets outside, demanding an end to seventy years of failed Communist rule, something strange began to happen. People started dropping dead.

There were no soldiers visible or bullets fired. The windows to the building were sealed, preventing the use of more exotic weapons by the faceless men hidden away inside. But still the bodies in the street piled up.

Some in the mob feared gas or some form of chemical weapon. Most dismissed this as unlikely, for whatever it was seemed to kill indiscriminately. A man would drop dead while his friends on either side were spared. And so an explanation was quickly decided on by the people of Kitai Gorod. The big sinister building with no windows and a chain around the only door was quite obviously haunted. During the days of civil unrest that brought an end to the Soviet era, the mobs began to cut a wide swath around the Institute and the deadly spirits that dwelled inside.

Anna had always found the superstitions embarrassing. Such ludicrous notions were the reason much of the world saw Russia as a backward nation. But when she returned three days ago to find the gates wide open to the street, she was thankful for the big ugly building's reputation. These days an open door in Russia was an invitation to looters and squatters and virtually everyone else in this crumbling, lawless society. Fear of the supernatural was the only thing that kept the people from sneaking in through the open door and stealing the nails from out of the very walls.

Not to say there was nothing to be afraid of at the Institute. It was only the fear of a building that she found ludicrous. After all, a building was just a building. For Anna Chutesov, the true thing to fear was that which had escaped into the world through that wide-open door.

After getting over her initial shock at the security breach, Anna realized she had to report this terrible news. On a good day it was a risky proposition to attempt to use the Moscow telephone system. On this day it could have been suicidal. Anna sped to the Kremlin.

She was ushered into a paneled conference room that would have been stylish in the early 1960s, but was now hopelessly out-of-date. She had left that old-fashioned room only one hour before. The president of Russia still sat at the desk where she'd left him, a celebratory vodka bottle at his elbow. His sharp eyes smiled up at Anna Chutesov.

"Ah, you have changed your mind," the president slurred. "You have decided to join me for a drink after all."

He fetched her a glass from a silver tray.

"No, sir, I have not," Anna had announced crisply. "I have come to report a danger. Perhaps the greatest threat to ever face our country."

The president's thin eyebrows rose skeptically. "Russia has faced down many threats," he said. "The Tartars, the Troubled Times, the *Narodnaya Volya*. The worst threat ever was stopped by you yourself just this week."

Anna didn't bother to explain to him that the things he had named from Russia's history were far worse than the recent events that had occupied her in America.

He waved his empty glass. Anna noted how small his fingers were. Like a child's.

"If this is your attempt, Anna Chutesov, to increase funding to the Institute, I am sorry to say that it is not possible. There is no more money to be found in all of Russia. Despite your stellar work in this crisis, you already receive a generous part of the secret budget."

Anna shook her head. "This is not about money," she insisted. "Only an idiot would use a crisis of this magnitude to attempt to extort a budgetary increase."

The president neglected to mention that he was forever hearing complaints from cabinet officials, each one declaring a greater crisis than the last, each assuring the president that this whatever-it-was crisis could only be solved by more money. Directed, of course, at each official's own agency.

He didn't say any of this because he was speaking to Anna Chutesov, one of the brightest minds he had ever encountered. Not only would she already know all this, it wasn't in her nature to state anything other than cold, hard facts. That was part of her appeal as an adviser.

Despite his earlier reservations, the president sat up straighter. He set his glass to his desk with a click.

"What is wrong?" he asked.

"Only the worst crisis to befall our country since our earliest wars with the Byzantine Empire."

As those dire words were sinking in, she quickly informed him of her discovery at the Institute.

"I scoured the entire building before coming here," she concluded urgently. "They were nowhere to be found."

At last beginning to grasp the nature of the problem, the president of Russia touched his tongue to his thin upper lip.

"As I understand it, you kept them confined for years. Perhaps they have gone to visit friends or family members. It is possible they will be back."

"No," Anna said firmly. "They were not prisoners. They were allowed several weeks of leave every year. And they knew where the special entrance was. The fact that they did not use it is not insignificant. Furthermore, the fact that the chain was broken and the gate was left open was a sign."

"From whom?" the president asked.

Anna shook her head gravely. "I do not know," she replied. "For security purposes there were no cameras inside, so I don't know what happened during my absence. I only know that which I found upon my return. And it puts not only me in danger, but you and the previous two occupants of your office, as well, for they knew of this. It is not an understatement, sir, to say that with them on the loose, our nation is at risk like never before."

But although the president appeared to understand the problem, he did not—could not—grasp its full enormity.

"World War II, Anna Chutesov," he said, shaking his head. "There were Germans within spitting distance of Moscow. That was a true threat to Russia. This cannot possibly be compared to the great dangers of our history."

But Anna's ice-blue eyes never wavered. "If that is your attitude, Mr. President," she insisted ominously, "you do not truly understand the peril we now face."

And with no further way to impress the gravity of this situation on the president of Russia, Anna gave up. She returned to the empty Institute building to sit in the shadows on the floor of the musty old gymnasium and listen to the workmen far away.

As she was staring into the dusty corner, she heard

the sounds of voices approaching. Two men came into the gym from the dark hallway. They carted with them an old dresser lying atop a rusted bed. Another man followed in their wake. The pushcart he rolled before him was stacked high with eight surplus Red Army footlockers. The wheels of the dolly squeaked as it rolled past Anna.

"Are you certain of this?" one of the men carrying the old bed asked Anna. He was no more than fifty, but looked eighty. Such was the toll taken on the human body and spirit in the modern Russia. The veins in his swollen nose were broken from years of too much drink.

Anna didn't even look up. She was staring somewhere near their shoes. She nodded.

"All of the beds, bureaus, nightstands. Take it all," she said darkly.

Anna didn't bother to tell them that she had removed and burned anything incriminating from the footlockers. Nor would they care. She had picked these men at random from the streets and offered them all of the furniture inside the Institute free of charge. They were eager to get the pieces out of the building and to the bazaar before she changed her mind.

Hurrying through the gymnasium, they headed out the far door. It led to the underground parking garage, which fed out to the street through the gate that was no longer locked.

As they were carting their prizes away, another man entered from the interior door.

He didn't move like the men with the furniture.

There was no huffing and puffing and stomping of feet. He walked with a more confident glide, like that of a ballet dancer. Indeed, he had been drafted from the ranks of the Bolshoi.

When he stopped before her, Anna's eyes rose reluctantly to meet his. He was thin and short, with delicate features and a slightly receding hairline.

"I may have found something," the man offered hopefully.

Anna didn't bother to mention how unlikely that was. It was too soon. No one—not even a man—would be fool enough to show his hand this quickly.

"Yes, Sergei?" she asked with a reluctant sigh.

"It is a news story from the Internet. A number of men have turned up dead in Alaska. Oil pipeline workers and soldiers. Their killers are unknown."

Anna considered his words. As she was thinking, the three men returned from the street. They wheeled the empty dolly into the gymnasium.

"More, Sergei," Anna said. "We need more than that."

The young man seemed to want to say more, but the three men with the cart were passing by. Sergei kept his mouth shut until they had squeaked back through the door into the main building. Once they were gone, he turned back to Anna.

"There is more," he promised. "There was a helicopter pilot who dropped off the soldiers. When he came back to retrieve them, he claims to have seen an army of ghosts."

This got Anna's attention. Blinking, she looked up

at the young man. "Explain," she insisted, her voice flat.

"He swears they were there, and then they were not," Sergei said excitedly. "He saw a group of soldiers briefly from the air, then they—poof—vanished from sight."

Anna's face steeled. Her jaw firmly clenched, she scampered to her feet.

Perhaps she was wrong. Perhaps whoever was behind this was dumber than she thought. Or mad to tip his hand so soon. One thing was certain: if this was genuine, whoever was responsible was most definitely a man. No woman on Earth would ever be so big a fool.

"Show me this story," Anna Chutesov commanded.

And her strained voice was filled with equal parts hope and dread.

7

So as not to lose the respect of the men under his command, Colonel Robert Hogue made a supreme effort to not vomit on the Eskimo's head. It wasn't easy.

As a young private, Hogue had served in Vietnam. He had seen plenty bad back then. But that was long ago. The inaction of the intervening years had dulled the horrors of youth. Time was apparently a great healer, even for a set of tired eyes that had seen as much as Colonel Robert Hogue's.

The rural town of Kakwik, Alaska, was bringing it all back with a vengeance.

The houses in the remote Eskimo village on the shore of the Yukon River were little more than steel drums. Fingers of thin black smoke still curled from chimney pipes, tickling the snowflakes that slipped down from the pale pink clouds. And all around the squalid village, the dead jutted from freshly fallen snow like gutted ice sculptures.

Colonel Hogue had nearly tripped over the first body as he and the eighty National Guard troops under his command were marching past the isolated town. The discovery of that one half-frozen corpse had led them here. Once in Kakwik, their routine maneuvers suddenly turned deadly serious.

Two dozen bodies were arranged in a gruesome tableau alongside the main road of the village. Stomach cavities were split open and throats were slashed. Blood froze black. Dead eyes, pried wide open, stared unseeing at the troops as they passed. Snowflakes collected on lash and lid.

At the sight of the bodies, a few of the National Guardsmen lost their lunch in the newly fallen snow.

Colonel Hogue forged on, fighting his own urge to vomit.

The bodies along the road had been arranged as if for review. Near a particularly dilapidated home, Hogue noticed another body, separate from the rest. He cautiously left the road, ducking between a pair of corpses.

The kitchen door was open on the nearest battered tin house. It looked as if the old man who lived there had been shot as he came out the door, then fell down the four wooden stairs of his small porch. Whoever had arranged the other bodies had simply forgotten him there.

The Colonel bent to examine the old man.

The Eskimo wore a pair of tattered red long johns and orange socks. Fresh snow, like a scattering of pixie dust, dulled the dark colors.

"Check the homes," Hogue barked as he stooped over the body. "And stay sharp."

Ever alert to danger, the National Guardsmen dispersed, moving in packs from house to house. As the men began fanning out, Hogue turned back to the lone body.

The Eskimo's milky white eyes were frozen glass. A single tap would shatter them into a million fragments. With his head tipped to one side and his arm extended, the dead man seemed to be staring at something. Almost begging understanding from beyond the grave.

With a frown Hogue got down in the snow next to the body. He followed the dead man's line of sight.

"What the hell?" Hogue whispered to himself.

Climbing back to his knees, he crawled around the body.

The dead man's blue hand extended to the base of the stairs. Colonel Hogue pulled out a flashlight. Lying flat on his belly, he directed the beam under the bottom step.

"Damn," he swore softly.

"Colonel?"

The voice came from above. Hogue rolled over onto his shoulder. A sergeant stood above him, his curious face framed by a drab ski mask.

"Take a look at this," Hogue said worriedly.

Confused, the sergeant got down on his belly, crowding in beside the Colonel at the base of the steps. He followed the yellow flashlight beam that Hogue shone on the wood.

The sergeant grunted in surprise.

"It looks like this man was trying to leave a message," Hogue said. "My guess is he didn't die right away and he heard his killers while they were doing that." He nodded back to where the rows of frozen bodies welcomed the stout of heart into Kakwik.

The sergeant frowned as he studied the bottom step.

A shape had been drawn in wet blood—now frozen—on the wood. A simple rectangle sat on a shaft, bisected at the midpoint by an arc.

"What do you think it means?" the sergeant asked.

Hogue shook his head. "It doesn't look like anything to you?" he asked leadingly.

"Well, sir," the sergeant said reluctantly, "I don't wanna sound like a paranoid product of the Cold War, but that looks like a hammer and sickle to me. I must be wrong, though. The Russkies haven't had a stake in Alaska in more than a hundred years."

Before the sergeant could even finish, Colonel Hogue was scurrying back to his feet, a fresh sense of urgency to his ruddy face. The sergeant had confirmed his worst fears.

"Get the men back here," he ordered urgently. "Get them back here *now*."

A sharp noise in the distance was followed by an angry shout. Hogue felt his stomach sink. He wheeled around.

The first gunshot was followed by others. The men under his command were yelling in panic.

The Colonel was helpless to stop it. Alone in an isolated Alaskan village facing an enemy from another age, Colonel Robert Hogue felt the youthful ghosts of Vietnam pounce from the recesses of his frightened brain.

And as the devil danced, Hell erupted anew on the slumbering streets of Kakwik.

8

His meeting with Smith went on for another hour after Remo and Chiun had left. When Mark Howard finally glanced at his watch, it was closing in on 9:00 a.m.

"I hate to interrupt, Dr. Smith, but I'll have to get going soon if I'm going to make that flight."

He was sitting in a hard, straight-backed chair across the desk from the CURE director. Smith looked at his own trusty Timex.

"I had not realized it had gotten so late," he said. Gripping the edge of his desk, he rolled back his chair. "Here is your identification." He took a laminated tag from his top drawer and slid it across the desk. "There will be no problem gaining admittance, especially at such a hectic time as this. Do your work quickly and get out. Once you are done, return to Folcroft immediately. Do not attempt to contact any old acquaintances while you are there."

"I understand," Howard said with a tight nod.

He half stood from his chair, leaning over to take the ID card. As soon as he'd gotten to his feet, he felt a sudden rush of blood to his head.

"Whoa," Mark said, grabbing on to the edge of the big black desk for support.

Smith's gray face puckered in concern. "Are you all right?" he asked.

"Yes," Howard nodded. "Yeah, I'm fine. Just stood up a little too fast, I guess." He shook the dizzy sensation away. "I'm sorry, Dr. Smith, but what were you saying about Alaska?"

Smith frowned. "Excuse me?" he asked.

"You said something when I was getting up, didn't you?"

"No," Smith said. "I did not."

A flush seemed to grow faintly in the young man's wide face. The generally confident demeanor he had displayed over the past few days seemed to erode before Smith's eyes.

"Oh," Howard muttered, vaguely flustered. "I just— Oh, okay." He picked up the ID, stuffing it in his breast pocket. "I'll...I'll give you a call when it's taken care of."

Across the desk, gaze suspicious, the CURE director pursed his lips. "If you do not feel equal to this, I can go myself," he said slowly.

"No, it's fine, I promise," Howard said, inching toward the door. "Besides, I don't think Remo is too crazy about me. It'd be safer for me to leave town for the day. I'll let you know."

With a reassuring smile he left the drab office.

Once Smith was alone, a dark notch formed behind the bridge of his glasses. His new assistant's sudden odd behavior probably wasn't anything to be concerned about. It could be chalked up to nerves. After all, this was all still very new to him. And his earlier encounter with Remo doubtless hadn't helped.

Dark expression fading, the old man booted up his desk computer. Banishing thoughts of CURE's personnel, Harold W. Smith quickly lost himself in the more manageable—and thus more agreeable—realm of cyberspace.

IN THE TIDY outer office of Smith's secretary, Mark Howard breathed a heavy sigh as he slumped back against the door.

Luckily, Mrs. Mikulka wasn't in the room. He tried to gather his fragmented thoughts.

He wasn't sure what had just happened in there. Something had come to him. A strong sense of...

Well, of what he didn't know. Not exactly, anyway.

His mind now clearing, Mark checked his watch.

He wouldn't have to leave to catch his plane for another twenty minutes. There was still time to do a little digging.

Mark pushed away from the door.

"Damn spider-sense," he muttered to himself.

Leaving the room, he hurried down the hallway to his office. To see what—if anything—was going on in Alaska.

9

Blind panic blazed like wildfire across the snowy streets of Kakwik. Forty of Colonel Robert Hogue's men had been slaughtered in the initial attack. The stink of blood swamped the frozen air.

As the dead multiplied, those still living loosed blind bursts of automatic-weapons fire into empty air.

There were no targets to hit. Between the shadows and the snow and the perpetual gloom of the swollen twilight sky, Hogue and his men were fighting ghosts.

At first it was gunfire. Blinding flashes like focused lightning screamed from out of the thinning snowstorm.

Barking orders all the way, Hogue and his remaining National Guard troops sought refuge behind the tin walls of the Kakwik hovels. Crouching, frightened, they waited as the gunfire stopped and silence descended once more on Kakwik.

The sergeant who had recognized the old hammer-and-sickle design squatted behind Hogue.

When the silence lingered too long, the two men peeked around the side of the house. Light dribbled onto the main drag from the shanty homes. Steam rose from freshly killed bodies.

"Maybe they're—" the sergeant whispered.

Hogue threw up a silencing hand. His ears were trained on the Alaskan night. For an instant he swore he'd heard the crunch of a foot on fresh snow.

A blur of movement. Something flashing through the snow just before his eyes. Almost simultaneously came a startled intake of air from the sergeant.

Hogue's head snapped around. One of the sergeant's eyes was open wide in shock. The other eye was nowhere to be seen. In its place was a dripping cavity where an invisible knife had plunged deep into brain.

With a hiss of air, the sergeant flopped to the snow.

And as he fell, the slaughter began anew.

Men screamed and bodies fell, trails of blood staining snow to red slush.

Guns vanished, yanked from hands by invisible demons.

No. Not invisible. As Hogue watched in impotent horror he saw a masked man here, another there. Spiraling, pivoting. Always away from gun or bayonet.

In no time the forty remaining soldiers were cut to twenty, then ten. When the white-haired man with the red-flecked brown eyes finally appeared from the dwindling storm, ten had become four. Including Colonel Hogue.

A terrified soldier lunged screaming at the apparition. His head bounced to the ground as his body made a beeline for a snowbank.

Colonel Hogue couldn't believe how fast the stranger had moved. His eyes had barely registered the death of the first soldier before the other two were rushing forward.

Another lost his head.

For an instant while the latest body dropped, the white-haired man seemed to lose his footing on the snow. But if that was the case, he quickly regained it.

The final Alaska National Guard soldier was thrusting with his bayonet when he became aware of a lightness to his hand. He quickly realized that the lightness stemmed from the fact that he no longer had a hand. His wrist now ended in a raw stump. His hand, still clutching his knife, lay in the snow at his feet. The soldier had no time to ponder the horror of what had just transpired. As he stared down numbly at his own severed appendage, he was finished off with a punishing blow to the forehead.

As the crumpled body fell, the white-haired young man turned slowly to Colonel Robert Hogue.

Behind him came the others, dressed now in snow-white fatigues. Black goggles and ski masks covering their faces, they swarmed in like ants around their queen.

The Colonel backed against the nearest shanty, breathing puffs of frightened white steam into the cold air.

"Who are you?" Colonel Hogue demanded.

The white-haired man smiled.

"I am the Master," he said in an accent that was unmistakably Russian. "You need know me by no other name. I have been sent to give you notice that your days of sowing decadence are over. Tell those

who hold your leash that the Soviet Union has re-
claimed Russian America.'' His eyes took on the demented glint of a zealot. ''Long live the new Sotsi-
alisticheskikh Respublik,'' the Master said coldly.

And as Colonel Hogue felt his blood run to ice, the
white-haired Russian flashed a toothy smile.

In spite of his great fear, the Army Colonel couldn't
help but notice that this fearsome fighter with the
flashing deadly hands was, at least in one small way,
a typical Russian. Even after ten years without communism, with access to all the bounty the West had
to offer, there apparently still wasn't one damn tooth-
brush or tube of Crest in the whole godforsaken Bol-
shevik country.

10

Mark Howard gained entry to the White House through the Old Executive Office Building. He followed subterranean corridors to the main mansion.

Men and women swarmed busily all around him. Some were hired guns who were still on hand to help with the transition from the previous administration, but most had the fresh-faced, starry-eyed look of political ideologues.

With his bland young Midwestern face, Mark fit right in. No one gave him so much as a second glance on his way through the labyrinthine tunnel system.

He clutched a small black valise tightly in one hand. It looked neither new nor old, just ordinary. His knuckles were clenched white, and the handle was slick with sweat.

His first visit to the White House had been just a few weeks before. That was as a CIA analyst, when he had gone to the West Wing for an Oval Office meeting with the outgoing President. This time everything was different: his purpose, the President, the agency Mark worked for, even his identity itself. The laminated ID tag Smith had issued him was clipped to his jacket.

The tag identified him as a telephone company official with high security clearance. The badge looked real enough. Mark hoped it was good enough to fool the pros.

Heart thudding, Mark followed the memorized route to the small West Wing elevator. A Secret Service agent stood at the closed door, a white wire threaded from collar to ear.

Mark did his best to hide his anxiety as the agent carefully studied his ID. After a glance at the nervous young man before him, the agent handed back the card.

"Open your bag, please, sir," the agent said. If he was suspicious, it didn't show. His voice was perfectly modulated, with not a hint of inflection.

Mark obediently thumbed open the tabs on the valise.

As the Secret Service man picked through the materials inside, Mark clipped his tag back to his jacket. After a perfunctory search, the agent handed the bag back.

"Left off the elevator, sir," he announced as he pressed the button. The elevator doors slid open. "Another agent will be there to accompany you."

"Thanks," Mark said with an anxious smile. Bag in hand, he stepped onto the car.

The agent followed him with his eyes. "First time at the White House?" he asked abruptly.

Mark was surprised at how easy the lie came.

The young man exhaled. "I guess it shows, huh?" Howard said.

The Secret Service agent nodded. "Sometimes I still find it intimidating," he offered. As the doors slid shut there was just a hint of a knowing smile.

Once the doors were closed, Mark took a deep breath. The car whisked him up to the First Family residence.

The agent downstairs was wrong. When the doors slid open there was no one waiting for Mark. An order to abandon the family quarters had been issued to all Secret Service personnel on this floor. The command had come from the highest level at the Treasury Department. All agents were to stay out for two hours while national-security experts updated the White House satellite system.

Of course it was a lie. Feeling like the only man inside the most famous residence on Earth, Mark followed the wide, empty corridor to the Lincoln Bedroom.

Going to the nightstand next to the bed, Mark opened the bottom drawer. He pulled out a cherry-red telephone that sat inside. Unclipping the cord from the back, he placed the phone on the bed.

Mark drew the cord through a hole in the back of the drawer and followed it to a silver wall plate behind the bed. Detaching the other end of the cord from the wall, he quickly retrieved a screwdriver from his bag. Removing the phone-jack plate, he replaced it with a blank one.

There would be no problem with someone removing the plate at a later date and tapping into this line. Once he removed the phone, the line had already been rerouted. The Lincoln Bedroom phone line was now officially dead.

Dropping the old plate and cord into his bag, Mark picked up both bag and phone.

Where he'd placed it on the bed, the dialless red phone had left a square imprint in the quilt. Sticking the phone up under his arm, Mark smoothed the wrinkles flat with one hand.

He glanced around the nightstand area. Everything appeared to be as he left it. He crossed to the door.

Casting one last look at the stately room that during the Civil War had been President Lincoln's cluttered office, Mark hurried out into the hallway. Unfortunately, in his haste to leave the Lincoln Bedroom, he collided with the man who was rushing into the room from the hall.

When the two men collided, the President of the United States went one way and Mark went the other.

With a grunt Mark fell against the door frame. He lost the red phone from under his arm. It struck the floor hard, the receiver spilling off the cradle. The bell inside gave a muffled tinkle as the phone bounced across the carpet.

The President had fallen to his backside. Lost in thought, he had been hurrying along with his head down. He seemed shocked that anyone was in the residence.

"Oh, it's you," the leader of the free world said.

"I'm so sorry, sir," Mark apologized. He hustled over, helping the President to his feet.

"What are you doing here?" the President asked.

He spotted the red phone on the carpet. "Where are you going with that?" he demanded.

"You requested that the phone be moved to your bedroom, Mr. President," Howard said nervously.

"Oh. That's right," the President said. "Well, hurry up and get it hooked up. I need to talk to your boss."

Fumbling the receiver back into the cradle, Mark scooped up the phone. With the President in the lead, the two men hurried down the hall to the presidential bedroom.

According to Dr. Smith, the phone had been in this room years ago. Even through various renovations and several administrations, the CURE director had been careful to issue circuitous orders that the old wall jack not be removed, lest it become necessary to reuse the old line.

Howard found the blank silver plate behind the bed. He reversed the process from the Lincoln Bedroom, installing a female plate on the wall. He ran the line through a hole in the back of the nightstand's bottom drawer before plugging the red phone back in.

Mark lifted the receiver to test.

There was no dial tone. For an instant he thought he'd broken the phone when he'd dropped it, but an abrupt ringing sounded on the other end of the line. It was answered before the first ring was over.

"Yes," said the lemony voice of Harold Smith.

"It's me," Mark said. "The phone's been moved."

The President held out an impatient hand. "Let me have him," he insisted.

"Very good," Smith said to Howard. "I have already deactivated the line into the Lincoln Bedroom. Please return—"

"Um, Dr. Smith," Mark broke in, "there's someone here who wants to speak to you."

The President was already pulling the phone out of Howard's hand. "Hi, Smith," he announced. His laconic nasal voice was eerily reminiscent of his father's, who had served as president a decade ago. "I realize we just got through that mess in Barkley, but there's something my advisers just mentioned that might need to be checked out by you folks."

"Yes, Mr. President?" Smith asked.

The President sat down on the edge of the bed. "As I understand it, there have been a number of deaths," he said seriously. "Now, as much as it pains me to say this, that's not what has me most worried. It's the oil. After the trouble with skyrocketing prices last year, we can't afford to have anyone tampering with domestic production."

"What is the problem, sir?" Smith asked.

"This is where it gets dicey," the President admitted. "We've got an eyewitness account, but I don't know how credible it is. Some helicopter pilot or something. His story is pretty crazy sounding. But no matter what, it's clear that someone, for some reason, has disrupted the oil flow through the Alaska Pipeline."

Kneeling on the floor, Mark Howard had been gathering up odds and ends into his bag. At the mention of Alaska, Mark's grip tightened on the screwdriver in his hand.

Before leaving for Washington, he had spent as much time researching as he possibly could. As it was, he had barely made his flight on time. For the little time he had managed to put in, he had come up empty.

Mark had hoped to do more searching once he'd returned to Folcroft. Now it seemed it wouldn't be necessary.

As he finished cleaning up, he listened carefully to the President's side of the conversation.

Apparently, there was a crisis brewing in Alaska after all. Mark only hoped that Harold W. Smith wasn't as attentive to detail as he seemed. With any luck, the CURE director would not even remember that Mark had mentioned Alaska that very morning. And if he did? Well, Mark would have to cross that bridge when he came to it.

As he knelt on the bedroom floor of the President of the United States, Mark only hoped that—if the time ever came where he had to make a confession—his honesty wouldn't get him a one-way ticket to a Folcroft rubber room.

11

Remo spent the long day driving aimlessly through the streets of Rye. When midnight came, he parked by the shore. For hours he stared blankly at the endless black waves of Long Island Sound.

At this point he no longer expected illumination for whatever it was that vexed him. Chiun had told him that enlightenment would arrive in its own time, and he trusted the old Korean on that count. But this knowledge alone wasn't enough to suspend the nagging feeling that he'd forgotten something of great importance. And this latest baggage certainly wasn't helping matters any.

Lately, everything seemed a complication for Remo. Smith's new assistant was just more piling onto the mess that had once been Remo's life.

It wasn't Mark Howard's involvement in the organization that was the problem. Remo had told the young man about the two others who had, at different times, briefly taken charge of the agency. But there were two more who had played roles at CURE in the past. Conrad MacCleary and Ruby Gonzalez had each assisted Harold Smith in different ways at different times. Remo had thought they were both okay. It was what Howard represented that most bothered Remo.

Change.

He wasn't ready to deal with it. Didn't want to think about it. Yet lately his life kept stubbornly coming back to that one word.

Alone with his thoughts, he stared into the waves of the Sound. Only when the light of dawn began to streak the sky did Remo realize he'd sat in his car all night.

With a troubled sigh he turned the key in the ignition.

He returned to Folcroft in the wee hours. Smith had not yet arrived for work when Remo parked his car and headed inside. Sneaking downstairs to his quarters, he was relieved to find the Master of Sinanju still asleep. The nightly buzz saw that was Chiun's snoring issued from beyond the old Korean's closed bedroom door.

Remo slipped through the dark communal room and into his own bedroom, shutting the door gently. He kicked off his loafers and settled to his simple tatami sleeping mat.

For a few seconds he listened to the soft sounds of Folcroft.

Nurses walked distant hallways. Toilets flushed and water sloshed through ancient pipes. Muted rumblings and bangs came from the cafeteria as the staff began the breakfast ritual. All these sounds carried to his sensitive ears. The same sounds might have been made at the sanitarium that fateful day three decades ago, when an idealistic young beat cop had awakened to a new life and a new identity.

In the quiet of his room, Remo took some small comfort in the timeless sounds of that old brick building. Embracing a rare moment of peace, he closed his eyes and allowed his body to drift off to sleep.

Ten seconds after he shut his eyes, the snoring in the next room abruptly ceased.

"Oh, crud," Remo groaned.

The light in the communal room snapped on, spilling under Remo's closed door.

Reaching up in the dark, he pulled a pillow from the unused bed that had been there when he moved in. He wrapped it around his head, pressing it tight to his ears.

No sooner was the pillow in place than the clanging began. Chiun banged around the stove for a time, slamming pots and rattling pans. After a few minutes Remo couldn't take it anymore.

"I'm trying to sleep in here," he complained loudly.

"Oh, is that you, Remo?" Chiun's disembodied voice called back. "When you did not come home last night, I assumed you had moved out."

"Very funny," Remo said. "You heard me come in."

"I thought that some vagrant flimflammer had won your room from you in one of the all-night gambling houses you frequent while prowling the mean streets."

"I wasn't gambling, I was thinking," Remo muttered.

"Believe me, the way you think, it's gambling," Chiun called knowingly. The banging resumed.

Remo took some encouragement from the fact that the old Asian was still talking to him. The way he'd left things yesterday, Remo had been sure he'd be getting the silent treatment for the next six months.

Moreover, it seemed as if Chiun wanted Remo to get up. This became clear when, over the course of the next forty-five seconds, the wizened Korean dropped the heavy cast-iron teapot seventeen times.

"A for effort, Little Father," Remo grunted, unwrapping the pillow from his ears. He rolled to his feet.

When he opened the door, he found the Master of Sinanju fussing with the small boom box that sat on the counter of their shared kitchenette. The old man raised a dull eye.

"Oh, you are up," Chiun commented.

"It's hard to sleep with you reenacting the Battle of the Bulge out here," Remo said. His eyes instantly alighted on the low kitchen table. Spread across the taboret were a dozen real-estate pamphlets. "Oh, brother," he exhaled.

Chiun followed his gaze. "Ah," he said, nodding. "I left those there, as you requested."

Remo offered him a gimlet eye.

"I didn't ask for those, so don't try to *Gaslight* me on this one, because I'm not in the mood."

"I am not surprised. After catting around all night, it is a wonder you can lift your head at all."

"It wasn't through any choice of my own," Remo said to himself as he gathered up the pamphlets.

With a flourish Chiun spun from the small stereo. As the device squawked to cacophonous life, the old man plucked the pamphlets from his pupil's hand.

"I will put these away for later," he said.

"Make it much later," Remo said. "And I'm already up. No need to torture me by playing Wylander Jugg."

This was the country music singer for whom the Master of Sinanju had recently developed a fondness. On the counter Wylander continued to yodel from the unlucky speakers.

"You would deny me this one pleasure? After all I have done for you and all you have done to me?"

"You bet," Remo said. He winced as Wylander tried to stretch her larynx for a note hopelessly out of reach.

"Too bad for you," Chiun said. "Breakfast is in ten minutes. Wash your hands, for I suspect I know where you spent your night." He turned to the stove.

Remo did as he was told without argument.

As he washed up in the bathroom sink he heard the sound of Smith's car wheezing and coughing its way into the parking lot far above. The old station wagon seemed to worsen with every winter, yet it continued to hang on.

Remo did his best not to read too much into that idle thought. Drying his hands, he returned to the kitchenette.

Chiun was tapping rice into a pair of stoneware

bowls with a wooden spoon. Two wedges of orange sat on each of their place mats. Remo took note of the fruit slices with a puzzled frown.

Their training limited them to a diet of rice and fish and, less often, duck. Vegetables were infrequent and fruit—which was high in natural sugar—was hardly ever eaten.

"Why fruit?" Remo asked, kneeling at the low table.

"I have not had any in several months," Chiun replied. "And you cannot remember the last time you had any at all."

Remo's frown deepened. The old Korean was right. He couldn't recall.

Placing the pot of rice on a pot holder, the Master of Sinanju knelt across the table from his pupil.

As they ate, the rising winter sun warmed the sleepy ivy-covered building on the shores of Long Island Sound.

Remo was grateful that Chiun didn't try to engage him in conversation.

The Master of Sinanju knew his pupil well. The few cross words they'd exchanged the previous day hadn't been taken to heart. This meal was a gift. A balm for the troubled soul of his adopted son.

Remo was actually starting to enjoy the moment when he heard the hurried footsteps approach from the hall.

Because of one arthritic knee, Harold Smith tended to favor one leg over the other, although it was undetectable in his gait to anyone but Remo and Chiun.

The person in the hall had no such problem. Whoever this was, it wasn't Smith.

Remo assumed it was someone on the regular Folcroft staff, until the person stopped outside his door.

A sharp knock.

Remo was enjoying his meal too much to be bothered.

"We're not here," he called.

"Remo?" a hushed voice said. "Remo, it's Mark Howard."

Remo's face soured. "We're even more not here," he said to the closed door.

But it was too late. Across the table from Remo, the Master of Sinanju's thin, venous eyelids fluttered wide.

"Please, by all means, honor us with your presence, Prince Mark," Chiun sang happily, rising like a puff of delighted steam. "Be civil," he hissed at Remo just as the door opened and Mark Howard's worried face peeked inside.

The young man took special note of Remo, still kneeling on the floor at the taboret, his back to the door. Standing at the table, Chiun bowed deeply.

"Welcome to my humble chambers, sweet prince."

Howard nodded as he closed the door. "Good morning, Master Chiun," he said anxiously.

"Your blessing is at once superfluous and inadequate," Chiun assured him, "for your being here with us does itself make a good morning great."

"He's not frigging Tony the Tiger," Remo complained.

It was as if Chiun didn't hear. "See, Remo," he said to his pupil. "Look and learn from a real nobleman. A true prince of the realm, he understands instinctively the value of his royal assassin, bowing and offering blessings on my day. Though barely weaned, he knows well the lessons of proper approbation."

Remo didn't turn around. "Not seeing. Caring even less," he said as he continued to eat.

His eyes trained warily on Remo, Mark took a few tentative steps into the main living room.

"I hate to bother you so early, but there's a situation in Alaska," the young man began.

"A most grave matter," Chiun intoned solemnly.

"Possibly," Howard said. "The details aren't entirely clear yet."

Chiun nodded, his wrinkled face a deeply concerned frown.

"Still, how considerable must this potential danger be for the future master of Fortress Folcroft to descend from his lofty perch rather than dispatch a footman. Your somber mien does augur great risk to the Eagle Throne and to the precious Constitution, which we are sworn to defend. Speak, dear prince, of the threat to our one lord, Emperor Smith."

Howard seemed somewhat put off by the Korean's flowery words and tone. "Um, it actually started a couple of days—"

Chiun's face suddenly brightened. "Do you want some tea?" he interrupted.

"What? No. No, thank you."

"I would like some," Chiun said firmly.

The Master of Sinanju promptly spun away from Howard, marching over to the gas stove.

Howard stood alone in the center of the room. "Um," he said uncertainly, clearing his throat.

"Go on," Chiun encouraged as he began fussing like a mother hen at the stove. "Your every word is a drop of rain upon the arid land of unworthy ears." In the cupboard now, he made an unhappy clucking sound with his tongue. "Have you seen my cup?" he asked Remo.

"Nope. There's a bunch more in the cupboard, though."

Chiun clearly wasn't happy with the idea of using an inferior teacup. He began scouring all the cupboards in the kitchenette.

Mark could see he wasn't making progress with the Master of Sinanju. Reluctantly, he turned his attention to Remo.

"There have been several—"

Remo didn't let him get any further.

"Save your breath, Howdy Doody," he said. "I don't go anywhere unless Smith says so."

Chiun had found his favorite cup. He returned from the stove with it steaming full of tea.

"That is true," the old Korean said, sinking to the floor near the table. "We are contractually bound to Emperor Smith and to Smith alone. However, do not let that stop you. You have such a lovely speaking voice. Very commanding, don't you think so, Remo?"

"We have any more rice?" Remo asked.

"Dr. Smith is the one who sent me to get you," Mark said, exasperated.

"Although your voice suddenly sounds strained," the Master of Sinanju said, concerned. "Are you sure you would not care for some tea? It is very soothing." He took a thoughtful sip.

"Can you two even *hear* me?" Howard asked.

"I'd like some," Remo said to the Master of Sinanju, ignoring Howard.

Chiun raised his cup to his wrinkled lips.

"It's all gone," he said.

HAROLD SMITH WAS scanning Mark Howard's most recent computer records—one curious eyebrow raised—when his office door sprang open. He glanced up as Remo marched into the room, his face a scowl. Chiun swept in beside the younger Master of Sinanju. Behind the two of them came Mark Howard.

Howard's youthful face was flushed as he closed the door behind them.

Before Remo could even speak, Chiun was interrupting.

"O gracious wholeness, Emperor Smith, who rules with virtuous majesty from within the mighty walls of Fortress Folcroft, Sinanju bids you good morning," he announced.

"Will you can that dippy ding-dong sucking-up already?" Remo said impatiently in Korean. "Smitty's indifferent to it, and the twerp's more weirded out than he is impressed by it."

"I am doing that which is necessary," the old man

replied in the same tongue. "Young princes like to hear pretty songs, especially when they are directed at the throne they one day hope to occupy."

As the Master of Sinanju sank cross-legged to the floor, Remo turned his full attention to Smith.

"Okay, what's the deal, Smitty? I think the kid was trying to ship us off to Alaska."

"That's not entirely true, Dr. Smith," Howard said, crossing the room. He angled the chair in front of the CURE director's desk so that he could see all three men.

"That is correct," Chiun interjected. "For he left out the part where I respectfully informed our young sire that we obey neither princes nor presidents. Sinanju is yours to direct and yours alone, Emperor."

"That remains true, Master Chiun," Smith nodded. "Our hierarchical structure is as it has always been. I merely asked Mark to get you because of a strange situation that is developing in Alaska. The President has filled me in on the broad details."

"Were not the details of females the concern of the roly-poly billhilly who preceded the current pretender to the crown?" Chiun asked.

"Figure of speech, Little Father," Remo said, sinking to the floor next to his teacher. "What's the story, Smitty?"

Smith placed his hands to his desk, his fingers interlocking. "Over the past few days there have been multiple attacks on both civilian and military targets in rural Alaska," the CURE director began. "The first was a group of Alaskan pipeline workers. The next was a state defense force team. They were slaughtered to a man by an enemy that, until yesterday, had not shown itself.'' Smith seemed to grow uncomfortable. ''At least not in such a way that I would be willing to trust a lone eyewitness account.''

''Why?'' Remo asked. ''What was it?''

''A small army,'' Mark Howard supplied.

Remo had been doing his best to ignore the young man. ''Good,'' he said. ''Send in our *big* army. I'll be at the tattoo parlor.''

He rose to a half squat but felt the pressure of a single bony finger on his thigh. With a sigh he dropped back to the floor.

''You're lucky I'm not in a body-cleaning mood,'' Remo said in a voice so low only the Master of Sinanju could hear.

''The first armed unit was put in place by helicopter near the murdered pipeline workers,'' Smith resumed. ''When the pilot returned, he saw what he has termed a, er, ghost army.''

''Ghost?'' Remo asked. He shot a look at the Master of Sinanju. The old Korean had grown more attentive.

Smith nodded gravely. ''He described a group of men who stood briefly among the dead as he flew over. He claims that, as he watched, the men vanished from sight. Fearing some supernatural force, he fled back to Fairbanks.''

''Sounds to me like he's got a couple of bent rotor blades,'' Remo said.

"Quiet, Remo," Chiun admonished. His alert hazel eyes were locked on Smith.

"My first impulse would be to agree with you, Remo," the CURE director said. "However, the ambushed ASDF unit wasn't alone. They were involved in joint exercises with the Alaska National Guard and the Army. A National Guard unit consisting of eighty men met a similar fate in the rural town of Kakwik. The sole survivor of that attack described a group of men who could hide in the open and kill at will."

"Hmm," Remo mused. "That sounds like us, doesn't it, Little Father?"

Chiun addressed Smith, not Remo. "We once encountered an invisible man," the old man said.

Remo was struck by the worry in his tone.

Smith nodded. "I considered that, too. But tests with the midnight-black paint were discontinued years ago. It was found that the molecular cohesion broke down over short periods of time. And we are not dealing with individuals who can hide only in darkness. Apparently, they can conceal themselves in daylight. Or, given the locale and time of year, partial light."

"You ever hear of ghosts that can kill, Chiun?" Remo asked.

"Well," Howard offered, reluctant to interrupt the comfortable dynamic of the three men, "it's obviously not ghosts, Remo." He waited for someone to agree with him.

Remo ignored Howard. His full attention was on the Master of Sinanju. Even Smith remained mute. Troubled, Howard turned his gaze to the old Korean.

His face unflinching, Chiun avoided Remo's eyes. "I would travel to this province alone, Emperor Smith," he announced levelly. "There is no reason for Remo to accompany me."

Remo's brow dropped. "Like fish," he said. "Why? What's wrong?"

"There is nothing wrong other than the fact that you are an obdurate contrarian," Chiun replied, his voice low. "Reserve one plane ticket, Emperor," he said, rising to his feet.

Remo got up, too. "Nothing doing. Make that two."

Chiun shot him an evil look. The old man's lips formed a razor-thin line of angry frustration.

"Sorry, Little Father," Remo said. "For you to get so jumpy, something must be wrong. If you won't spill the beans, I'm not letting you take off on your own. *Two* tickets, Smitty," he said emphatically.

"I'm not certain what your concern is, Master Chiun, but it is too soon to make any assumptions," Smith said reasonably. "We could merely be dealing with some kind of new technology at work here that allows these men to remain unseen until the moment of attack."

But the old Korean slowly shook his head. "It is not too soon," Chiun said, his voice ominous. "It is long overdue."

And the look on his face was such that both Smith and Remo knew enough at this point not to press further.

Remo exhaled. "Okay. Dead end there for now."

He returned his attention to Smith. "We'll find out the skinny on your ghost guys, Smitty. And I'm gonna keep a good thought that they're with the Eskimo branch of the Crips or the Bloods. I've been up to my fanny in ghosts lately."

"Actually," Smith said seriously, "if the lone survivor of Kakwik is to be believed, they are of a corporeal nature. It would be more accurate to say they are lost in time." His lips pursed unhappily. "He swears that the men who attacked his National Guard unit were Russians."

Remo blinked. "You're kidding, right?"

Smith shook his head. "Moreover, he seemed to think they were Soviet-era Russians. According to his eyewitness account, they were mired in the iconography of that time."

Remo threw up his hands. "Great. Perfect," he said in disgust. "Twice in one week. Geez Louise, Smitty, what is it with them? Is it the fuzzy hats? The 800-proof grain alcohol they pour on their Brezhnev-Os? How many times we gotta rub their noses in it before they stop pooping on the red, white and blue carpet, for chrissakes?"

"The Russia connection has not been confirmed," Smith said quickly. "Although those seeds have been planted, they may have been done so as a smoke screen." As he spoke, his hands sought the edge of his desk.

"Yeah, well, it better not be them," Remo said as the CURE director began typing at his special keyboard. "I've pasted enough hairy-mole and double-

chin snapshots in my Memories of Pottsylvania scrap-
book lately.''

"I have arranged a military flight to Alaska for the
two of you," Smith said. "It will be faster than a
commercial airline. A taxi will be arriving at the main
gate in fifteen minutes. It will take you to your rendezvous with an Air Force transport. Begin in Kakwik. That is the site of the most recent attack."

"Fine," Remo said, his expression still displeased.
"But I'm warning you, if I see one more Eastern
Blockhead this week, I'm not responsible for my ac-
tions."

Remo was turning to go when Howard broke in.

"That's it?" the young man asked, confused. All
eyes turned to him. "It just—it seems like there
should be more. At the CIA—"

"Love to stick around and hear how you, Larabee
and the rest of the Control guys escaped from Camp
Gitche Gumee Noonie Wa-Wa," Remo cut in, "but
we've got big-boy work to do. C'mon, Chiun."

The Master of Sinanju was still deep in thought.
Offering only the slightest of nods to the director and
associate director of CURE, he padded quietly out the
door.

Once they were gone, Howard turned back to
Smith, a questioning look on his wide face.

"There is no need to weigh them down with mi-
nutiae," Smith assured him absently. The older man
was fussing at his keyboard once more.

"If you say so, Dr. Smith," Howard said. "If we're
done here, I'll be in my of—"

"Please sit."

Mark was halfway out of his chair. The coldly precise words of the CURE director froze him in place. It was clear by his tone that something was wrong. Unsure what he'd done, Mark slowly lowered himself back to his seat.

Behind his desk, Smith had taken on the disapproving look of a strict boys-school headmaster. His mouth pinched in a thin frown, he scanned his monitor briefly before raising his eyes to meet Howard's.

"How did you know of the situation in Alaska yesterday?" Smith asked. His gaze never wavered.

Just a moment's hesitation. "Well, the President—"

"You knew of it before you left for Washington," Smith interrupted. "I have been going over your computer records. You used the time just before leaving for the airport to search for any anomalous activity there. What's more, in our meeting yesterday you suddenly seemed to think that I had mentioned something about Alaska when I had not. Now, under different circumstances I might assume you were involved in whatever is happening there. However, you are well above average intelligence. You would know that I have full access to your computer. And it seems highly improbable that, were you involved, you would blurt it out in front of me. Therefore, I must conclude that you are innocent but were somehow still possessed with the knowledge that something was wrong. So I will ask you again, *how* did you know?"

The CURE director's eyes were hard gray truth detectors, boring straight through to Mark Howard's soul.

Mark considered lying. After all, he had successfully done so on this topic for almost his whole life. But he could not escape the penetrating gaze of Harold W. Smith. Shoulders sinking, Howard shook his head.

"I don't know how," the young man said, exhaling. "I just had a feeling."

Smith's lemony face grew interested. "Explain."

"I really can't, Dr. Smith," Mark said. "It came to me while we were talking yesterday. Just a sense that something might be wrong. I wanted to check to confirm, but I couldn't find anything before I went to Washington. Then Kakwik happened, and it turned out I was right. But I still don't know how it came to me in the first place."

Smith didn't see anything deceptive in the younger man's body language. He seemed certain of what he was saying, yet simultaneously frustrated by his own claim.

"It came to you," Smith said evenly. "Are you suggesting that this is some form of psychic phenomenon?"

Howard's head snapped up. "No, sir," he insisted. "It's just some weird thing that happens sometimes."

"You are saying that this is not the first time?"

Howard's reluctance seemed to return. "No," he said hesitantly. "I've been able to do it a long time. It's sort of a sixth sense, I guess."

Smith considered Howard's words. "It is possible

that your mind simply works differently," he ventured after a thoughtful pause.

Mark's face showed cautious relief. "You believe me?" he asked.

"When I was your age, I probably would not have," Smith admitted. "However, I have seen enough that I no longer dismiss such claims out of hand. How do these episodes manifest themselves? In words? Images?"

"Both," Mark said. "Sometimes neither. With that Raffair business a few weeks back, it was mostly newspaper articles and on-line stories. It's sort of an instinct that directs conscious thought."

The CURE director nodded. "If you indeed possess such an ability, I would assume that this is precisely the case," Smith said. "Every minute of the day, the human subconscious is bombarded with much more information than it could ever possibly process. A natural filtering absorbs data that is necessary while at the same time disregarding that which is not. Perhaps your subconscious is better able to detect what others might ignore. It then forces the data up into the conscious realm in what you describe as a sixth sense."

Howard offered a wry smile. "I've been through all the possible explanations before, Dr. Smith," he said. "That one's always been the most comforting. It still doesn't go far enough, though."

His brow creasing, Smith leaned back in his chair.

"That will be all for now," the older man said. "However, if you have any further insights that might be considered out of the norm, do not keep them to yourself."

Mark nodded. "Yes, sir," he said. As he got to his feet he was now clearly relieved. "Thanks, Dr. Smith."

He was at the door when Smith called to him.

"And, Mark, it would be wise if you did not share your intimate involvement in the Raffair matter with either Remo or Master Chiun. They lost their home during that assignment. Since it was you who initially called attention to the criminal activity at that time, I would not want them to ascribe any misplaced blame to you."

Howard gave a lopsided smile. "You and me both," he said, and slipped out the door.

When the door had closed and he was alone once more, Smith took the arms of his battered leather chair in both gnarled hands. He turned slowly.

Beyond Folcroft's sloping rear lawn, Long Island Sound sparkled in the winter sunlight. Smith gazed at the water without seeing. Lost in thought.

Lately, he had been contemplating more and more the end of CURE. For Harold W. Smith, that end would bring down the final curtain on a life that had been almost exclusively dedicated to country.

In the watch pocket of his gray vest was a coffin-shaped pill. When his last day as director of CURE finally arrived, that small capsule would insure that any secrets Smith possessed would die along with him. And, Smith had generally assumed, CURE as an agency would die, too.

But in the past few days the world had changed dramatically. And with it, for the first time in a long time, Harold Smith felt a touch of unaccustomed optimism. It was possible that he and his agency would no longer die together. CURE's life span could conceivably be open-ended.

With that realization came a surprising irony. For a long time now, Smith had been exhausted. His advancing years and the constant pressure of his demanding job had been taking their toll. But these past few days had been different.

Oddly, the addition of Mark Howard to the CURE staff seemed to be having an invigorating effect on Smith. He could feel it in his stride, in his mind. Smith still felt the pains in his joints and the inevitable slowing down that came naturally with age, but it was not the distraction it had been these past few years. With a protégé, Smith now had a new purpose: to impress on Mark Howard the seriousness of their work here at Folcroft.

Nothing at CURE could be taken lightly. Smith had been a relatively young man when he was first drafted into the agency. A CIA analyst like Howard, Smith was about to retire from the intelligence game to take a position teaching law at Dartmouth, his alma mater. But history beckoned and Harold Smith heeded the call. His life before that time had not been without difficulty, but it turned out that it was only a prelude to what was to come. Only when he became director of CURE did Smith finally feel real pressure.

At first the task to save America seemed insurmountable. But eventually he found the help he would need. The moment the Master of Sinanju stepped off that first submarine so many years ago, things changed. When Remo was shanghaied into the organization not long after, CURE seemed complete. The secret agency had lucked into a tight group of three men who, by an amazing quirk of fate, complemented one another.

But perhaps it wasn't luck after all. Mark Howard seemed possessed of a gift that could be a positive boon to the organization. Smith was not a religious man. Such ideals would be hypocritical for someone who had sent so many to their deaths. Yet part of him could not help but wonder if there was some larger force at work here, guiding his agency, his nation.

If Mark Howard was to succeed, he would need a strong hand to guide him. There was much the young man had to learn. And much Harold Smith could teach him.

Smith's eyes came sharply back into focus. Out beyond the one-way glass of his office window, the February wind continued to tear at Long Island Sound.

Although in the winter of his own life, Smith no longer felt the beckoning of the waves.

With a steely resolve, he spun back around.

Surprised at the renewed vigor in his own arthritic fingers, Smith attacked the keyboard at the edge of his desk. He was quickly absorbed in his work.

Behind him, the comforting siren song of the Sound faded to silence.

12

A yellow cab brought them from Rye to the airport in White Plains. Thanks to Smith's string-pulling, an entire runway had been shut down. An Air Force transport squatted like an impatient bird at the far end.

At Remo's direction, their driver steered them through a gap in the chain-link hurricane fence and out to the waiting plane. The driver had barely slowed before they were out of the cab and scampering aboard the plane. Before the taxi had even left the tarmac, the aircraft was screaming skyward.

The Master of Sinanju had remained silent since they'd left Smith's office.

Over the years, Remo had cataloged sixty-two distinct variations to the old Korean's silences. Most of these fell under different subheadings in the overall ticked-off-at-Remo category. This was different, however. This was the Master of Sinanju's contemplative silence, which was always the most worrisome because it usually had to do with something else and only marginally reflected the old man's customary irritation with Remo.

Remo let it go on for twenty more minutes. The airport had long disappeared behind them, replaced by wispy clouds and featureless land, when he finally opened his mouth.

"I know you're probably cheesed off at me for countermanding you back there," Remo said, "but I wasn't gonna let you fly all the way to Alaska by yourself. Plus we don't know what's even going on there."

The Master of Sinanju didn't turn his way. "Speak for yourself, white man," he said, his voice flat.

"Okay, so *you* know," Remo said, exasperated. "Why don't you let *me* know so that *we'll* know? That sound like a plan to you, or are you gonna leave me in the dark till we get there?"

Chiun considered for a long moment. Finally reaching a reluctant inner decision, he turned to face his pupil.

"You are avatar of Shiva, the Hindu god of destruction," the old man began, "the dead night tiger made whole by the Master of Sinanju."

Remo had heard this many times over the years. Chiun had been convinced for ages that Remo was the fulfillment of some ancient Sinanju legend.

Even though Remo had experienced too much in his life to totally discount the claim, he still found some small comfort in offering at least token resistance to Chiun's assertions on the subject. To do otherwise would be to accept something that Remo preferred not to even think about.

The younger man shook his head. "Chiun, I—" he began.

"Do not argue," the old Korean cut in, his tone sharp.

Remo could see by his severe expression that his teacher would brook no argument. "Sorry, Little Father," he said quietly, sinking into his seat.

The hard lines of Chiun's wrinkles softened. "Your Masterhood was prophesied by no less than the Great Wang himself," he resumed. "He of the Sun Source, the first Master of the New Age. Wang said that a Master would find among the barbarians of the West one who was once dead. This Master, who we now know is I, would prepare his disciple for the coming of Shiva."

"I heard all that before, Chiun," Remo said. "What's it got to do with Alaska?"

"You heard only part of the story. Wang also spoke of the time of hardship, when Shiva's avatar would be put to the test." He folded his hands in his lap, and his voice took on the familiar cadence of instruction. "'And in this time will be reborn one of the dead, but beyond death, of the Void and not of the Void, of Sinanju, yet not of Sinanju. And he will summon the armies of death and the war they wage will be the War of Sinanju, the outcome of which will decide forever the fate of the line of the Great Master Wang and all who have followed him.'"

By the end, the old man's voice was barely a whisper. His wrinkled lips puckering in a frown of concern, he waited for his pupil's reaction.

Remo carefully absorbed the Master of Sinanju's words.

"You think this is happening now?" he asked quietly.

Chiun nodded. "I have seen the signs," he intoned. "As have you, for it was prophesied to you that you would face hardships in the coming years. Some have already occurred, others have yet to pass. Yet this is the time. *Your* time."

Though he felt for his pupil, the wizened Asian didn't let the emotion seep to the surface. His face was etched in stone.

Remo's own expression had darkened. He dropped a frustrated hand to his knee. "Well, ain't that just a turd in the water tank," he exhaled. A sudden thought came to him. "Hey, wait a minute. You just said you think this is what's going on now. This dead, undead whoever-he-is leading his corpse army to wipe out Sinanju."

Chiun nodded. "The false Master is to be of Sinanju, but not of Sinanju. Although it is unclear the form the armies of death will take, you yourself said that these beings Smith spoke of appeared to have abilities similar to our own. They appear and vanish at will. Those who have seen us would say the same of us."

"Okay, so what the hell did you think you were doing running off by yourself?"

The old Korean's eyes flicked to the window. "I was not certain," he said, smoothing a wrinkle in his brocade kimono. "Nor am I now. Rather than waste all our time, I thought it would be wise to first reconnoiter alone."

"Baloney," Remo said. "You were trying to protect me."

Chiun arched an eyebrow. "Someone has a high opinion of himself," he sniffed. "If you must know, what I was trying to do was give myself a few hours of time alone. Since moving into Smith's palace, you have been underfoot every waking minute of the day. I was welcoming the solitude afforded by this trip. And then you had to come along and ruin it all with that big nosy mouth of yours."

"Right," Remo mumbled, crossing his arms. "I believe you about as much as I believe all that bilge water you were pumping up what's-his-face's blowhole."

Chiun's hands retreated to his kimono sleeves. "I will say whatever is necessary to garner the goodwill of Smith's heir," he said.

"No kidding," Remo said blandly. "I'm surprised you weren't volunteering me to wax on, wax off his car. Which reminds me. After the way I left yesterday, I figured you'd rip me a new one when I got back this morning. I'll probably live to regret asking, but you wanna tell me why? Maybe I can do whatever it is I did again."

The old man's face was flat. "That is extremely unlikely," he said.

"Why?" Remo asked. "What'd I do?"

It was clear from the way he shifted in his seat that the Master of Sinanju did not welcome this direction in their conversation. Chiun looked not at his pupil, but dead ahead. When he spoke, his voice was low.

"It is possible, Remo, that you were correct," he said. Each word had to be bitten off. His jaw trembled at the painful admission.

At first, Remo had no idea what to say, so shocked was he by the tiny Asian's statement. He blinked.

"Oh," said Remo.

"Oh," he repeated.

"Oh," he said a third time after a prolonged pause during which he still had no idea how to respond.

"*Oh,*" he said, suddenly more brightly than the first three times. "What was I right about?"

Chiun gave him a withering look. "How many opportunities have you ever had to be right in your entire misspent life?"

Remo frowned. He could remember being right lots of times. So many times that he couldn't narrow down this particular time.

Glancing over, Chiun saw the confusion creeping into his pupil's face. The old man rolled his eyes impatiently.

"I am referring to our discussion about the Master Wo-Ti, imbecile," he said.

"Oh, *that,*" Remo said, nodding. "I know I was right about that one." He scrunched up his face. "Hey, not only was that one of the many times I've been right, but for those of you keeping score at home, that makes you wrong."

"I did not— Will you wipe that stupid smirk off your face? I did not say that. I believe in this instance we were both correct."

"Nope," Remo said firmly. "You're not gonna

square that circle. I'm the one who's right this time. You said so yourself. And as soon as we get back home, I'm calling the Guinness people to see if they'll put it in print.''

"If they did not give you an entry for the world's biggest feet or for that summer squash you call a nose, I doubt they would be interested.''

"Didn't mean it that way,'' Remo said. "I meant put *you* in for finally admitting it. So, when was the exact moment you realized I was right? Was it at the actual moment I was right, or did it come later, a few minutes after I was right?''

Chiun's brow was a flat line. "Will this craft never land?'' he complained, leaning toward the window.

Western New York State was far below.

"We've still got a ways to go,'' Remo said.

Fussing unhappily with his kimono, Chiun sat back in his seat. "You may suspend your self-congratulations for the duration of this trip,'' he grumbled. "There is little enough room in here for your other comically swollen features without having to surrender space to your swelled head. I merely meant that in interpreting the scrolls of Sinanju it is possible the conclusion you reached was correct.''

Remo wasn't buying it.

"It's right there in black and white,'' he insisted. "'Sinanju will never serve a succeeding emperor.' That was the lesson of Wo-Ti.''

"There is more than just that to the story,'' Chiun said. "In foolishly agreeing to safeguard the life and throne of Pepi II for all of that pharaoh's natural life,

Wo-Ti was stuck in Egypt until Pepi died at the age of ninety-six. Afterward, Wo-Ti's successor declared that Sinanju does not guarantee life, but only death. This could be considered the greater part of his lesson. If so, he has his legacy and we would be safe to dispense with that other trivial part.''

"I think Wo-Ti would have something to say about that," Remo warned. "When I met his spirit a few years back, he was under the impression that the 'no successor' lesson was the big one.''

"Wo-Ti has been dead for three thousand years," Chiun clucked. "He has likely not kept up with the modern demands of our ever changing craft.''

Remo shook his head. "This reeks of a dodge, Little Father," he said. "I know you've cooked the books before, and most of the time I didn't care because I didn't really think it mattered. But this one's too big to let slide. We work for Smitty until he's gone. After that, we're done and that pimple-faced twit assistant of his can go pound sand.''

"We have just had this discussion recently," Chiun said. "America is the only nation that can afford both of us.''

"Well, maybe we should—I don't know—maybe we should split up, then. Find two countries next door to each other and go there. I'll take England and you can have France. We'll holler insults across the English Channel. Or maybe we could just go home for a while and veg out.''

"Home where?" Chiun said suspiciously.

"To Sinanju," Remo said. "I could go baby shopping for an apprentice. You could lock yourself away like Monty Burns in that bank vault you call a house, counting and recounting every nickel Smitty's ever sent you. It'd be fun."

"When, Remo, did you develop this affection for Sinanju?" Chiun asked, his hazel eyes hooded.

"I haven't," Remo said. "I can't get all gaga like you over a pile of shit-smeared rock. But if we're checking out options, we have to consider them all, because tradition dictates that we can't work for Smith's successor."

"And who is the current guardian of our traditions?" Chiun asked haughtily.

Remo opened his mouth to answer, but stopped abruptly. "Wow," he said, blinking surprise. "Déjà vu."

"What is wrong?" the Master of Sinanju asked.

"Huh? Oh, nothing," Remo said. "I just flashed back to California. That thing that I ought to remember, but can't." He shook his head in an attempt to dislodge the strange sensation. "Weird. I almost had it, I think." He glanced at the Master of Sinanju. "You sure you don't wanna tell me what this is all about?"

Chiun shook his head. "I have spoken too much as it is, my son," he said. "It will come in its time. As for returning to Sinanju, I may do so to visit, but at this stage in my life, to move back there for any extended period of time would be to move back there forever. And I am not yet ready to enter that final phase of my life."

The old man closed his wrinkled eyelids, settling in to sleep for the rest of the long trip to Alaska.

Remo shook away the residual effects of this latest odd episode. Whatever was trying to break through, he hoped it did so soon. "Smitty's helper is a drip," he offered.

"Sinanju has worked for worse," Chiun replied, his eyes still firmly shut. "I could tell you stories about Victor Emmanuel I of Sardinia that would whiten even your fair skin. As long as their gold takes proper teeth marks, nothing else matters. Now get some rest."

His final command delivered, the old man fell asleep.

When the snoring started a minute later, Remo hardly heard it. His troubled eyes were directed out the window. His thoughts were far away.

Beyond the glass the gossamer clouds continued to slip silently by.

13

The cold wind carried a faint odor from the vast Pripet Marshes and across the wide, cracked tarmac. Even the frigid Russian winter wasn't cold enough to keep the stench down. In the summer the smell was powerful enough to make a strong man retch. Anna Chutesov ignored it.

Sergei stood behind her, the hems of his coat flapping in the wind. Fanned out around him were five others.

Six men. All that was left.

The men moved, stopped, even seemed to breathe in unison.

A warm hood was pulled up tight over Anna's blond hair. Her hands were stuffed deep in the pockets of her down parka. Blue eyes impatiently scanned the sky above the vast tracts of empty land that abutted the airfield.

"This is absurd," she muttered as she checked her watch for the twentieth time.

When she spoke, Sergei shifted guiltily. She shot him a deeply displeased look.

Only after she had read the news report he had found online had the young man reluctantly admitted something to her. It turned out to be an item of vital importance that he, in his stupid male loyalty, had kept from her far too long. Not wishing to betray the others, Sergei had waited to tell her with whom they were truly dealing.

The terrible truth only fueled Anna's fear.

Behind Anna and her Institute men, an abandoned flight tower scraped the sky. An empty barracks squatted below it.

The airport buildings were all in various states of decay. Tar paper hung from roofs in sheets. Broken windows howled forlornly in the gales. Chunks of concrete littered the ground where once had trodden the boots of many a Red Army and Soviet air force soldier. On the field, wind whistled through the rusting hulks of three old MiG-23s.

The old base was a shadow of its former self. Anna would leave it to the poets and the hard-line zealots to draw from its condition whatever conclusions they might like to make about the Russian nation as a whole.

Anna's ride sat near the flight tower. The remodeled Kamov helicopter, called a Helix in the West, resembled a giant wheeled fish. Above the fuselage, two rows of silent rotors—both upper and lower—shuddered in the desolate wind.

Anna's ice-blue eyes continued to impatiently rake the weak white sky.

To the west was Poland. Northeast was Moscow. And farther east—well away from Russia and its former client states—was the place where Anna Chute-sov should be.

"Men," she muttered to herself.

The moment she said the word, her ears tickled with the distant hum of a plane engine. With darting eyes she found the aircraft. The Ilyushin was a tiny speck in the sky.

Anna crossed her arms tightly. "It is about time."

It took an agonizing few minutes for the big aircraft to land. The Ilyushin bounced across the ruts and holes in the runway, finally rolling to a stop near the tower. The pilot didn't cut the engines.

Anna ran across the tarmac to the waiting plane. Sergei and the other men ran with her, cold, silent shadows.

The Russian presidential plane was nothing like America's Air Force One. The poor Ilyushin looked to be on its last legs. The fuselage was dull and grimy. The tires were nearly bald. A thin, almost invisible stream of white smoke slipped from the starboard nacelle. The pilot had been assuring Russia's worried president for weeks that white smoke wasn't anything to worry about. They could go all the way through the various shades of beige to black before it became necessary to take the plane in for expensive servicing. Fuel drizzled to the tarmac from a pinhole leak.

As soon as Anna reached the plane, a door popped open behind the left wing and a retractable ladder extended. She kicked the bottom rung so that the metal ladder locked in place and scurried up. At the top a hand reached out and helped her inside.

The man's copilot uniform was faded and worn. Ragged threads hung from the cuffs. Since he hadn't been paid in three months, he had recently been forced to sell his insignia to some visiting American teenagers to buy food.

"That way," the copilot said, pointing.

Anna had already pushed past him. Even as her entourage of six began boarding the plane, she was hurrying down the aisle to the lounge.

The engine sounds were muted inside. Wind buffeted the plane, rocking it from side to side.

She found the president of Russia sitting in a tatty seat. The seat belts had apparently been stolen from the presidential plane. Cords of nylon clothesline hung in their place.

There was very little that ever surprised Anna Chutesov. But when she saw the two men sitting with the current Russian president, she felt her brow sink.

One was a big man. Tall, with no neck and a large belly that seemed to go from pelvis to chin without taking the time to form a chest. In comparison, the other man was small, although his wide cherub's face and rounded body gave him the appearance of a teddy bear come to life.

Both men had led Russia at different times. The smaller one had accidentally taken the country away from the Communists. The larger one had—through corruption and mismanagement—turned it over to criminals.

The latter man had escaped the presidency when no one was looking on New Year's Eve of the new millennium with a presidential pardon and a pair of suit-cases crammed to overflowing with American foreign aid. His looted wealth had done nothing to remove him from his path of personal destruction. His skin was waxy, and his crown of white hair crashed in great uneven waves across the top of his big head. Around his ankles three empty vodka bottles rolled with the jostling movements of the wind-tossed plane.

The two former leaders along with Russia's latest president looked up as Anna entered the lounge.

The current president quickly got to his feet.

"Forgive us for being late," the little man said. "It is not easy to get away these days. I do not believe introductions are necessary." He held a small hand out to the other two men.

The bigger one wasn't even paying attention. He was rooting around with one paw under his frayed seat for a fresh bottle. This apparently required all his concentration. He bit down on his jutting tongue.

The other ex-president answered for both of them. "We know Anna Chutesov well," he said soberly.

The man scratched his forehead. Even though it was warm enough on the plane, he still wore a hat, pulled down low. Just the bottom of his world-famous wine-stain birthmark could be seen peeking out from under the wool. The part that Anna could see looked as if it had mutated somehow.

"I decided to check with my predecessors after our last meeting," the current president explained to Anna. "They convinced me that the danger might be greater than I originally feared. For *all* of us. I have extended presidential protection to them both, for Russia cannot run the risk of appearing weak. If something were to happen to them, it could open us up to even more dire security threats."

Anna didn't bother to tell him that, short of a full-scale nuclear war or a comet flattening Moscow, they were already facing the greatest threat imaginable.

"Presidential protection is an empty phrase," she said. "What we need goes beyond mere words."

As she spoke, the first of her entourage began filing into the lounge. The men were so silent Anna had not heard them. She knew they were there only by the look of relief that bloomed on the face of the hat-wearing former president.

The current president raised an eyebrow, as if he had expected more.

"Are they good?" he asked.

"They are trained," Anna replied.

"They had better be," the ex-president with the hat said. "It is bad enough when vandals can break into your house in the dead of night and permanently disfigure you. Now I find out my *life* might be in danger." His pudgy fingers scratched once more at his birthmark.

When his hat shifted, Anna could see that the mark now resembled the number one.

"Forgive me, Mr. President," Anna said frostily, "but I would remind you that it is *you* who started us down this road more than ten years ago. Pandora's box has been opened now, but you are the one who made certain it was full."

The former president bristled. "Do not forget your contribution in all this," he growled.

Anna's spine stiffened. "I won't," she said. "Nor could I if I tried."

The current president wasn't interested in squabbling. "These men will accompany us back to Moscow," he said, indicating Sergei and the other five. "Four will guard me. I will assign one each to the two of you."

The big bear of a man was oblivious. He was draining dry a half-filled vodka bottle. A shaking hand tapped the last drops onto his eager, bloated tongue.

When the hat-wearing president objected to the inequitable division of guards, Russia's current leader shook his head angrily.

"It is *your* fault we are even in this predicament," the latest president snapped. "You started us down this road to insanity."

"What I did was for the sake of national security," the ex-president argued.

Anna had heard enough. "Every stupid thing that has ever been done in Russia has been done in the name of national security," she said impatiently. "And I do not have time for this. These are the men you requested. Do whatever you want with them. I am leaving."

Only Anna Chutesov could get away with speaking in such a way to one—let alone three—Russian heads of state.

She turned from the three politicians.

"Be careful," she advised Sergei and the others,

knowing the foolishness of the wasted words even as she spoke them.

She hurried through the men and down the side aisle of the plane. At the still open door, her foot sought the ladder. When she turned to climb down, she found that the president had hurried out behind her.

"You still have some new recruits, do you not?" Russia's diminutive leader asked. "You should bring them with you."

Anna almost laughed in his face. The poor fool still didn't understand.

"I will go alone. Skachkov might still listen to me. Where he goes, the others will follow."

Across the crumbling tarmac, Anna's helicopter pilot saw her on the ladder. The wobbling rotors of the Kamov spluttered to life.

"And if he does not listen to reason?"

"Then, Mr. President, we are in real trouble," Anna said somberly. "For the only two men who might be able to stop him will want an explanation, and they will not stop until they get one. And they, unlike Skachkov, have never had any particular loyalty to Russia, its politicians or its spies."

Her final word delivered, Anna began to descend.

The president quickly disappeared inside the plane.

Anna had barely reached the ground before the ladder was being pulled back inside. The ladder vanished and the door thudded shut. The plane began to taxi almost immediately.

As Anna ran toward her waiting helicopter, the Ilyushin's engines whined in pain and the four big turboprops began to drag the plane slowly forward.

Accelerating rapidly, it reached the end of the runway by the time she made it to her helicopter. Engines screaming, it was pulling into the air as she climbed aboard the Kamov. A thin stream of white smoke trailed the presidential plane into the cold sky.

Anna's helicopter rose from the battered runway a moment later. As the Ilyushin banked toward Moscow, the helicopter turned east.

A military flight in Tambov would bring her as far across Russian Asia as the Kamchatka Peninsula. Another Kamov would be waiting for her there.

Settling back in her seat, Anna Chutesov pulled off her hood and stuffed her hands in the pockets of her heavy coat.

The three Russian politicians had been given the illusion of safety. Anna Chutesov had no such illusions.

She was flying into the grinning teeth of Death himself. And though she had cheated him before, she had her doubts that she could succeed this time. After all, if she was right, this time Death would come to Anna Chutesov wearing a familiar face.

She closed her eyes. Despite the din of the rotor blades, Anna quickly fell asleep. For the time being, there was nothing else for her to do.

14

Instead of offering an igloo control tower and a terminal staffed by walruses and polar bears, the Fairbanks Airport proved to be as modern as any Remo had ever visited.

Outside, the climate left a lot to be desired.

"It's kind of chilly," he commented as he and Chiun walked through the parking lot to pick up their rented Jeep. "I think we might be underdressed."

The cold wind made the hair on Remo's bare arms stand on end. He looked down at his flimsy cotton T-shirt and tan chinos. His pants flapped in the sub-zero wind.

The Master of Sinanju nodded agreement. "Our current attire would be sufficient for a short trip," he said. "However, we do not know how long this will take. We should plan for an extended stay."

They were at their rental car. Remo popped the locks with a button on the key chain.

"Got you covered," Remo said as they climbed inside the Jeep. "Two sets of Admiral Bird casual outerwear coming up."

Trailing cold exhaust, the rental headed out into the streets of Fairbanks.

BOOTSIE KLEIN WAS talking on the phone behind the counter of the clothing store where she worked in downtown Fairbanks when the bell over the front door tinkled to life.

As she took a good look at the pair walking in off the street, she dropped her voice low.

"I've gotta go," Bootsie whispered to her girlfriend. "No, I'll tell you later.... Yeah. Bye."

She quickly hung up the phone.

"Can I help you gentlemen with something?" she asked the two men.

It was clear that she could. When Bootsie had driven to work that morning, the digital thermometer on the bank had read eight degrees.

The old one wore a yellow kimono that looked as if he'd swiped a pair of curtains from a Chinese brothel. The young one was dressed to unload shrimp boats in Key West, not traipse around the streets of Fairbanks.

"Hi, Boobsie," Remo said, reading her name from the tag on her ample chest. "We need some winter gear. Something to keep us from freezing to death for a couple of days in the tundra. What do you think, Chiun," he said, turning to the Master of Sinanju, "windbreakers?"

"The lining cannot be too thick," Chiun sniffed. "My precious pores must be allowed to breathe."

"You got windbreakers?" Remo asked Bootsie, leaning his bare forearms on the glass countertop. "The early-spring kind, with the liners?"

"You're kidding, right?" Bootsie asked.

"Oh, and we're gonna need hats," Remo added.

"I, um, think your friend's already found one he likes," Bootsie suggested, pointing. "I'll have to check out back for windbreakers."

As the sales clerk ducked through a nearby door, Remo glanced over to the Master of Sinanju.

"Oh, brother," he muttered.

Chiun was standing at a narrow door mirror. Nestled over his bald head was a red plaid winter hat. Long flaps hung down like lazy dog's ears. Happy hazel eyes peeked out from under the pinned-up brim.

"Should I even try to talk you out of it?" Remo sighed.

"Of course, Remo," Chiun replied. "You may do so after I have convinced you to trade in that undergarment you wear as a shirt for a proper kimono." He wiggled his head. His hat flaps flapped.

"Figured I'd be on the losing end," Remo said. He leaned back on the counter to wait for the saleslady.

Bootsie returned a few minutes later with a pair of spring jackets. By then, Remo had a plain wool ski cap for himself on the counter.

Chiun immediately plucked one of the coats from the young woman's hand. His arms vanished, turtle-like, up the sleeves of his kimono, dragging the jacket inside. With a few wiggling contortions, he slipped into the windbreaker. His bony hands reappeared a moment later.

"Pay the woman, Remo," he commanded.

Spinning, he marched out the front door.

Remo had tugged on his own coat. It was a snug fit around his thick wrists.

"Did you mean what you said?" Bootsie asked as she rang up both coats and hats. "Are you really going outside the city dressed like that?"

Remo stuffed his hat into his pocket. He pulled out his wallet.

"You bet," he said, slapping a credit card on the counter. "And if we find a nice ice floe, a certain lucky someone might just be taking a one-way Eskimo cruise."

Bootsie's face darkened. "That's not a very nice thing to say," she scolded as Remo signed for his purchases. "He seems like a nice old man."

Remo's eyes met hers. "Who said I meant him?"

Dropping her pen to the counter, he turned and left the small store.

REMO PICKED UP a map from a gas station rack and called Smith from a pay phone. Between the map and Smith's directions, he was able to find the rural route to the Kakwik settlement.

Word had spread of the massacre, keeping highway crews from clearing the road after the recent storm. Luckily, a strong wind had blown snow to both shoulders. Remo's Jeep sped up the middle of the lonely road.

At one point, a crooked sign sprang up from a snowdrift to announce that Kakwik was five miles away. Remo saw something else printed in an unfamiliar language just below the English words.

"What'd that say?" he asked as they raced by the sign.

Chiun's face was bland. "How should I know?"

"I thought you were Sinanju's universal translator," Remo said. "You know every language known to man, including two dozen that everyone else has forgotten about."

"Languages, yes," Chiun admitted. "However, that was nothing I recognized. Those scratches were no doubt caused by a passing bear sharpening his claws."

"Didn't look like Gentle Ben scratches to me," Remo said. "Probably some kind of Eskimo dialect. Since I never saw any piles of whale blubber stashed away back in Sinanju, I guess the natives here never needed to hire an assassin."

The Master of Sinanju tugged at his hat flaps. "I have truly gone from one barbarian land to another," he grumbled.

Three miles shy of Kakwik, an Army blockade rose from beyond a pile of drifting snow. A few trucks and military jeeps were parked across the road.

Remo stopped his rental near a wooden sawhorse.

A young soldier hurried to the driver's-side window, an M-16 clutched to his chest.

"This area is off-limits, sir," the soldier announced.

"Remo Leiter, CIA," Remo said, holding up a laminated card for the soldier's inspection.

The young man looked from the ID to the two men in the car. Remo wore only a light windbreaker. Beyond him Chiun was playing with the flaps of his hat. He was holding them out like wings while making vrooming airplane noises.

"He's CIA?" the soldier asked.

"You bet," Remo said. "Right now he's practicing for his spy school pilot's exam. Makes you feel confident that America's ready to face the counterintelligence demands of the new century, doesn't it?"

"*Rat-a-tat-tat,*" said the Master of Sinanju, as he and his hat strafed the dashboard.

The skeptical soldier found an officer who confirmed Remo's identification. Ten minutes later the two Masters of Sinanju sped up the main road to Kakwik.

There was really only one real road in town. The rest were merely glorified driveways. The main drag ran up between a pathetic collection of rusty tin huts.

The snow-clogged road became impassable at the edge of town. Remo and Chiun left their Jeep and continued on foot.

The fires inside the dilapidated homes had long ago burned to ash. The huts had grown cold in the day since the massacre. After Colonel Hogue's escape from town and the incredible story he had related of events there, federal and state authorities had descended on Kakwik like a human blizzard. Somber-faced men picked around bodies that lay frozen in the snow.

Some of the tin homes were doubling as makeshift morgues. With no need for refrigeration, some of the dead had been removed from the snow and stacked inside.

There was enough carnage still outside for Remo and Chiun to get a sense of what had happened. As they walked along, Remo noted a few of the National Guard corpses.

"Looks like you can breathe a sigh of relief, Little Father," he commented. "These guys were shot. Since we don't use guns, no Sinanju ghost army to worry about."

The tension on the old man's face never faded. "And if you would use your ears half as much as you use your mouth, you would have heard me say that the one who is to be of Sinanju but not, will summon the *armies* of death. The prophecy does not say that they themselves will be of Sinanju, nor of what form they will even take."

"Oh," Remo frowned. As he spoke, he noted a group of men clustered near the side of a small house. "Looks like the fun's over there."

He and the Master of Sinanju headed for the crowd.

A middle-aged man with an FBI tag spotted them as they approached. "Hold it," he ordered. "You can't be here."

Remo flashed his CIA ID at the FBI agent.

"Any idea what happened?" Remo asked as the agent studied first Remo's identification, then the clothing the two new arrivals wore.

"Not really," the FBI man said. "Nothing beyond what you probably already know. The only witness is an Army Colonel. He was kind of out of it when they found him. Kept saying something about a Russian ghost army. I don't think we can put much stock in that. Aren't you guys cold?''

Remo didn't hear him.

There was an outdoor oil tank behind the nearest house. A body lay beside it. Leaving Chiun, Remo crossed over to the dead man. He crouched next to the body.

The man's head had been removed. It had rolled through the snow until it was facing the tin wall of the hovel.

''Uh-oh,'' Remo said quietly as he peered at the neck stump.

''Yeah,'' the FBI man said, walking up beside Remo. ''A real mess. There's a couple like that. Weird thing is, there's no one from the other side dead. All this mess you'd think some of our guys would have taken out at least a couple of theirs. I'm thinking that whoever did this might carry off their dead and wounded with them.''

''Or maybe their dead are already dead,'' Remo said grimly. He ignored the puzzled look the FBI agent gave him. ''Chiun,'' he called.

The Master of Sinanju had been studying the ground around where the greatest concentration of men were working. He padded quickly over to Remo.

''What do you make of this?'' Remo asked worriedly, gesturing to the decapitated corpse.

Chiun cast a wary eye at the body. ''This was accomplished with a single stroke,'' he pronounced.

"No tools, right?" Remo said. "It looks to me like it was done by hand. And I don't know many people who can lop off a head with a single palm stroke, present company excepted."

Chiun nodded thoughtful agreement. "Here," he beckoned ominously.

Leaving the baffled FBI agent, Remo crossed with Chiun to the spot where the old man had been studying the snow. A long fingernail extended, aimed toward two separate sets of tracks that hadn't been stomped on by authorities.

Remo saw that one pair was deep and clumsy. A normal man's tread. It was the second set that made his stomach sink.

They were light. Virtually invisible to the untrained eye.

The faint footprints seemed to have danced and moved around the victim, hiding in every blind spot that would have been offered by a moving opponent. With footwork like that, the dead soldier whose boots had made the deeper impressions would never have even seen his killer.

More tracks touched the snow near the first. Many more kissed the periphery of the killing field.

There were only two men on Earth capable of such subtle movements. At the moment, they both were staring into the tracks of a killer who, though unknown, remained disturbingly familiar. With a sinking feeling, both men now knew without doubt that they were facing an enemy in control of an army trained in a deadly art forged in blood on the rocky frozen ground of a tiny fishing village on the West Korean Bay.

15

Remo looked up from the tracks. His eyes as he stared at the Master of Sinanju were dull. "I don't know about you, but right now I'm feeling real nostalgic for the day our house got incinerated," he exhaled. "Guess this clinches it. We're dealing with a bunch of guys trained in Sinanju."

Chiun nodded seriously. The carflaps of his winter hat bobbed in the chill air. Alert hazel eyes scanned the area.

The desolate town of Kakwik was a slaughterhouse at the top of the world. And somewhere out there lurked an enemy with knowledge of the most deadly killing art to ever brush Earth's frail mantle.

"Hey, what about the Dutchman?" Remo asked suddenly.

The Dutchman, whose real name was Jeremiah Purcell, was one of the most dangerous adversaries Remo and Chiun had ever faced. Skilled in the ancient art of Sinanju, he had spent the past decade in a coma, confined to Folcroft Sanitarium's security wing.

"I checked on him before we left," Chiun replied. "He is still asleep in Smith's dungeon."

"So this is somebody new. Swell," Remo grumbled. "The tracks lead that way," he added as he dragged his ski cap out of his pocket, pulling it down over his ears.

The footprints headed away from the investigators, threading between two tin houses. Others had fallen in line with the path of the leader. Though not as light-footed as their leader, they were far more graceful than ordinary men.

"We better get a move on," Remo announced glumly. "Another few hours and we'll lose them completely."

Even to their trained eyes, the tracks weren't easy to follow. Wind pushed the powdery snow.

The FBI agent in charge watched the two men wander off alone, their eyes downturned as if following some invisible trail. Shaking his head, he returned to his work.

The two Masters of Sinanju passed between the last hovels at the edge of the tiny village and continued into the snow-blanketed field beyond. In the deceptively close distance, blue snow-capped mountains held up the sky. Nearer, snow-brushed hills rolled up from the vast plain.

They lost the tracks at the midpoint to the low hills. Punishing wind had erased all traces of the men they were following. Rather than turn back, they forged onward.

Four miles out of Kakwik, the faint trail became visible once more at the mouth of a narrow gorge. By now there were only ten of them. At some point on the plain, the others had to have veered off in another direction.

Up ahead, a small range of frozen hills rose from the canyon floor. Beyond them, a thin thread of smoke touched the sky. Exchanging tight glances, Remo and Chiun scampered up a hill, assuming a cautious crouch near the top.

In a shallow canyon below, white shapes scurried around a small fire.

The Master of Sinanju's face grew worried. "They *are* spirits," he hissed.

With narrowed eyes, Remo studied the figures below. At first glance they did look ghostly. The ten men wore off-white jumpsuits. Masks of cream white covered their faces.

Training his ears on the valley below, Remo quickly found the supernatural give way to the painfully ordinary.

"Unless somebody's changed what makes ghosts tick, those are just guys, Little Father. At least the last ghost I met didn't have a heartbeat."

The Master of Sinanju tipped his head, listening to the sounds of the valley. Ten distinct heartbeats carried to his sensitive eardrums.

"They live," Chiun said in soft surprise.

"Live, breathe and stink like Russians," Remo said, his face fouling at the scent that had just carried to him on the breeze.

Chiun had caught the distinct odor, as well. Abandoning all pretense of stealth, he rose to his full height. His lips puckered in displeasure.

"If they are not spirits," he said, planting hands to hips, "why are they dressed to make us think they are?"

"Winter camo," Remo suggested, getting to his feet, as well. "It'd give them an edge in the snow."

"True Sinanju does not rely on parlor tricks to deceive the eyes of men," Chiun dismissed. "Therefore this whatever-it-is is false and stolen." He hiked up his kimono hems. "Come, Remo," he declared. "These brigands are already dressed for the Void. Let us dispatch them to the place where thieves dwell eternal."

He started down the hill. Remo ran to catch up.

"We save one for questioning," Remo insisted.

"As you wish," Chiun said with crisp impatience. Eyes of hazel doom were directed on the men around the fire.

Their last words carried to the group of commandos. Ten sets of black goggles turned to the hill.

If there was shock beneath the masks, it didn't show.

Remo and Chiun hit the valley floor at a sprint. Near the fire, the ten ghostly figures jumped to their feet. A few managed to grab guns. Almost in unison, all ten shifted their weight just as Remo and Chiun caught up with them.

To any other eyes on the planet, it would have seemed as if they'd disappeared into the ether. Remo proved to the nearest man that he could still see him. He did this by planting the barrel of the man's own AK-47 deep into the center of his masked face. Both mask and face puckered. The man reappeared, harpooned on the end of his gun.

"Peek-a-boo, I see you," Remo said as he tossed the body onto the fire. Sparks shot into the air.

Near Chiun, a white-clad figure threw out a sloppy power thrust, palm forward, fingers curled.

The cobwebs of Chiun's mouth drew tight at the affront.

"You dare?" the Master of Sinanju cried, his voice flirting with the fringes of outrage. A downward stroke of his own arm severed the offending hand of the commando. As the hand fell, a long talon slid deep into the man's occipital lobe.

The soldier fell like a cold white fog.

A thrill of panic coursed through the remaining eight.

One man tried to shoot Chiun. His smoking gun joined his steaming severed arms in the snow.

"That is how Sinanju deals with thieves," the Master of Sinanju proclaimed, swirling into the midst of the men.

Near Remo, one commando attempted a familiar Sinanju attack stance. One balled hand floated like a feathery mallet before his blank white face.

"This one's not so crummy, Chiun," Remo called as he dodged a lightning blow.

When he missed his intended target, the man's shoulder snapped from its socket. He fell screaming to the ground.

"Okay, so I've seen better," Remo mused as the Russian rolled in agony in the snow. "But the pantry shelves ain't exactly stocked these days. Maybe I should keep him. In ten years he might be able to learn something.''

''Take a Russian for a pupil and I will disown you,'' the old Korean warned.

Razorlike fingernails swept across a nearby pair of black goggles. Gashes raked the plastic. The eyes beneath popped like viscous balloons, sending streams of milky inner ocular fluid streaking through the air.

''Why?'' Remo asked. ''Hasn't there ever been an alcoholic Master of Sinanju before?'' With a sharp toe to the forehead, he finished off the commando with the dislocated shoulder.

''Do not be ridiculous,'' Chiun snapped, eliminating the blinded soldier in the same way. ''And pay attention.''

Another soldier leaped into the fray.

Remo made an effort not to be distracted by the poetry of movement that was Sinanju. It had been a long time since he'd seen anyone other than Chiun or himself ply the art.

When the commando attacked, Remo bent back at the waist, his spine forming a backward forty-five-degree angle as a sweeping hand attacked the spot where his chest had been.

Another shoulder was dislocated as the commando's forward momentum carried him over Remo. Muscles and tendons strained and snapped, and he flew face first to the snow.

''These guys know about two moves,'' Remo frowned. A pirouette ending in a crunching loafer heel to the back of the prone man's head sent the soldier to sparkling eternity.

"It is two more than they have the right to know," Chiun replied, advancing on the next man like a vengeful dervish.

The latest soldier shed his goggles in panic. His eyes grew wide at the old man's approach. A muffled shout issued from the flexible white mask that covered his mouth.

Chiun's flashing fingers flew at the commando's neck. With nails strong as a lion's claws and as delicate as a surgeon's scalpel, he pierced the soldier's throat. A sharp twist snicked the spinal cord in three separate places.

His strings cut, the soldier dropped limp to the snow.

As displaced snow rose sparkling into the air, Chiun was already bounding over the corpse.

Behind him three men were charging Remo. Frightened now, they'd abandoned their basic Sinanju training. Knives drawn, they lunged in unison at Remo's flimsy windbreaker.

Before they could make contact, a thick-wristed hand flashed forward. The side of Remo's flattened palm snapped three successive knife blades.

"Lesson number one," he instructed as the shards of tempered steel rocketed skyward. "Weapons cheapen the art."

The three men slammed on the brakes. Eyes invisible behind goggles stared blankly at their naked knife hilts.

"Lesson number two," Remo continued, aiming a single index finger straight in the air. "Don't look up."

One of the men numbly followed Remo's finger rather than his advice. The returning knife blades shredded his upturned face to hamburger.

There was a sharp intake of air from the remaining two as their bloodied comrade slipped from between them. Panicked heads twisted back to Remo.

"Lesson number three—die with dignity."

He gave them no time to do otherwise.

Hands darting forward, he grabbed a fistful of ski mask in each and brought them sharply together. Waterproof masks quickly became home to a pair of misshapen masses that had formerly been human skulls.

"Lesson number four," Remo said coldly as the bodies slipped from his hands. "Steal from the rest or face the wrath of the best."

He heard a slippery hiss behind him. Wheeling, he was just in time to see the steaming red sack that was the tenth and final commando's internal organs slopping from out a yawning incision in his abdomen. The man joined his insides on the ground. Chiun stood above the gutted body, a look of deep disdain on his leathery face.

"Dammit, you didn't save one," Remo groused.

"Neither did you," the Master of Sinanju replied. He flicked an imaginary dollop of blood off his index fingernail as he padded over to his pupil.

"Perfect," Remo scowled. "We better start figuring out a schedule for whose turn it is to save one, 'cause we sure as hell can't keep doing this all the time.'' He pointed at one of the dead men. "That one yelled some Russian claptrap at you before you finished him off. What'd he say?"

Chiun folded his hands inside his kimono sleeves. "'It is you,'" he replied, his voice betraying mild curiosity.

Remo looked from the body to the Master of Sinanju. "What the hell's that supposed to mean?"

"I am Reigning Master of Sinanju. Perhaps my reputation has preceded me," the old man speculated.

"Right," Remo said skeptically. "Probably has your Topps rookie assassin trading card in a plastic collector's case on his bureau back home."

He squatted to pull the mask off the dead man. It wasn't easy, given the fact that the man's eyes were oozing down his face like a pair of runny two-minute eggs.

"Yuck," Remo complained as he tugged the mask free. He flung it to the snow. "You ever see this guy before?"

After peering at the dead man for but a moment, Chiun shook his head. "Whoever he is, he is unknown to me."

Standing, Remo surveyed the small encampment with a frown. There was no sign of how the men had gotten there. They might as well have been actual ghosts, dropped in the middle of nowhere like this.

Stooping, Remo checked a few pockets. He came up empty.

"Well, ain't this just hunky-dory," he groused.

When he glanced at the Master of Sinanju, he found that the old man wasn't listening to him. Lips puckered, Chiun had turned a shell-like ear to the south.

Remo cocked an ear the same way. The faint sound of a distant helicopter carried to his ears.

Chiun was already marching back toward the hill.

"I hope it's their ride," Remo grumbled, following. "And if it is, question first, eviscerate second, got it?"

"Do not blame me if you can't keep track of your own silly plan," the Master of Sinanju called back.

Up the hill and back down into the narrow gorge, they retraced their steps back out to the plain. By the time they emerged from the low hills, the helicopter had swept in close. A few hundred yards distant, it flew back and forth through the night sky.

The helicopter almost seemed to be lost. But when Remo and Chiun emerged from the hills, it suddenly found focus. Banking right, it steered a beeline for them.

"Infrared," Remo commented as they walked across the surface of the ankle-deep snow. He had detected the telegraphing signals directed from the approaching chopper.

The helicopter was of an unfamiliar design. An extra set of rotor blades rose into the sky above it. Furiously chopping at air, the helicopter quickly ate up the distance to them, coming to an angry hover above the two lonely men on the desolate plain.

Swirling clouds of snow blew out all around.

"You think we're just gonna stand here looking at

each other until the spring thaw?" Remo called to Chiun over the roar of the rotors.

His eyes had left the helicopter for but a moment. The instant they did, he saw a sudden look of tight concern appear on the wrinkled face of the Master of Sinanju.

Remo followed the old man's gaze back to the helicopter.

A face now peered out the small rear window. A fringe of blond hair peeked out from under a furry parka hood.

Remo's stomach sank.

An instant after he'd seen her, the face of Anna Chutesov disappeared from view and the helicopter began to descend from the frigid black sky.

Remo shot a hard look at the Master of Sinanju. "It's official," he called over the roar of the rotors. "We have a new winner in the Suckiest Week of My Life Sweepstakes."

His words swirled away in a vacuum of wind-tossed snow.

16

Remo could tell by the grave look on Anna Chute-sov's face when she emerged from the Kamov that things were even worse than either he or Chiun imagined.

She hurried over to them, the wind plastering the fur fringe of her heavy parka against her forehead. Her delicate face—used to freezing Russian winters—was bare. A scarf was knotted at her neck, spilling up around her pale chin.

"Are you gonna start showing up now every time we kack a Russian hit squad?" Remo asked her. "Because at the rate we've been going lately, you're gonna be racking up some major frequent-flyer miles."

"You killed some of them?" Anna asked by way of greeting. "Where are they?" Her tense voice was urgent.

"Nice to see you, too," Remo said dryly. "And since we've dispensed with the pleasantries, you mind telling me just what the hell you people think you're doing here?"

"The last time I checked I was a single person," Anna said thinly.

"Why buy the cow when it gives its milk away like a barnyard harlot?" the Master of Sinanju volunteered. His hands in his kimono sleeves, he appraised the Russian with bland distaste.

"I don't mean *you* you," Remo said to Anna. "I mean Russia you. We've got more dead Russians back there than you had running that backward country of yours back in the early eighties." He stabbed a thumb at the hills behind him.

"They are there?" Anna said, her voice intent. "How far? How many?"

"Ten," Remo replied. "About a mile and a half in."

Before he could say any more, she had turned on her heel and was marching back through the snow to the Kamov.

Remo gave Chiun a questioning look.

"Do not look at me," the old Korean sniffed. "She is your scarlet woman."

Turning wordlessly from his teacher, Remo dogged Anna back to the helicopter. Chiun padded alongside him.

"Where are you going?" Remo demanded.

"I must examine the bodies," Anna answered. "You may come along if you wish."

"That's mighty white of you," Remo said aridly. "And don't waste your time. I checked them already. No ID."

"You will forgive me, Remo, if I question your thoroughness?" Anna droned as she boarded the Kamov.

Remo's face fouled. "Who swiped your Pamprin?" he said. He tried to board the helicopter but the Master of Sinanju pushed past him, settling into the seat behind Anna's.

The Kamov was lifting off the ground even as Remo was pulling the door shut behind him. At Anna's direction, the pilot steered for the low hills.

"So what's the big Russian deal here?" Remo demanded as they swept across the plain.

"My government is not responsible for what is happening if that is what you mean," Anna replied. She was looking out the window. The first low hills dropped away behind them. "These men are renegades. There are more than just the ten you say you stopped. With any luck, this group can offer us some clue where the others might be."

"Yeah, well, we'd kind of like to know, too," Remo said. "Seeing as how these guys have somehow gotten hold of some bogus, watered-down version of Sinanju."

Anna's heart rate quickened. Both Remo and Chiun noted the change.

"I know," she admitted darkly.

"No, you don't," Remo said. "Sinanju the discipline is Sinanju the village's bread and butter. If someone steals from Sinanju, they're stealing food out of my people's mouths."

"*Your* people," Anna stressed.

"Yes, *my* people," Remo nodded. "They might be a pack of ugly, ungrateful backstabbers, but they're our pack of ugly, ungrateful backstabbers. We're responsible for them, and if someone else gets hold of Sinanju skills—any Sinanju skills—they dilute the market for the real deal. Not to mention making us look bad with their sloppy techniques. Back me up here, Little Father.''

The old man's face was unchanged. "I do not have to, for you are doing well enough on your own," he said.

At the Korean's words and tone, Anna raised an eyebrow.

''There, you see?'' Remo pressed. ''So where the hell'd these guys learn their moves?''

Anna started to speak, but something out the window caught her eye.

''Wait,'' she said.

The helicopter was sweeping up the ravine, lights from the belly illuminating the terrain. They might have missed the bodies if not for the blood. The pilot managed to settle the Kamov in a small adjacent valley. As he cut the engines, Anna was popping the door.

She hurried through the ravine, coming into the encampment in the direction opposite the one Remo and Chiun had first used. The two Masters of Sinanju followed.

The first body was of the man Chiun had eviscerated. Stepping gingerly around the gore, Anna pulled off the man's goggles and mask.

The face beneath was ghostly pale in death. The Russian's hair was dark. That was the extent of her examination. Anna threw down the mask, moving quickly on to the next body.

"You know, someone of a suspicious nature might wonder what you were doing way out here," Remo suggested as she tugged off another mask.

"Since these men are Russians, I was sent by my government to stop what could become an international incident," Anna explained as she worked. "We were flying near the village where the slaughter took place when a radio transmission we intercepted said that two very unusual CIA agents had set off on foot through the snow. They said the men were underdressed and ill-equipped to survive in such a hostile environment." She raised a thin eyebrow beneath her fringe of hood. "However did I know it was the two of you?" she said with dull sarcasm.

Finished with that body, she moved on.

Remo shot a glance at the Master of Sinanju.

Chiun was playing once more with his hat flaps, supremely uninterested in both Remo and Anna.

"You might work up a head of steam on this one, Chiun," Remo said. "It's your village these guys stole from."

"It is *our* village," Chiun replied. "You have just said so. And nothing of any real value can be stolen from the village. We are Sinanju's greatest resource. Well, *I* am. But you are a close second. Third or fourth at the most."

There was an odd undertone to the old man's words. As if his apathy were feigned.

"Thanks for the vote of confidence," Remo droned.

Turning from his teacher, Remo found Anna in the process of pulling off yet another mask. She grunted displeasure at the man's brown hair.

"I can't help noticing you're not patting down pockets," Remo observed. "Care to tell us exactly which Russian you're looking for up here in the Great White North?"

"Great Frontier," Anna corrected tensely, wiping blood from her hands on a white jumpsuit. She used the toe of her boot to roll over the next man. His belly was burned black where he'd landed on the campfire. "The Great White North is Canada," she explained as she pulled off the latest ski mask.

"You sure?" Remo asked. "I thought Great Frontier was space."

"In that case, the Great Frontier is what exists between your ears," the Master of Sinanju offered.

"Ha-ha," Remo said dryly. "Say, Anna," he called, one sly eye on the old Korean, "gimme the name of one of these Russians. I'm in the market for an assassin's helper."

He saw a flash of silk just before a whizzing snowball caught him square in the back of the head.

"No? Okay, maybe a Frenchman," Remo muttered as he went to retrieve his hat from a snowbank near Anna.

Anna was at the tenth and final body. It was the man whose mask Remo had earlier removed. She looked down on the face of the corpse, her own expression one of disgust.

"Lavrenty Skachkov," she announced.

Remo was knocking snow from his hat. "God bless you," he said.

She fixed him with a dull eye. "You asked for the name of one of these," she said, waving a hand across the field of Russian dead. "Skachkov is one. The most dangerous of all these. And he is not here."

She spun away, marching past Remo.

"So is this Crotchcough the guy in charge here?" Remo asked, following. Chiun fell in behind.

"Unfortunately, no," Anna admitted as she walked. "Skachkov is a follower, not a leader." She quickly amended her own words. "Or, rather, he is leader to a select few. Whatever is going on here is not his doing."

In the valley at the mouth of the narrow ravine, Anna's pilot saw them approaching. The Kamov's twin rotor stacks spluttered to life.

"All right," Remo said. "So whose doing is it?"

Anna stopped dead, turning on the two Masters of Sinanju. Snow thrown up from the helicopter's downdraft whipped the fringe of fur on her parka.

Her ice-blue eyes were deadly serious.

"An utter madman," Anna Chutesov insisted with cold certainty.

Jaw locked in grim determination, she turned, hurrying for the waiting helicopter.

17

Crazed. Demented. Mentally unbalanced.

When being kind, that was what they said about him.

Insane. Psychopath. Sociopath.

These terms filled psychological profiles stashed away at intelligence agencies all around the world.

But informally, when they were discussing Vladimir Zhirinsky, men and women from all shades of the political spectrum, both at home and abroad, often found themselves agreeing with the private assessment of an American State Department official: "It is my sincere opinion that Vladimir Zhirinsky is a raving, ranting, slobbering, foaming, nuttier-than-a-fruitcake loon—with a capital *L*."

For Vladimir Zhirinsky their words had no sting. After all, it was only natural for the weak to attack the strong. And if strength could be judged by the viciousness of verbal attacks, then he was by far the strongest man to stride the face of the planet since Hercules.

Not that he believed in ancient myths of gods. Vladimir Zhirinsky knew with a certainty as deep as the marrow of his Russian-born bones that there were no gods. No heaven. No hell. Eternal judgment was a bedtime story.

There was only man and his environment. Or, as he liked to put it, the Worker and the State.

A truer Communist than Vladimir Zhirinsky had never been born. Even after the Iron Curtain collapsed and communism became as hopelessly out of fashion as last year's bourgeois French fashions, Zhirinsky remained a rabid believer.

The State, he argued to anyone who would listen, was supreme. The Worker existed to benefit the State. And when the State prospered, so did the Worker. Russia, Zhirinsky screamed from atop soapboxes in Moscow's Gorky Park, *needed* communism. It was dead without it.

The world would never respect a Russia lacking the ideological purity of communism. The Soviet philosophy was the unifying force that had kept the nation strong for seven decades after the October Revolution. Without it, Russia was nothing more than a Third World country. A husk. A pathetic shell of its former glorious self.

In the early 1990s the Russian experiment in democracy was still new. Luckily for Zhirinsky, the changes were frightening to enough old-fashioned zealots. When election time came, his brand of fiery finger-waving and venomous rhetoric gained him a seat in parliament. He attacked both his job and the new Russia with demented glee.

It wasn't unusual for Vladimir Zhirinsky to get into fistfights in the great senate chamber of the Kremlin.

One representative from Belorussia who disagreed with him wound up with a bust of Stalin to the side of the head. A Moldavian senator who accidentally sat in Zhirinsky's chair went home that night to find his apartment broken into and his cat, Buttons, drowned in the toilet.

Trying to steer clear of Zhirinsky did no good. Even when he had no specific ax to grind, Vladimir Zhirinsky still tripped colleagues down the Duma stairs, slammed doors into people's faces and keyed cars in the Kremlin parking lot.

Everyone knew that when a smile appeared beneath the crazed senator's great bushy mustache, it was time to run back and see if the office or the wife and kids were on fire.

For a time his unorthodox behavior made him a hero. Zhirinsky the iconoclast challenged authority, ironically by seeking restoration of a government that would crush such challenges. He had even run for the Russian presidency.

Alas for Vladimir Zhirinsky, his brief popularity bubble among the Russian people had burst unexpectedly. It happened during a nationally televised debate. On the live broadcast, Zhirinsky's opponent had said something that the senator couldn't counter and, in rebuttal, Zhirinsky had done the first thing that came to him. He bit off the man's nose.

Worse, when the hapless moderator demanded he spit the nose back out, the ultranationalist smiled a blood-smeared smile before swallowing visibly. His great Adam's apple bobbed, and the screaming politician with the hole in his face lost his nose forever. It was little comfort to him as he was led, bleeding, from the Moscow studio that the night that robbed him of his nose was also the night that ended the career of Vladimir Zhirinsky.

In the wake of this event, the crazy nationalist lost not only the presidency but also his senate seat. And around the world was quiet relief that a man so unstable was no longer a serious candidate to assume the leadership of Russia.

Soon Vladimir Zhirinsky was forgotten.

It was the lowest time in his life, this public exile. To be forgotten while stuck in some faraway Siberian labor camp was one thing, but to be shunned on the very streets of Moscow was worse than any gulag.

His life for the past several years had been lived in shadows. But as he rode through the streets of Moscow this bleak February day, Vladimir Zhirinsky no longer felt the heavy depression of days past. His time of public exile was now, at last, coming to an end.

The sky over the capital was a sallow gray. Here and there snowflakes whispered to the pavement.

Frozen pedestrians scurried past piles of dirty snow. Scarves and collars met in tight fists as men and women hurried home to cold walk-up flats.

Winter in Russia was a depressing season. One could feel it in the air. But that same cold made weak men strong.

Vladimir Zhirinsky sat bundled in his greatcoat in the rear of his battered Zil limousine. The rusted old car coughed and spluttered through the cold streets of Moscow.

Through careful eyes he studied the city as it passed his tinted windows.

They had just driven by McDonald's. Burger King, too. Radio Shack, Dunkin' Donuts and Pizza Hut all had franchises in Russia's capital. A few days before, Zhirinsky had traveled on business to San Francisco. It sickened him to see the same capitalist logos adorning buildings in his beloved Moscow as he'd seen in America.

An old Russian proverb spoke of the land of his birth as "not a country, but a world." If that was true, then in his lifetime, Vladimir Zhirinsky had seen the world grow smaller.

For the Communist it had been a waking nightmare.

Poland, Czechoslovakia, Romania, Hungary, Yugoslavia and Bulgaria were gone overnight. They were followed by Lithuania, Latvia, Estonia, Kirghizia, Georgia, Uzbekistan and a hundred other puny states no bigger than a mile across.

All of them were ingrates. And they would each one pay.

The Soviet Union was gone only temporarily. If Vladimir Zhirinsky had his way, Mother Russia would rise again.

As he drove through the cold streets, the Kremlin rose up under the gloomy sky, its great onion domes touching the gray clouds. When he saw the buildings from the rear of his car, a smile curled beneath Zhirinsky's drooping mustache.

"Pray to your capitalist gods," he said with low menace, "for your end is near."

"Comrade?"

The nervous question came from the front seat. Even though the term was long out of fashion, Zhirinsky insisted his people use "comrade," the old Soviet form of address.

When he looked up, he found the fearful face of his young driver staring back at him in the rearview mirror.

"Nothing," Zhirinsky grunted with an impatient wave of his hand. His brow sank low in thought. "Their lackey president has a small nose," he mused as the Kremlin disappeared behind them, replaced by the bland facades of Moscow's downtown buildings. "Not like the last president. Now, *there* was a big Russian nose."

As he considered the nose of the last Russian leader, a thin dollop of drool rolled from the corner of his mouth.

He was patting his belly hungrily when the Zil pulled to the curb minutes later.

Zhirinsky's building was a good, solid Soviet-era affair. This was clear by the chunks of broken concrete on the sidewalk. Zhirinsky had to dodge hunks of falling mortar on his way to the cracked front door.

Inside, the elevator wasn't working. Even though it had never worked since it was installed in 1968, Zhirinsky blamed the capitalists who now owned what was rightly state property. He took the stairs.

Those people he met on his way up ran for the

nearest exits when they saw the wiry, middle-aged man with the pale complexion coming toward them. Even while running, they kept their hands clamped firmly to their noses.

On the third floor, Zhirinsky steered down the dingy corridor. A crude hammer and sickle was outlined in red on the cracked veneer of one warped old door. Zhirinsky grabbed the wobbly doorknob, flinging the door open with a vengeance.

As the former Russian senator stomped into his cramped office, a pair of startled eyes shot up across the room.

"Comrade Zhirinsky," said the breathless young man from behind an overflowing desk.

Ivan Kerbabaev had been assisting Zhirinsky ever since he'd lost his job as a file clerk in the office of the chairman of Material Reserves.

Ivan jumped to attention, knocking a stack of pamphlets to the dirty floor. Mouth locking open in horror, he shot a look at his employer. Luckily, Zhirinsky seemed distracted.

He pulled off his hat, flinging it to his own desk. A tousled mess of brown-turning-to-gray hair spilled out.

"What is the latest intelligence?" Zhirinsky barked.

Ivan's eyes grew wider. "Oh. The intelligence," he stammered. "About that..."

Fearful eyes darted around the office, but other than his desk drawers there was no place to hide. Ivan had a sudden mental image of Vladimir Zhirinsky stuffing his dismembered body parts into his desk. He shivered.

"Well," Ivan continued carefully, "everything seems to be going along perfectly. *Better* than perfectly. It is fan-socialist-tastic."

When he smiled weakly, Zhirinsky fixed Ivan with cold black eyes. His demented gleam sparkled with flecks of gray.

"So the capitalists have surrendered Russian America to us?" Zhirinsky said, his voice flat.

Ivan hedged. "Not yet, comrade," he admitted. "Not technically surrendered. I suspect they are getting things together. Packing, phoning ahead to see if there are hotel rooms ready, that sort of thing."

As he spoke, he pretended to scratch a persistent itch on the bridge of his nose.

"There should have been something by now," Zhirinsky said to himself. "I have crippled their oil pipeline and destroyed an entire village. Not to mention the demonstration against their army. I— Take your hand away from your face!" he snapped, suddenly distracted.

Jumping, Ivan slapped his hands to his sides.

"The Soviet Union must be rebuilt piece by piece," Zhirinsky continued. "Russian America was lost even before the Revolution. By retaking it, we will signal the start of the new Revolution. The new age that will bring order back to this nation of thieves and whores."

Before Zhirinsky, Ivan's hands quivered at his sides.

"Actually, comrade, there may be a slight problem.'' Ivan hated to admit it, but he feared the repercussions if he did not. His eyes were fixed squarely on his employer's sharp teeth. ''The Kosygin Brigade has not reported in.''

Black eyes narrowed. ''Where were they last located?''

''Near Kakwik,'' Ivan explained. ''There was not enough room to airlift them out with the rest. They were to be collected tomorrow.''

Zhirinsky's next word was a hiss. ''Skachkov?'' he asked.

''He was not with them, comrade,'' Ivan promised.

The brief flash of concern faded. ''Is it a communication problem?'' he suggested.

''There was some snow in that region of the Alyeska Republic,'' Ivan said, visibly relieved at his employer's calm acceptance. ''The storm could have affected communications.''

All remaining tension drained from Zhirinsky's bushy eyebrows. ''Then that is what happened,'' he insisted. ''Given their abilities, there is no other explanation.'' He frowned as he took a seat at one of the desks. ''I do not like the fact that the Americans are ignoring us. Contact Skachkov. Tell him to purge another village. If they will not evacuate our property willingly, we will remove them one by one.''

Ivan almost tripped over his own feet in his haste to leave the office. He couldn't use an office phone to call. The Moscow telephone company could rarely get them to work. He'd have to run around the corner to Arby's.

He was bounding out into the hallway when Zhirinsky's voice boomed behind him.

"Ivan!" the ultranationalist bellowed.

When the terrified young man turned, the former Russian senator was thoughtfully stroking his bushy mustache.

"Tell him to save the noses," he commanded. There was a hungry look in his demented eyes.

As Ivan left, shuddering, Vladimir Zhirinsky bowed his graying head and began sorting through the day's mail.

18

The ground flew by beneath the belly of the racing Kamov, a blanket of soothing white stretching off to the horizon.

Remo, Chiun and Anna were in the back of the helicopter. The two Masters of Sinanju were side by side. Anna sat across from them.

"What the hell's a Zhirinsky?" Remo was asking Anna.

"He is an ultranationalist," she explained. "He was a senator in my country at one time. He is also one of many who would like nothing better than to see a return to the old Soviet totalitarian system."

"So much for my first guess," Remo said. "I thought it was one of those shitty kerosene-powered Eastern European cars with the bicycle tires. So where'd these guys of his get Sinanju training?"

"It is not Sinanju," Chiun interjected firmly. "Whatever it is they possess was not given them by a true Master and is therefore false. Since it is not Sinanju, it is less than Sinanju. These are no different than the thieving ninjas or Sherpas or all the others who would steal embers from the flame that is the true Sun Source."

"Sherpas?" Remo asked.

"Not now," Chiun intoned. "Your prostitute is about to speak."

"These men *do* have a Master," Anna said, ignoring the old man. "Lavrenty Skachkov is the most skilled of them all. He has guided the training of the rest of the men, who look on him with awe. They even call him *Mactep.* 'Master.'"

Chiun's face grew concerned. "This is true?" he demanded of Anna.

She nodded. "Skachkov is a true danger," she said. "He is not like the rest. I caution you to be very careful if you encounter him."

Remo's brow furrowed. "That Mactep thing sounds familiar," he said. "Where did I hear that word before?" He snapped his fingers. "I know. That whacko general with the death wish in California. Fraidykov."

"Yes," Anna said, nodding. "He apparently mentioned the word to you before he died. I told you that it was the name of the program General Feyodov led that was intended to bring Sinanju to Russia."

"Yeah, but you said it was just to get me and Chiun to work for you. And that was years ago. You didn't say anything about any other recruits."

"I am afraid I was not completely truthful with you," Anna admitted. In her blue eyes was a hint of genuine shame.

"There's a surprise," Remo said with a scowl. "I suppose I shouldn't have expected any more. This from a woman who managed to make a full recovery from being dead for thirteen years."

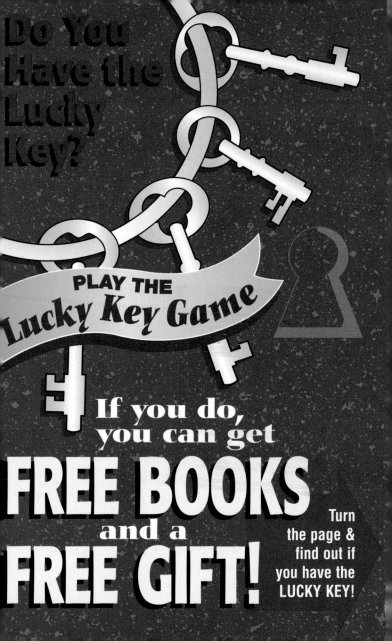

PLAY THE Lucky Key Game and get

HOW TO PLAY:

1. With a coin, carefully scratch off the gold area at the right. Then check the claim chart to see what we have for you — **2 FREE BOOKS** and a **FREE GIFT** — **ALL YOURS FREE!**

2. Send back the card and you'll receive two hot-off-the-press Gold Eagle® novels. These books have a cover price of $4.50 or more each, but they are yours to keep absolutely free.

3. There's no catch. You're under no obligation to buy anything. We charge nothing — ZERO — for your first shipment. And you don't have to make any minimum number of purchases — not even one!

4. The fact, is thousands of readers enjoy receiving books by mail from the Gold Eagle Reader Service™. They like the convenience of home delivery…they like getting the best new novels before they're available in stores…and they love our discount prices!

5. We hope that after receiving your free books you'll want to remain a subscriber. But the choice is yours — to continue or cancel, any time at all! So why not take us up on our invitation, with no risk of any kind. You'll be glad you did!

YOURS FREE!
A SURPRISE MYSTERY GIFT

We can't tell you what it is…but we're sure you'll like it! A **FREE GIFT—** just for playing the LUCKY KEY game!

© 1999 GOLD EAGLE.

The Gold Eagle Reader Service™ — Here's how it works:

Accepting your 2 free books and gift places you under no obligation to buy anything. You may keep the books and gift and return the shipping statement marked "cancel." If you do not cancel, about a month later we'll send you 6 additional novels and bill you just $26.70* — that's a saving of 15% off the cover price of all 6 books! And there's no extra charge for shipping! You may cancel at any time, but if you choose to continue, every other month we'll send you 6 more books, which you may either purchase at the discount price or return to us and cancel your subscription.

*Terms and prices subject to change without notice. Sales tax applicable in N.Y. Canadian residents will be charged applicable provincial taxes and GST.

"Forget her," Chiun said in Korean. "We have a danger far greater here."

"What danger?" Remo asked. "These guys are no great shakes. We just took out ten of them without breaking a sweat."

"Did you not hear the woman?" Chiun insisted. "Or did you forget so soon the prophecy of Wang? 'Of Sinanju, yet not of Sinanju.' And what are these night tigers if not an army of death? We must beware this Master, Remo."

"I don't know, Little Father," Remo said. "I figured the false Master would be Korean, not Russian. After all, just saying you're a Master of Sinanju doesn't automatically *make* you a Master of Sinanju."

"That is not entirely true, either," Chiun said, his lips pulled tight, as if relating some painful truth.

"What's that supposed to mean?" Remo asked, noting the sudden stiff posture his teacher had affected.

"It means listen to this woman's advice," the Master of Sinanju said. "We must both exercise great caution, for the future of the line of the Great Wang rests on both our shoulders. And it is *you* who must ultimately face the false Master alone."

"Who says?" Remo asked.

"It was part of Wang's prophecy. I may assist you to remove his night tigers, but the Master must be dealt with by the youngest of the line. That is you."

Remo exhaled. "No pressure there," he muttered to himself. He turned his attention back to Anna.

"What was that all about?" she asked. Since she

could not speak Korean, she had been unable to follow their conversation.

"Same old, same old," Remo sighed. "Last train for sanity's already left Removille, and I'm not on it. So where'd these soldier guys learn their moves?"

She looked from one man to the other, her brow knotted, before answering.

"In Moscow there is a training facility," Anna replied. "For more than a decade men have been recruited. Skachkov was one of the earliest. He, like many of the others, was a former athlete. Those who showed natural physical abilities were enrolled in the program."

"That's the what, but not the who," Remo said. "Someone had to have trained Scratchcop, right? If he's the almighty false Master, who taught *him?*"

Chiun also seemed interested in her response.

"That is something you will have to ask him," Anna said.

There was a hint of vagueness in her tone. Although Remo missed it, Chiun did not.

Before she had even finished, Remo was turning to Chiun. "Nuihc was dead ages before this."

"Do not speak that name to me," Chiun said, his face fouling at the mention of his traitorous nephew and former pupil.

"I'm just saying we can eliminate him is all," Remo said. "The Dutchman might not be out of the equation, though." He glanced at Anna. "You said ten years, right?"

"Perhaps a few more," she admitted.

"The time frame fits," Remo said. "He could have hired out to Feyodov to train this Scratch guy before that last time we beat him."

"It is possible," Chiun replied. He was studying Anna Chutesov through narrowed eyes.

"Only explanation," Remo insisted. "Unless you've got another undead Master of Sinanju stashed up your sleeve, it'd have to be him. So let me guess," he said to Anna. "These guys along with Zhirwhosie were with Feyodov in the black market. But when we bumped off their sugar-daddy general a couple days ago they all snapped. Am I close?"

"Zhirinsky had been dealing with Feyodov and others in the black market a great deal lately," Anna admitted carefully. As she spoke, she stared out the helicopter's side window. The dark sky and light ground formed a fuzzy, perpetual twilight. "The SVR was interested in his transactions," she continued. "He has been receiving a great many donations lately from others with political leanings like his own. He was spending the money on a rather exotic collection of black-market items. Some feared he might be staging a coup to take back the Russian government for the hard-liners."

"No such luck," Remo said. "Instead of rooting through your own garbage, he's got to come kick over our cans. What's he think he's going to accomplish in Alaska anyway?"

"Why does a man do anything?" Anna asked. "They are insane. Strutting and crowing to prove their worth. If Zhirinsky is worse, it is only a matter of degree.'' She seemed to be harboring some secret anger. Her icy eyes flashed hot as she stared out at the night.

"Okay, this time let's try to answer leaving out all the NOW rhetoric, shall we?" Remo said reasonably.

She glanced at him. "Zhirinsky wants Alaska," she said simply. "He is a madman with a mind to act. And this twisted mind doubtless thinks a stunt like this will be met with public approval back home. Given the present state of my country, he is probably correct."

"Does the phrase 'World War III' mean anything to him?" Remo asked.

"Zhirinsky is a true Communist," Anna said bitterly. "He would be willing to sacrifice the lives of millions in order to gain power."

"Happy days are here again," Remo grumbled. "You know, a lesser man might take this opportunity to point out that if you'd shared some of this information with us like our original agreement all those years ago instead of pulling that disappearing act of yours, we might have been able to nip this in the bud."

She shook her head. "Zhirinsky only just made his intentions known," she said, her voice distant. "As it is, he is free somewhere in Russia. I could not trust the SVR to apprehend him, for they might have decided to join him. I am the only person I trust to stop him, and when I heard what was going on here I had to leave him at large in Russia to travel to Alaska. I am alone, Remo. And I have been alone for a long,

long time. I told you already what it would mean to share information with you. I was not willing to sacrifice my life, which is what would have been the result had I broken my silence.''

It was Remo's turn to shake his head. ''I know you think I would have killed you, but I wouldn't have,'' he insisted. ''Smith would have thought you were a security risk, but I know better. I don't know why you're so sure about this, but you're wrong, Anna. I would not have killed you. Period.''

She turned to him once more. A hint of warm sadness melted the iciest depths of her deeply intelligent blue eyes.

''You *would* have,'' she said quietly.

And the seriousness of her tone seemed to leave no room for argument.

The lights of Kakwik appeared to the far right of the helicopter.

''Should I have my pilot change course so that you can retrieve your vehicle?'' Anna asked.

''Let's ditch it,'' Remo said. ''We'll see this through together.''

''Yes,'' the Master of Sinanju said, breaking his studied silence. ''Let us remain close.''

Remo saw that he was watching Anna with suspicious hazel eyes. He automatically chalked it up to the old man's distaste for the relationship Remo and Anna had shared in the past.

''The events have been confined to this region of the state,'' Anna said. ''We should assume that the troops are near here.''

"Alaska's a big town," Remo said. "But I guess we're stuck till they make their next move. In the meantime I'll give Smitty a call."

Anna's features tightened. "Remo," she warned.

"I know, I know," he promised. "You're still dead. But it'd be nice if someone kept track of this Zhirinsky while we're cooling our jets, don't you think?"

The tension drained from her face. "Agreed," she said reluctantly. "Just please think of a plausible lie to explain where you learned the information I have given you."

"Don't sweat it," Remo promised. "I'm on it."

And the smile of self-confidence he flashed her was such that Anna Chutesov regretted more than ever her participation in the events that had led her here, to the end of the world.

19

Though he knew he was in Folcroft, Mark Howard didn't know exactly where.

It was a hallway like any of the others. Apparently, night had fallen. At least there was no sign of daylight beyond the barred windows.

Funny, as he walked he couldn't remember seeing bars on any of the windows before. But there they were. Solid steel, preventing escape. The world beyond the thick panes was as black as death.

A cold wind snaked up the hallway, icy fingers brushing Mark's shivering spine.

A voice. Soft. More a plaintive moan than spoken words. It stopped abruptly.

For an instant he thought he'd imagined it. He paused to listen.

Nothing. Just the forlorn sigh of the wind and the creaking of the sedate old building.

He strained to hear.

And as he listened to the shadows, he swore he saw something moving in the darkness before him. The flicker of movement turned to a flash. Whatever it was had flown to his side at a speed impossible even for his mind's eye to reconcile. And the voice that was the wind and the dark and everything else in this lost place bellowed with rage and pain and hate in his ear.

Come for me!

"WHAT?" Mark called, snapping awake.

It took him a moment to orient himself.

He was alone in his small Folcroft office. The blinds were open. Gray daylight bathed the naked trees beyond his one window. The thin snow that had been spitting down since he'd come to work early that morning continued to drop to the ground. Where it struck, it melted on contact.

Mark rubbed the sleep from his eyes.

A dream. He'd been dreaming. Somehow he had fallen asleep at work.

"Great," he mumbled, annoyed with himself. "Just the right way to start a new job."

Shaking away the weird feeling of dread the strange dream had given him, Mark turned his attention to his computer.

The monitor wasn't high tech like Dr. Smith's. A simple old-fashioned screen and keyboard sat before him. When not in use, a concealed stud lowered the monitor into the surface of the scarred oak desk, hiding it from prying eyes.

According to Eileen Mikulka, the desk had belonged to Dr. Smith. Mark assumed it had been with the older man for much of his stewardship of CURE. With a somber appreciation for the history that the battered desk represented, Mark reached for the keyboard.

After only a few moments he had banished all thoughts of the disturbing dream.

Dr. Smith had asked him to look into the Russian angle of what was taking place in Alaska. Since the survivor of the Kakwik massacre had mentioned an old Soviet rather than a modern Russia connection, Mark had begun by searching for known ultranationalists. He quickly found that the list of unrepentant hard-liners was discouragingly long. The names on the screen seemed to scroll forever. There were far too many to go through them all.

Dumping the list, Mark altered the search parameters. Reasoning that whoever was behind this would almost certainly have to be unbalanced, he instructed the CURE mainframes to limit the search to Russian ultranationalists with known or suspected mental problems.

When the list reappeared after a few scant moments of analysis, Mark was troubled to find that it was nearly identical to the first roster of names.

His search had once more been too broad. The vague category of mental problems he had used was too all-encompassing to isolate those who would restore Communist rule and enslave the Russian population.

He leaned back in his chair to think, careful not to bump his head on the wall. Almost as soon as he'd tipped back, a thought came to him. Deciding that whoever would launch such an attack on American soil would have to be insane, Mark returned to his keyboard, typing something more straightforward.

"L-O-O-N," he said aloud as he entered each letter.

The word he'd typed on a whim yielded instant results. A single file appeared. At its top was the name Vladimir Zhirinsky.

Mark remembered the unreformed Communist from a few years back. In fact, one of his first suggestions as a CIA analyst had been to warn his superiors of the threat Zhirinsky presented. As he scrolled through the profile, he found the term "loon" had been applied to the ultranationalist by a State Department official.

"Score one for the State Department," he said as he reacquainted himself with Zhirinsky's biographical data.

Mark was surprised to learn that Zhirinsky was no longer a member of the Duma. He typed in the Russian's name, executing a quick search through CURE's most recent files. He was surprised to find Zhirinsky mentioned in a file dated that very day.

Upon accessing it, Mark found that the file had been routed from the FBI. One of the Bureau's agents had been brutally assaulted in San Francisco earlier in the week. He had been found in a closet at the airport, and had only just regained full consciousness that morning.

When Mark read the details of the assault, he felt his heart trip.

The man's nose had been torn off in the attack. Worse, there was every indication that it had been bitten off.

Even before reading it a few minutes ago, Mark had remembered well the incident where Vladimir Zhirinsky had chewed off his debate opponent's nose on live Russian television.

All at once, Mark Howard was beginning to get a very strong feeling.

Hands moving swiftly across the keyboard in a vain attempt to keep pace with his racing mind, Mark allowed his intuition to take over. Unmindful of where it might lead him.

20

Remo left Chiun and Anna to oversee the refueling of the Russian agent's Kamov. At a pay phone in the Fairbanks airport terminal, he stabbed out the multiple 1 code that automatically rerouted the call to the CURE director's office. Remo was relieved to hear Smith's tart voice on the other end of the line. For a moment he had been afraid the older man's new assistant might answer.

"More bad news, Smitty," Remo announced. "The problem here might be bigger than we bargained for."

"Explain," the CURE director said tightly.

Remo quickly told him about the ten men he and Chiun had encountered. "So that's it," he concluded. "Except Chiun's all wigged out that we're facing down some renegade Sinanju Master. Oh, and I think the Dutchman might be to blame."

The tension in Smith's tone was evident. "Has Purcell escaped?" he asked, voice growing sick.

"Not unless he took off after we left. I think he trained these guys before he took a permanent powder from sanity at Folcroft. It's the only explanation."

Smith cleared his throat. "Perhaps not. Remo, Master Chiun has been known to on occasion—" he paused, searching for the right word "—*solicit* outside work. Could he—"

"I know where this is heading," Remo cut in, "and the answer is no. Chiun doesn't have time to train any armies. He's got too much on his plate as it is, what with catalog shopping for a house and brownieing up to the new guy."

"Army? Remo, how many of these individuals are there?"

"Oops. Forgot to ask her. I'll have to get back to you on that one, Smitty."

Smith's voice suddenly seemed to drop. His acid tone took on a worried edge. "Her who?" the CURE director asked.

Remo hadn't even realized he'd misspoken. His eyes darted around the airport terminal as if searching for a convincing lie among the thin crowd of travelers.

"Um," he said. "Just someone we—" Inspiration struck. "You know that FBI agent that helped us out in Barkley a couple of days ago?"

"Brandy Brand," Smith supplied, his voice perfectly even.

"Yeah, her," Remo said. "She's here, too. She must get all the 'When Good Russians Go Bad' cases these days."

"You are saying that she has been assigned to this case and is working in Alaska right now?" Smith asked. By now his voice had grown distinctly dubious.

Remo suddenly got the impression he was being set up. But he'd come too far to bail out now. "Yes?"

he said cautiously. It came out sounding too much like a question.

"That is odd," Smith said. "Because my information has Agent Brand still in California. She is directing the FBI's follow-up investigation into those individuals at Barkley University and elsewhere in town who were involved in smuggling and assembling the device that was used to wreak havoc on the global satellite network earlier this week."

He let the words hang between them.

Caught in an obvious lie, Remo didn't know what to say. He shook his head in tired annoyance. "What are you even doing checking up on Brandy, Smitty?" he asked wearily.

"It would seem the situation that involved her is tied to events in Alaska," the CURE director explained. "While conducting research, Mark linked an assault on Agent Brand's partner at San Francisco Airport with a Russian nationalist by the name of Vladimir Zhirinsky. Apparently, her partner recognized Zhirinsky but did not know from where. He remembered when he recovered this morning from the shock and heavy sedation he had been under."

"Bully for the prince regent," grumbled Remo, who now had a new reason to dislike Mark Howard. "Zhirinsky's the guy who's pulling the strings on the soldiers up here," he said. "I was calling to have you keep tabs on him."

"I have already issued orders to put Zhirinsky under surveillance," Smith said. "And you still have not answered truthfully my original question. Since it is not from the woman you claimed, from whom did you get this information?''

Remo's mouth thinned. ''Trust me on this one, Smitty. You don't want to know.''

''I fear I already do,'' Smith said gravely. ''Remo, is Anna Chutesov still alive?''

Remo felt his heart sink. ''Oh, boy,'' he said. ''How long have you known? You must've just found out with that mess in California. Just do me a favor, Smitty, and make sure you don't say I'm the one who told you. She's gonna kill me when she finds out.''

For a few seconds there was nothing but dead air on the other end of the line. When the CURE director at last spoke, his voice was a barely audible croak.

''My God, so it *is* true,'' Smith said.

A continent away, in his Spartan Folcroft Sanitarium office, Harold Smith gripped the edge of his black desk with his free hand. His arthritic knuckles grew white.

''Oh,'' Remo said over the blue contact phone. ''You mean you didn't know for sure already?''

Smith's grip on the desk did not relax. ''No, I did not. Have you known this all along?'' he demanded.

''No, Smitty,'' Remo said. ''We all thought she died on that assignment years ago. She just popped up and said 'hi' this week when we were in Barkley after that screwy Russian general. I'm lucky I had my nitroglycerine tablets on me.''

''How did she escape this time?'' Smith asked.

A pause. ''I don't follow,'' Remo said.

"Obviously she escaped from you. Otherwise she would not be alive now."

"Oh. That," Remo said slowly. "I kind of let her go."

"Let her go," Smith said, his voice perfectly flat. "Given the knowledge she possesses of this agency. In spite of the danger she represents to everything we do, you let her go?"

"Well, if you put it that way, sure it's gonna sound bad," Remo admitted. Before the CURE director could speak, Remo forged on. "Look, Smitty, she kept our secret for more than ten years. The proof's in the pudding on that, otherwise we wouldn't still be in business. Anna was afraid you'd send me to kill her, so she took the only way out she thought was open to her. And before you try to get me to bump her off, the answer is no. And Chiun's on the same page because he knows I'd be pissed at him if he kills her."

"Then I will do it myself," Smith said.

"Try it and you can find yourself a new enforcement arm," Remo warned.

Smith relaxed the tension in his fingers. His hand slipped from the desk, falling wearily beside his worn leather chair.

"Remo, this is an untenable situation," he said tiredly.

"Why?" Remo asked. "Anna worked with us before. Why can't we just go back to where we left off?"

"Because things have changed drastically in the intervening years," Smith explained. "There is no Soviet Union. We were arm's length allies while our countries were both superpowers. Our pact at that time benefited both nations. With Russia in its current state, however, Anna Chutesov simply is not needed any longer."

"Don't be so sure on any of that, Smitty," Remo said. "If this Zhirinsky guy gets his way, the old-line Commies might be back singing 'Hail Freedonia' while splashing around naked in the celebratory vodka fountain."

Smith was loath to leave the topic of Anna Chutesov, but for the moment they were at an impasse. And Remo was right. Right now Vladimir Zhirinsky was the more immediate threat.

"I will issue orders to the Moscow police to pick up Zhirinsky," Smith sighed.

"You might want to hold off on that," Remo suggested. "Anna seemed pretty sure that a lot of people might throw in with him, including law enforcement. She was afraid to even have the SUV come in on this."

"SVR," Smith said. "They are successor to the KGB."

"Whatever they are, they can't be trusted," Remo said. "You better let me and Chiun take care of him. Except we can't go right now because we've got a bunch of Sinanju thieves and their Master to track down up here, and maybe a moldy old Sinanju prophecy to deal with in the bargain."

"Huh," Smith mused. "It was the SVR that I had

ordered to watch Zhirinsky. Ms. Chutesov is probably correct about their divided loyalties. I will pull them off.''

Even as he spoke, he reached for his desk. An alphanumeric keyboard appeared as if by magic beneath his summoning fingers. Typing swiftly, he began issuing the surreptitious orders that would suspend the surveillance orders on Vladimir Zhirinsky.

"See, Smitty?" Remo said as the CURE director worked. "She's coming in handy already."

Smith allowed the remark to pass.

"We cannot allow a lunatic like Zhirinsky to excite militaristic passions in the Russian people," the CURE director said as he typed. "The former Red Army is a shambles. For defense, Russia is relying almost exclusively on its nuclear arsenal. Even a small force operating on American soil could cause a destabilizing chain reaction with cataclysmic effects."

"Not a problem," Remo replied. "The first ten weren't anything special. Some glorified karate moves and camo suits to help them hide. We'll pull the plug on however many are left and then take a spin back to Russia for Zhirinsky."

Smith was only half listening. Peering down at his angled desk monitor, his gray face had grown troubled.

"That might prove difficult," he said. "Zhirinsky has apparently disappeared." Eyes of flint-gray scanned the translated report he had accessed from the SVR's Moscow mainframes. "It would seem he became aware of SVR interest in him and fled. His whereabouts are currently unknown.''

"Sounds like they tipped him off," Remo said.

In the silence of his office, Smith nodded. "So it would seem," the CURE director agreed. Determination clenched his jaw. "We will attempt to find him from here. Mark has discovered the alias he used to travel to San Francisco earlier in the week. Perhaps he will use the same name again. In any event you and Chiun have work to do."

"Smitty?" Remo said as the older man was hanging up.

Smith returned the phone to his ear. "What?"

"You didn't know Anna was still alive," Remo began. "You didn't even know we bumped into her in Barkley, right?"

"That's true," Smith conceded.

"So what made you even think it after all this time?"

Smith placed a cautious, flat palm to the surface of his desk. "While conducting research into Vladimir Zhirinsky, Mark accessed some of our old Russia-related files. He found Anna's name among the data."

"So what?" Remo asked. "That still doesn't mean anything. She should have just been a name on a page to him. How did he know she wasn't really dead?"

The CURE director grew uneasy. He was grateful Remo was thousands of miles away and unable to see the disturbed expression that had taken root on his patrician face.

"Upon reading the details of her death, Mark had

a hunch,'' Smith explained. He quickly added, "Now please excuse me. We both have work to do."

Before Remo could pry any more, the CURE director hung up the phone.

A shadow of concern formed a brief knot in the old man's brow. Feeling sudden empathy for the lifelong efforts Mark Howard had gone through to hide his gift from the world, Harold Smith turned slowly to his computer, a thoughtful expression on his lean face.

21

The Master of Sinanju posed imperiously on the airport tarmac. Beside him, Anna Chutesov watched the fuel line that was feeding the Kamov's hungry tanks.

No one seemed interested in the odd-looking helicopter, which was licensed to a private geological surveying company.

Chiun had been careful not to make his suspicions about Anna known to Remo, lest some misguided sense of chivalry cause him to come to the defense of his former concubine. When Remo left to phone Smith, the old man waited until he was well out of earshot before turning his attention to Anna.

"You know more than you are admitting," Chiun announced bluntly. His eyes beneath the brim of his hat were accusing.

Anna was studying the helicopter refueling. "Why am I not surprised that you would be suspicious of me?"

"Because you are not stupid," Chiun replied. "And it is in your nature to lie when it suits you. Just as it is in my son's nature to be too trusting. Especially when it comes to you. You blind him to your deceptions."

The smile that brushed Anna Chutesov's pale cheeks was sad. "You invest too much power in me," she said softly. "The time when that might have been true was long ago."

Years before Anna Chutesov had been able to manipulate the many men who worshiped her. But by rejecting her, Remo had changed all that. Blue eyes grew wistful at the memory.

"It is not your wiles, but Remo's sentimentality that is the problem," Chiun insisted. "He sees you for what he thinks you were. If only he could see you for but a moment through my eyes." His face remained impassive. "He would blame me if any harm were to befall you by my hand, so I cannot force the truth from you. Therefore you may keep your silly secret, on one condition. Tell me if Remo is at risk."

Anna considered for a long moment. At last she relented, her shoulders sinking almost imperceptibly. "The only immediate risk to either of you is that which I have already told you," she admitted quietly.

Chiun could see she was telling the truth. Accepting her words with a nod of his bald head, he turned back to face the helicopter. Wind whipped the skirts of his kimono.

Anna was relieved when he pried no further. Eyes of ice turned from the Master of Sinanju, facing once more the Kamov.

"You have both changed since last I knew you," she said softly. As she spoke, she still did not turn to the old man.

Chiun took a few seconds to reply.

"Remo is no longer the child he once was," the tiny Asian admitted. "He has achieved the level of full Master."

"Ah," Anna said, nodding. "That is why you cede authority to him. How long ago did he succeed you as Reigning Master?"

Chiun's jaw clenched. His sliver of beard whipped wildly in the wind. "He has not yet assumed the mantle of Reigning Master," he admitted tightly.

Anna glanced, curious, at the old Korean. "I do not wish to offend, but should he not have done so by now? After all, at your age..." She let her voice trail off.

But Chiun was through answering her questions. "These are private matters, not to be discussed with outsiders," he said stiffly. "Remo's former concubine or not, if you wish to keep your tongue, I would advise you to keep your theories of Sinanju succession to yourself."

He offered the Russian agent his frail back. The old man stared out across the airport, a figure of ancient wisdom lost in deep thought. The darkness of the long and lingering Alaska winter night weighed heavy on his bony shoulders.

It was clear she had inadvertently struck a raw nerve. Biting her lip, she left the old man to his private thoughts.

Ten minutes later the fuel line was just being detached when Remo appeared through a side door in one of the low terminal outbuildings. He hurried to rejoin Anna and Chiun.

"I talked to Smith," he said, his voice tense. "Looks like Zhirinsky's pulled a disappearing act."

Anna's expression made it clear that this was in no way good news. "How long has he been gone?" she asked.

"Don't know. Didn't ask. Does it matter?"

"It does, depending on where he is going," she said, her tone troubled. "You were careful to keep me out of your discussions with your Dr. Smith?"

Remo grew sheepish. "Well..." he said.

Anna's voice grew flat. "You didn't," she accused.

"*I* didn't," Remo said quickly. He just as quickly reconsidered. "I guess I sort of did. But only after he did it first. Smitty's got this new assistant, Anna. Somehow the little nit figured out you weren't dead."

Chiun's curiosity was piqued. "How did Prince Mark divine such a thing?"

"I dunno." Remo shrugged. "Probably just dumb luck." When he turned to Anna, he found that the Russian agent's beautiful face had taken on a caved-in look. "Don't sweat it, Anna," he said. "I told him that Chiun and I are hands-off in the killing-you department. When this is over, I'll talk him into letting us go back to our old arrangement."

Anna shook her head. "Things have changed too much since then," she said. Her soft words seemed spoken only for herself. Ice-blue eyes sought the imperious face of the Master of Sinanju.

Remo would have said more, but they were interrupted by the Kamov's pilot. The man was scurrying down from the helicopter cockpit. His face urgent, he approached Anna, spouting a stream of Russian while he ran.

He was barely finished before she was turning on the others. Her face remained without a hint of emotion.

"There has been another massacre," Anna said dully. "A small town to the west of here."

"How long ago?" Remo demanded.

"Apparently it is happening right now," Anna replied. "One of the townspeople has radioed for help."

Expression still flat, she turned to her pilot, issuing a few brief Russian commands. The man turned and ran back for the Kamov.

"I forgot to ask before," Remo said as the engine coughed to life. "How many of these guys are there?"

He was surprised by her answer.

"Nearly 150," Anna said, her tone lifeless.

"Looks like our work's cut out for us, Little Father," Remo said tightly.

The Master of Sinanju offered a sharp nod of agreement. Hiking up his kimono skirts, he hurried to the waiting Kamov.

The wobbly rotors had just begun to slice the chill air.

Remo began to follow his teacher, but paused.

Anna still appeared to be shell-shocked.

"Don't worry," he vowed softly to her. "You're safe as long as I'm around." Giving her a reassuring smile, he turned and ran for the helicopter.

Alone for a moment, Anna shut her tired eyes.

Blocking out the cold, the wind and the growing roar of the Kamov.

"No, Remo," she said quietly to the night. "That is when I am at the greatest risk."

Shoulders hunched against the freezing wind, Anna Chutesov hurried to the waiting Kamov.

22

Anna's pilot dropped them a mile outside town. The Russian agent and the two Sinanju Masters made their cautious way down to the village.

The small Inuit settlement of Umakarot was a snowcapped junkyard. Half-scavenged cars and trucks rose from the drifts like the bones of frozen metal beasts. Sheets of tin on tumbledown homes rattled in the wind.

And amid all the squalor lay the bodies.

In spite of the pervasive gloom, Anna could still see well enough to note that the first body they passed had been mutilated. The villager's nose had been removed. A gaping red triangle sat beneath the dead man's wide-open eyes.

The others they saw were like the first.

"Zhirinsky," Anna hissed knowingly. With a tear of Velcro, she pulled her automatic from the pocket of her parka. Her eyes studied the washed-out grays and blacks that shadowed the village.

Remo and Chiun were proceeding cautiously. There was nothing in their movements that indicated either safety or danger. Anna pitched her voice low.

"Are we alone?" she asked.

"Nah," Remo replied. "We're pretty much surrounded."

From where they were walking, Remo and Chiun took note of eighteen commandos, all dressed in the same concealing off-white uniforms.

"Hey, be careful where you point that thing," Remo said.

Anna's gun barrel had strayed to his back as she studied the blank shadows. She quickly shifted it away.

"What are they doing?" Anna asked.

"Standing," Remo said. "If it wasn't for the guns they've got pointed at us, I'd say they kind of looked like snowmen. Albeit smelly, skinny Russian snowmen, one of which I think is carrying a beach pail full of noses. Yuck." His brow lowered. "Why do you suppose they haven't opened fire?"

"Perhaps they want my autograph," the Master of Sinanju sniffed as he padded along.

"Huh," Remo said. "That's weird."

"What?" Anna whispered. She had yet to see a living soul.

"One of these guys is kind of moving his hands funny," he said, making a point not to appear too interested in the soldier who loitered in the shadow of a fix-it shop. "Chiun tells me I move my hands like that, don't you, Chiun?"

The old Asian nodded. "There," he said, with a subtle chin motion. "Another does the same."

When he followed the old man's gaze, Remo found a Russian standing in shadow near a tall stack of useless snowmobile chassis. To Remo's surprise, this soldier was also rotating his wrists absently.

"Now that's freaky," Remo mused. "You think Purcell taught them that to try to throw me off guard?"

"We do not know who taught them anything," Chiun cautioned. "Nor do we know how much they know. Therefore we must remain cautious."

"Fiddlesticks," Remo said. "Guy uses a gun's a guy who ain't so tough. Look, I'll prove it."

They were in the process of passing within a breath of one of the soldiers. Remo reached out casually, clamping on to the man's black goggles. With a yank he pulled them a foot away from the startled soldier's face and let them fly.

The goggles shot back much faster than they should have. With a thwack they struck his face, burying deep back in bone and brain.

The soldier appeared as if out of the ether, flopping to his back in the snow. He didn't move again.

"See?" Remo pointed out with a knowing nod. "I told you."

Anna met the sudden appearance of the soldier with shallow shock. Her brain didn't have time to fully absorb what had happened before she felt herself being hoisted in the air. As the guns of the remaining soldiers abruptly blazed to life, Remo flung Anna to safety behind the nearby heap of half-dismantled snowmobiles.

"Stay put," Remo suggested as he twisted and twirled around the incoming spatter of screaming lead.

Leaving Anna crawling on her knees in the snow, Remo and Chiun swirled into the center of the small village. Like moths drawn to a flame, the soldiers converged.

The men continued firing even as their shielded eyes told them that they had to already have hit their targets. Any doubts they might have entertained were quickly settled by the Master of Sinanju.

Chiun launched himself at the soldiers. A flying kick to the forehead of a charging commando sent the man's head back like a swatted tennis ball. It struck the face of the man directly behind. Skull met skull in a fusion of bone that instantly turned the two soldiers into Siamese twins conjoined at the head.

"Remember, we keep one for questioning this time," Remo warned as the two men fell.

He slapped a gun barrel up into a soldier's chin. It sprang like the first spring dandelion from the top of the man's head.

"It is your turn," the Master of Sinanju replied, tossing aside a pair of kidneys. The man to whom the kidneys belonged fell to the snow, a gaping hole in his lower back.

"Sez who?" A pulverizing forearm sheered the top clean off a soldier's head. The bucket of noses he carried spilled to the snow.

"Do you recall who saved one for questioning several months ago on another of Emperor Smith's errands?" the old man asked indignantly.

Remo couldn't recall. "No," he admitted.

"In that case it is definitely your turn," Chiun concluded. With that, he swirled away in a flurry of kimono skirts.

"I think I've been had," Remo said as he wheeled into the next tight group of four Russians.

They aimed their guns at Remo's chest and fired. He danced around the blast, coming up beside the startled men.

"Eenie, meenie, miney, moe. One of you has got to go," Remo sang.

His hand flashed forward and he tapped one commando dead center in the forehead. Behind thick goggles, Moe's eyes rolled back in his head. Before the other three knew what had happened, Remo had picked up the unconscious soldier and thrown him behind the pile of snowmobile chassis.

Eenie, Meenie and Miney swirled to Remo. There was a grunt of muffled Russian from beneath one ski mask.

"*Mactep*," the man breathed fearfully.

Remo had already been exercising greater caution with these soldiers. But with mention of the Russian word for "Master," his senses tripped higher.

Straining alertness, he tried to detect any concealed signs of life or stealthy movements in the area, anticipating the approach of Chiun's false Master of legend.

None was evident. In fact, as the soldiers raised their guns once more—now in shaking hands—their goggles were aimed squarely on Remo.

"Maybe they just know quality work when they see it," Remo mused with a shrug.

Before the men could fire, he smacked the barrels of the two on either side. Already squeezing their triggers, the two outside men blasted the man in the middle to ribbons even as they were mowing each other down in the cross fire.

As this latest trio was falling, Remo skipped on to the rest, the promise of doom writ large on his cruel face.

ANNA WAS KNEELING in the cold snow, her pistol still clasped tightly in her hand. She was forced to scramble out of the way when the soldier Remo had knocked unconscious came sliding back to join her.

Moe slid to a stop, a soft mound of snow gathering like a pillow beneath his head.

Tearing her eyes from the battle in the street, she crawled cautiously over to the man. When she saw he didn't stir, she sat her gun on her thigh and—very delicately—tugged off his ski mask and goggles.

The soldier had black wiry hair and harsh features. When she saw that it was not Skachkov, her face grew darkly disappointed.

Behind Anna, the crack of bones rose from the street. Remo and Chiun would be finished soon.

She dropped the mask to the snow, picking up her gun once more. She cast one last look over the unconscious man in the snow.

"I am sorry, Yuri," she whispered softly.

Jaw determined, she raised her automatic to the face of the slumbering man.

REMO WAS in the process of disarming his last soldier. As the armless man fell screaming to the snow, Remo finished him with a sharp toe to the bridge of the nose.

He twirled on the Master of Sinanju. Chiun, too, had only one soldier left. The commando was lunging at the old Korean, knife in hand.

"Have you saved one?" Chiun asked tersely as he dodged the sharp blade.

Remo nodded even as he tossed away the arms of his final soldier. "We're covered this time. The rest are baggage."

Chiun nodded sharply. "I have enough luggage," the old Asian sniffed.

Long-nailed hands raked the last startled Russian's throat. The man died not with a scream, but with a gurgle.

The two Masters of Sinanju were turning from the last Russian body when they heard the crack of a single gunshot. It came from where Remo had left Anna and the soldier he'd saved.

Fearing the worst, the two men raced back down the street, ducking around the pile of scrap metal.

They found Anna climbing to her feet, gun still in hand. Lying in the snow was the man Remo had kept for questioning. A gaping bullet hole decorated the dead soldier's forehead.

As they rounded the snowmobile heap, something near the corner of the adjacent house caught the Master of Sinanju's eye. Leaving Remo's side, the old man padded beyond Anna, stopping a few yards away.

Remo stopped before the Russian agent.

"Dammit, Anna, what did you do that for?" Remo complained, waving a hand at the soldier's body.

"Forgive me, but are we not here to stop them?" Anna asked blandly. She dusted snow from her knees.

"Yeah, but I wanted to question that one. Why do you think I tossed him over here?"

Her face grew impatient. "If, Remo, your secret code involves flinging bodies, you two are constantly sending messages. What is the key? The way they fly through the air, or the way in which they land?"

"Har-de-har-har," Remo scowled. Hands on his hips, he looked down at the dead man. "This is just peachy. Next time you wanna help, count to ten and then *don't.*"

"We haven't the time for this," Anna said, shaking her head. "Did any of these men offer any great resistance?"

Remo sighed. "No. Same as the last batch. Couple of moves here and there. That's it."

She seemed grimly satisfied. "Then it is unlikely any of them was Skachkov. He is better than the rest by far. Nevertheless, I had better make certain."

Turning, she headed out to the street where the Russian soldiers lay.

Remo glanced one last time at the dead man before spinning away in disgust. It was then that he spied the Master of Sinanju standing alone in the snow. The old man was peering down at something near his feet.

Puzzled, Remo walked over to his teacher. Before he'd even reached the tiny Korean, he saw what the Master of Sinanju was looking at.

A small body lay in the snow. It was a young girl, no more than nine years old.

Remo saw by the way the body was positioned that the child was the victim of a Sinanju floater stroke. It had been sloppily executed, but was effective just the same.

Chiun's face was unflinching. He stared down at the young girl with eyes of hazel stone. Remo's own expression mirrored that of his teacher. They stood there for a moment, side by side. Neither man said a word.

It was Remo who broke the silence.

"We're getting the guy who's behind this, Little Father," Remo vowed quietly. His tone was enough to chill the already frigid air.

No more words were needed. With sad and steely resolve, the only two true Masters of Sinanju slowly turned away from the tiny body.

23

The Hind might as well have been purchased from a junk dealer. When it was delivered, it had been rusted and moss covered, with rotten wiring and missing seats. The parts needed to restore the helicopter to its former military specifications had taken forever to acquire on the black market. But acquire them he did.

The fact that Vladimir Zhirinsky could buy Red Army hardware in this new Russia was convenient to the cause. Still, it disgusted him. All would change soon enough.

The old Mil Mi-24 squatted now in the snow behind him, painted with cold-climate camouflage. His troops stood around it. At the moment they were six dozen strong. And that number would grow over the next few hours. Greater still in the days ahead.

Some had only recently joined the cause. A few of the SVR men who had warned him he was under surveillance in Moscow were here. Ready to fight for the motherland.

The other men he was bringing with him were all good, faithful Communists. All had been unable to forge lives in this new, sham Russia. Of course, they weren't trained like his special force in Alaska. Not yet. But they were loyal.

To the east behind both helicopter and men, the Anadyr Range was a blurry blue streak against the pale winter sky.

Zhirinsky stood in the cold of the Chukotsky Peninsula. He was at the very edge of Mother Russia, the end of the world for his nation for far too many years. Just a few miles away from the spot where he now paced were the frigid black waters of the Bering Strait. And on the other side of that, Vladimir Zhirinsky's destiny. And that of the new Soviet Union.

"They tried to stop me," Zhirinsky said to himself. "But my comrades would not allow it. History is on my side. I smell victory in the air!" he announced as he marched back and forth in the powdery snow. A path had been stamped flat beneath the squeaking soles of his long black boots.

Ivan Kerbabaev jumped. "Victory, comrade!" he parroted nervously.

Zhirinsky slapped an enthusiastic paternal palm to the younger man's raw cheek. In the intense cold, the hand stung like fire.

"You smell it, too, eh?" Zhirinsky boomed. He pounded a balled fist to his own chest. "You have a strong Russian sense of smell. Like me."

The last thing Ivan Kerbabaev wanted his ultranationalist boss to talk about was anything that had to do with smelling or sniffing or picking or anything even remotely associated with noses.

"Uh, no. I mean. No. I mean..." A flash of desperation. "I must get going." He waved vaguely in the direction of Alaska. "There are preparations there that the others cannot be trusted to do."

Zhirinsky waved an angry hand. "They are Russian!" he proclaimed. "Of course they can be trusted."

"I did not mean—" Ivan said, shrinking from his employer.

But Zhirinsky didn't seem interested. Arms dropping to his hips, the ultranationalist studied the eastern sky with eyes of black.

Standing in the snow behind Vladimir Zhirinsky, Ivan dared not press the issue. But the truth was, more concerned him than just the work that was waiting for him in Alaska.

Ivan had only recently learned that the team left behind near Kakwik had not arrived at the designated rendezvous. Before breaking this news to his employer, he wanted to make sure Zhirinsky was in a good mood. A full stomach might help, so Ivan was anxious to hear back from the men who had been sent to gather Vladimir Zhirinsky's Eskimo take-out at Umakarot. They, too, were late in calling in.

Ivan gave an anxious smile. "The men in Fairbanks—" He cringed at the glare Zhirinsky gave him. "*Zhirinskygrad*," he corrected. "I really need to get over to them."

Zhirinsky threw his arms up. "Skachkov is there, is he not?"

"He will be arriving soon."

"There is no one better. We are poised to succeed.

The Americans are weak. They haven't the will to fight back. After we reclaim Russian Alaska, our people will rise up to overthrow the whores in the Kremlin. Is anyone else hungry?''

The last words took Ivan off guard.

As he spoke, Zhirinsky seemed to have become fixated on Ivan's face. Hypnotized by sudden fear, the young man stood locked in place.

"Comrade?" he gulped.

When the broad smile flashed sharp, yellow teeth beneath Zhirinsky's bushy black mustache, Ivan suddenly realized that it was already too late.

Growling savagely, Zhirinsky lunged.

Ivan fell back, stumbling into a line of waiting soldiers.

"Comrade, it's me!" Ivan pleaded.

But Zhirinsky didn't hear. Blood lust sang in his ears.

"Hold him," Zhirinsky commanded.

The men grabbed on tight. Strong hands forced the thrashing aide to the ground. When Vladimir Zhirinsky knelt in the snow, a warm frothy drool was already forming at the edges of his great mustache.

"Do you *really* smell victory, Ivan?" he hissed. "I must see for myself."

Ivan jerked his head to one side. A set of unseen hands clamped firmly to either side of his head, twisting him straight. Zhirinsky loomed above. Eyes wild, he pressed in close.

"Comrade!" Ivan begged. "Your Eskimos! Do you want to spoil your supper?"

Zhirinsky's mouth was open, his tongue brushing the tip of his assistant's nose. His breath was warm and rancid as he considered. All at once, Vladimir Zhirinsky drew back, his teeth bared now in a thoughtful smile.

"I did order supper," he agreed.

"Yes, *yes*," Ivan insisted, relieved.

"Still, I think I can sneak one little appetizer."

Ivan had closed his eyes in panting relief. They sprang open just in time to see Zhirinsky lunge.

Sharp incisors snapped on tight. With a mighty chomp and a twist, Vladimir Zhirinsky ripped off his screaming assistant's nose. He gobbled it greedily, his Adam's apple bobbing appreciatively above the stiff neck of his Red Army greatcoat.

When Zhirinsky stood, blood streamed down his chin.

On the ground at his back, Ivan lay in shock. Watery blood bubbled from the gaping holes of his exposed nasal cavities. No one moved to help him.

"More addictive than American potato chips," the ultranationalist observed as he licked the blood from his teeth. His expression was deeply thoughtful. "You cannot eat just one."

Patting his slight paunch, Vladimir Zhirinsky raised his black eyes. To once more study the cold eastern sky.

24

Remo called Smith from the counter phone at the Umakarot general store.

"Just me again," he announced when the CURE director picked up.

His face and tone were lifeless. The gruesome scene outside was too strong an image to casually dismiss.

"Remo, thank God," Smith said. "There may have been another attack. Someone in a small village radioed for help."

"Been there, killed that," Remo said. He gave a quick rundown of events in Umakarot. "So that's it, Smitty," he finished. "Except that it is definitely not my fault we don't have one for questioning this time. I saved one, but—" He hesitated.

Anna stood near the entrance to the store. Her proud face was unapologetic.

"Well, our signals got crossed, that's all," Remo said. He cupped the phone. "You could at least look sorry," he snapped at Anna.

"That is unfortunate," Smith was saying. "I have been unable thus far to track down Zhirinsky."

"What, did Little Lord Fauntleroy blow a circuit in his magic eight ball?"

"Mark has been quite helpful in this crisis, Remo," Smith said, his tone growing vague. "And his input should not concern you. It is Zhirinsky who is the problem. Given what we already know, it seems clear that he wishes to absorb Alaska into the Russian federation."

"A guy after Chiun's own heart," Remo grunted. "Doesn't he have enough freezing weather back home?"

"Do not compare the creature responsible for this destruction to me," intoned the Master of Sinanju. He stood near Anna. His lifeless eyes were directed out the frosted front window of the general store.

"Sorry," Remo called. To Smith he said, "I just don't know why he's not trying to take over Hawaii instead."

"According to his published views on the topic, he considers Alaska to still be Russian property. After all, other than the convenience of its geographical proximity, Alaska was once part of Russia."

"Yeah, right," Remo scoffed. "So was Pittsburgh. Sounds like he's an even bigger nut than he's getting credit for."

"It's true," Smith insisted.

Remo frowned. "Get outta town. When did this happen?"

"Secretary of State William Seward purchased the territory in 1867," the CURE director said dryly.

"You sure about that?" Remo asked. "Or is this one of those things like the Japanese buying Manhattan or the Chinese buying a U.S. president? Because that Japanese one wound up not being true.''

Across the room came a hiss of annoyance from the Master of Sinanju. Even Anna was rolling her eyes.

''How little *did* you learn in that Christian poorhouse?'' Chiun asked.

''So sue me for cutting American-history class,'' Remo groused at them. ''Sister Mary Elizabeth stunk like cheese and spit like a sprinkler.''

''I wish you had managed to save one of the commandos, Remo,'' Smith said, steering them back to the topic at hand. ''Did you at least find out how many there are?''

''Yeah,'' Remo said. ''Somewhere in the neighborhood of 150.''

''That many?'' Smith asked. By his tone he was clearly troubled by the potential problem a number that large represented.

''Tell me about it,'' Remo agreed. ''And by the looks of it, Purcell trained them to copy our mannerisms and everything. He's probably sitting with his crayons and bathrobe right now having a mountain of yucks at our expense.''

''About that,'' Smith said. ''To be safe, I checked on Purcell after our last conversation. He is still under heavy sedation. If he is to blame, then it is as you said. He trained these men prior to his hospitalization here. Have you had any luck establishing a more certain link?''

''No, Smitty,'' Remo admitted. ''But it's him. Even Nuihc wouldn't have given away Sinanju wholesale.

He'd know it's too precious a commodity in a few hands. This has the fingerprints of a happy-farm reject all over it.''

At his words Chiun spun from the window, deep annoyance creasing his parchment face. ''It is *not* Sinanju, Emperor,'' he called. ''They do not even have the basic breathing techniques that are mastered by Korean pupils in the first months of training. What they have are tricks and deceptions. Things to fool the eye and nothing more.''

''Tell Master Chiun that is only somewhat of a relief,'' Smith said.

''Chiun, Smitty says—''

''I heard,'' Chiun sniffed, turning back to the window.

''Anyway, we took out another eighteen of those guys here in Ustinkalot, or whatever the name of this place is. So we're up to twenty-eight we've packed on ice.''

''It's a start,'' Smith said, exhaling. ''If Zhirinsky's intention is to foment terror, cutting into his forces will make that more difficult to do.''

''Still don't know what he's thinking with all this,'' Remo said. ''He can wave the hammer and sickle till the cows come home, but there's no point. It's not like there's even a Soviet Union anymore.''

''In Zhirinsky's mind there is,'' Anna chimed in. Since her secret was now out, there was no point in remaining silent. ''Just because it has been shattered into pieces, that does not mean those pieces cannot be put back together. Zhirinsky sees himself as the glue that will make the old Soviet Union whole once more.''

Her eyes were dull as she watched Remo from across the store.

Smith tried not to react to her voice. ''Ms. Chutesov's analysis is correct,'' he said evenly. ''However, without further information to go on, we are in a holding pattern. You cannot remain there. The authorities will be arriving shortly. Call me when—''

A muted beep sounded from the other end of the line.

''Please hold,'' Smith said crisply.

Remo heard the sound of Smith's fingers drumming the edge of his desk as the CURE director accessed whatever information the mainframes had just flagged for him.

It took but a moment before he was back.

''My God,'' the CURE director croaked. The words barely registered over the line. His throat had turned to dust.

''What's wrong, Smitty?'' Remo asked, instantly wary.

Smith's breathing was a pained wheeze.

''Zhirinsky's men have surfaced in Fairbanks,'' Smith said woodenly. ''And if the claim they have just made is true, he may well have the means to take over a large portion of inhabited Alaska.''

And his voice was as hollow as a tomb.

25

Lavrenty Skachkov was the product of the improbable union of a grubby Sevastopol tractor mechanic and a retired Bolshoi ballerina.

In Soviet Russia the best that could generally be hoped for in life was eventual work as a KGB *komendant* in some out-of-the-way posting. That was the best. More than likely someone like Lavrenty would apprentice with his father, following not only in his footsteps as a mechanic, but modeling his entire life after the senior Skachkov. Endless grimy days would feed bitter drunken nights. There would be smoking, cancer at an early age and, mercifully, death.

This was the likeliest life for young Lavrenty because it had been the life for millions in his social class for generations. But fate had something different in store for Lavrenty. Something odd had happened in the strange genetic cocktail from which this young man of destiny had sprung.

"Stop running inside!" Lavrenty's grandmother would yell at him when he was only three.

"Get out of that tree!" Lavrenty's mother would shout into the courtyard they shared with a dozen other families.

More than once his father needed to borrow a ladder to get his son down off the gabled tile roof of the small apartment building in which the Skachkovs lived.

Lavrenty's youthful energy translated into a talent for sports. So good was he at nearly everything he tried that at the tender age of six he was taken from his family.

Olympic athletes were always in demand. Lavrenty Skachkov would win many gold medals for the motherland.

Lavrenty's trainers didn't need to experiment on their young protégé with dangerous doses of chemicals—either legal or otherwise. Lavrenty came by his skills naturally.

He was an accomplished swimmer and diver. He was graceful enough to be a gymnast, though he was a bit too large and had not begun the formal training at an early enough age. When it came time to decide on what skills would best serve his country, his speed won out. The Olympic coaches chose to groom young Lavrenty as their greatest track and field star. And one day soon he would win gold medals.

He trained hard and long. And when his time finally came, Lavrenty Skachkov—the prodigy that everyone said could not lose—lost to an opponent no one expected. History.

December 25, 1991, brought an end to the Soviet Union. The entire Russian Olympic training program collapsed with the old Communist regime.

Lavrenty had bought into the promises of the state

and of his coaches. When Russia collapsed, Lavrenty Skachkov saw his dreams collapse, as well.

For years his creature comforts—though few in number—were supplied by the state. But with little money offered by this new democratic government, Lavrenty was forced to find a job to subsidize his own training. The strain on his regimen dashed forever his Olympic dreams.

It was too humiliating to bear. After twelve years away from home, he returned in defeat to Sevastopol, where he crawled inside a vodka bottle. There he marinated.

Lavrenty might have followed—albeit belatedly— the pattern established by all preceding Skachkov males if not for one fateful day.

He was in the squalid apartment he shared with a raunchy Russian techno-punk band. When the pounding started at eight in the morning, Lavrenty, who was still hungover from the night before, assumed it was the band rehearsing. It took several bleary moments to realize that someone was at the door.

Head spinning, Lavrenty staggered to answer it.

The impatient figure standing in the filthy, urine-soaked hallway wore a look of haughty disdain.

"You are drunk," his visitor said in introduction.

Lavrenty didn't remember much after that. The effort to open the door had been too much for him. As the stranger's face soured, Lavrenty's world spun crazily around his head. Spewing vomit, the former Soviet star athlete passed out.

When he awoke on his torn sofa it was afternoon.

The apartment had only one window. Brilliant yellow sunlight streamed in through the torn black shade.

Lavrenty tried to blink the pain from his eyes. When he rolled his head to one side, he found he wasn't alone. The threadbare easy chair across from the couch was occupied.

"You are disgusting," his visitor sneered. "You live like a pig. This apartment is filthy."

"Who the hell are you?" Lavrenty snarled. Hand pressed to his forehead, he sat up.

"I am the person who is about to give you an offer that you do not deserve."

Bloodshot eyes suspicious, Lavrenty pushed to his feet. "It sounds like I'll need a drink for this," he said.

"Don't bother. I dumped all the liquor down the sink while you were unconscious."

Already halfway to the tiny kitchen, Lavrenty stopped. The apartment continued to spin.

"You what?" he demanded.

"Alcohol is not permitted in your new training regimen," his visitor said calmly.

With those words it was suddenly all very clear.

Lavrenty's shoulders drooped and he fell against the nearby wall for support. "No, not again," he moaned.

"I am not with the Russian Olympic team. I have nothing to do with your silly running games. I am offering you something new. Something that you might not deserve and that you certainly do not now have. I offer you a life, a future. Both rare commodities in Russia at the present time. You need only say yes and your life changes today.''

Lavrenty was still leaning against the wall. It was greasy. The floor was worse. Moldy and rotted. Rats scurried around it at night.

"I have heard this promise before," the former athlete said weakly. There was surrender in his voice.

His visitor leaned forward. "No, you haven't. Before when they came for you, you could not decline.''

The truth of his visitor's words hung heavy in the fetid apartment air.

The stranger stood. "You will have food and shelter. There is no drink, and the training is difficult, but it is a better life than you will ever have here.''

Lavrenty dragged his eyes around the dirty apartment. His gaze finally settled on his guest.

"What is the name of the person for whom I will be working?" he asked with tired acceptance.

There was not a hint of satisfaction on his visitor's pale, chiseled face. "My name is Anna Chutesov," she said crisply. And a glimmer of something that might have been regret touched the depths of her blue eyes.

A BLACK VAN WHISKED Lavrenty Skachkov to the airport that afternoon. By nightfall he was in Moscow. His training at the Institute began the next day.

Those first two years were a living nightmare.

Everything he had learned as an Olympic athlete had to be unlearned. The lessons were endless. The instructors far more demanding than those in the Olympic training facilities.

He watched them in action a thousand times. A thousand times a thousand times.

The two men carried themselves with a grace of movement that was impossible, nearly inhuman. The first few hundred lessons, he couldn't unravel the complexity. When at last he saw the truth, he realized that it was simplicity disguised as complexity. At the same time the opposite was true. And in that paradox was their secret.

They never spoke. Never said a single word to Lavrenty. Yet they became his greatest teachers. One moved with a skittering grace, the other with a confident glide. They seemed able to appear and disappear at will.

"May I speak with them?" Lavrenty asked Anna Chutesov one afternoon after his first few months of training.

Anna glanced at Lavrenty's two teachers. A strange expression settled on her beautiful face. "No, you may not," she said quietly, as if afraid they might overhear.

"Then *you* tell me," Lavrenty whispered in awe. "How do they do what they do?"

"I don't know," Anna admitted. "But if you follow their example properly, you may one day be able to do the same."

Lavrenty couldn't believe it. Yet he had signed on to the program, called Mactep, and so had no choice.

In an underground training chamber, Lavrenty was covered with grease-smeared electrodes. His silent teachers joined him. Technicians were in a sealed booth above the chamber to monitor his progress. Success went unrewarded. Failure was punished with excruciating electric shocks. Lavrenty received many shocks during his first months of training.

It was frustrating beyond belief. Much harder than the training he had endured in his youth. Most times he was certain that he could never succeed.

Then one day, when he least expected it, he actually matched a move.

Lavrenty was shocked. It was a small thing. A mere baby step compared to the abilities of his teachers. But to Lavrenty, it was life-changing. In that moment the impossible became possible.

A few more arduous years followed, during which Lavrenty eventually matched every move made by his teachers. When he was done, he couldn't believe how easy it had been. There was an obviousness to it all that should have been evident to him on that very first day.

A handful of others had preceded him in the program. These, he learned, had used their skills to protect the Institute from the mobs at the end of the Communist age. They had christened their skills in blood.

Lavrenty was better than them all. He surpassed the skills of all who came before or after him in the program. His superior ability inspired awe in the men with whom he shared quarters in that big, ominous building in Kitai Gorod. So revered was he that the others bestowed the program designation on him. Lavrenty became *Mactep* to them. Master.

Yet all his awesome skills were for naught. While some of the others had been able to put their lesser talents to use during the prodemocracy uprising, the great Master Lavrenty Skachkov was given no such chance.

When his training was complete, Lavrenty had gone to see Anna Chutesov.

She was in her small basement office. The big floor safe in the corner was open. As Lavrenty stood before her desk, he noted the rows of videotapes lined up on the shelves at the back of the safe.

"What is it, Lavrenty?" Anna had asked.

"I was wondering, Director Chutesov," he said, "when I would be allowed to test my skills." As he spoke, he rotated his wrists absently.

"We already test your skills daily," Anna had replied.

"Not here," he insisted. "I mean in the real world. Others have been used before me. When will I get my chance?"

Anna set her hands to her desk, her fingers interlocked.

"When will I permit you to kill—is that what you want to know?" she asked.

The twitch of one eye told her that this was his desire.

"We are agents to be deployed, are we not?"

"No," Anna answered evenly. "You are something else entirely. And if I have my way, you will never see active duty." Before he could object, she plowed on. "The men you have spoken to were sent by me to disperse the crowds during the days of civil unrest. It was an action not undertaken lightly and done only for the specific purpose of protecting the secrets of the Institute. Once the crowds left us alone, the men were withdrawn."

"So we are a counterinsurgency force," Lavrenty said, still wrestling with his confusion.

Anna shook her head. "You are a mistake, Lavrenty," she replied. "One for which I am responsible and one that the idiot men in power have seized upon." Her voice softened as she considered what had brought them to this point. "Before I became director of this agency, there was a plan to bring a pair of American agents over here to work for the Institute. That plan failed. Unwittingly, I offered those in the Kremlin another chance. Over my objections, they seized on it. All you have been through—all the pain, the sweat, the endless training—is the product of a stupid idea."

As she spoke, Lavrenty could feel his world slowly shrinking. "But what is our purpose?" he asked.

"To keep our idiot leaders happy," Anna replied. "Perhaps to keep them from making any rash decisions when dealing with America, although I think that time has long passed. We continued to do what we do here now because things were set in motion ten years ago and it is impossible to get a man to stop doing a stupid thing if he believes it to be smart. Ultimately, Lavrenty, you and the others are weapons that will never be used."

Harsher medicine Lavrenty Skachkov had never

taken. All of the years, the electric shocks. All for nothing.

When he returned to the barracks to tell the others, morale at the Institute collapsed more completely than had the old Soviet system. All the men there had assumed they were being prepared for some higher purpose. The truth was almost too much for them to bear.

For the next few months, Lavrenty and the others went through the motions. They engaged in their training—much of which was now handled personally by Master Lavrenty—but it was hollow exercise. Life without purpose.

Lavrenty considered escape. They were meant to be enrolled in the Mactep program for life, but with the skills he now possessed it would be impossible for them to stop him. Yet these men belonged to him and he to them. They were part of a fraternity like no other. And so he stayed.

His pointless life at the Institute had begun to feel much like his life of drunken despair in Sevastopol, when fate once more intervened to rescue Lavrenty Skachkov.

He was on summer leave from the Institute. Instead of going home, he remained in Moscow. On the first evening of his vacation he went for a stroll through Gorky Park. Walking along a winding path, Lavrenty came across a small crowd. Men and women formed a circle around a speaker who stood on an upended Absolut crate. The man had wild graying hair, a big bushy mustache and unblinking black eyes that seemed to target every member of his audience like twin rifle scopes.

Lavrenty listened to Vladimir Zhirinsky rant and rave for over three hours. The sun had long fallen and the last of the crowd dispersed before the ultranationalist finally climbed down from his makeshift stage. By then he had already won over a new convert to his cause.

Zhirinsky wasn't entirely accepting at first. In fact, when Lavrenty went to introduce himself, the former Russian senator snapped his teeth like an angry dog. Only when the man who had been standing before him vanished and Zhirinsky found that he was not savoring a mouthful of nose did he start to get an inkling that there was something odd about this late-night encounter.

"Where did you go?" Zhirinsky asked the shadows of the park. His black eyes were slivers. "Trotsky?" he questioned softly. "Kosygin?" His voice grew awed, as if he scarcely dared entertain the notion. "*Stalin?*"

A tap on his shoulder. He wheeled.

He saw the young man again. Short white hair. Delicate features. Like a woman's. This was not one of the great leaders of days long past, come back to aid him in his struggle against the lapdogs of the West now in the Kremlin.

If he was not going to get help from the heroes of the Revolution, he was at least going to get a meal.

His brief moment of hope dashed, Zhirinsky lashed out again. Again the man vanished.

Only the second time did Zhirinsky realize something large indeed might be going on here. When he reappeared this time, the young man's delicate face was serious.

"Comrade," Lavrenty said, surprised by how happy it made him to use the old form of address, "we need to talk."

That night Lavrenty broke the most important rule of the Institute. He told an outsider precisely what was going on in that somber building with the bricked-up windows.

For his part Vladimir Zhirinsky had a hard time controlling his drool, let alone his joy.

Together that very night, the two men hatched a scheme that would liberate the others from the Institute. Zhirinsky already had plans for Mother Russia. With the addition of these specially trained forces to the mix, he was more certain than ever that he could achieve his goals.

The only real problem would be Anna Chutesov. She was never away from the Institute for more than a few hours at a time. While Zhirinsky suggested they kill the pesky woman and leave with their heads held high, Lavrenty could not bring himself to do the deed. Director Chutesov had been the only person in his life who had ever made clear promises to him without ever breaking a single one.

With Anna there, they could not just up and leave, for she apparently had ties to the highest level of government. She would alert the army were they to defect.

And even his men might have difficulty against the entire Russian army.

The solution came as a surprise nine months after Lavrenty's first chance meeting with Vladimir Zhirinsky.

Anna Chutesov had summoned Lavrenty to her office to tell him she was going away. An assignment had come up, and she had been ordered to leave at once. Since the other men looked up to Lavrenty as their leader, she put him in charge of them during her absence. The way she spoke that day, it sounded almost as if she expected not to return.

She was gone no more than an hour when Vladimir Zhirinsky's rusted-out Zil pulled to a coughing stop before the Institute building.

Lavrenty met the ultranationalist at the curb. With a simple downward stroke of his hand, the Institute's reigning Master broke the chain on the driveway fence and led the former senator down into the heart of modern Russia's most closely guarded secret.

The others didn't know of his betrayal. They were shocked when he walked into their barracks with an outsider.

They all recognized Vladimir Zhirinsky. Many there agreed with his political views. Jaws dropped. Eyes looked to Lavrenty for an explanation while the ultranationalist silently toured the rows of worn beds and battered bureaus.

At the far end of the barracks, Zhirinsky had stopped, turning slowly. His black eyes were dully accusing.

"Is this a kennel?" Zhirinsky had asked quietly.

No one said a word. Initial confusion was slowly giving away to a sense of creeping hope.

Zhirinsky's bushy eyebrows formed an angry V.

"Have they removed your tongues as well as your will to fight for Mother Russia?" he exploded.

Fire lit in his dark eyes, igniting sparks in their own. Without even realizing it, they snapped to attention.

"No, sir!"

The fire in his eyes grew cold.

"I am not a 'sir,'" he spit in contempt. "I am your *comrade*. Your equal. And together we comrades will make them all fear once more the might of a united Russia!"

When they saw Master Lavrenty cheer, the others knew they had finally found their special purpose. In the person of Vladimir Zhirinsky, they had their savior.

A cheer rose up from the buried basement of the Institute building, like a chorus of lost souls, muffled by dirt and concrete and the hum of passing cars.

And through it all, a smile remained plastered to the delicate face of Lavrenty Skachkov. He was finally going to be able to fulfill his purpose in life. The Mactep program had bestowed on him the powers of a god. With them, Lavrenty Skachkov was at long last going to be allowed to kill.

THEY WERE GHOSTS. Shadows upon shadows, slipping silently through the streets of Fairbanks.

Master Lavrenty led the Institute army. Here a

lonely car moved. There a streetlamp sliced the night. The Russians avoided it all. Of the world, but not.

According to Zhirinsky, the city of forty thousand would be an easy target. By the standards of the contiguous United States, it was a small town. But it was along the pipeline route, and so served a strategic purpose.

They had abandoned their trucks and helicopters well outside of town, coming in from the north.

Fort Wainwright lay sleeping beyond the Chena River on the east side of town. The Russians steered clear of the Army base. The clock had long struck midnight by the time they made their cautious way along First Avenue.

Lavrenty found the flatbed trailer precisely where it was supposed to be. Parked along the side of the road. Smuggled in so easily. Like all of their equipment.

Comrade Zhirinsky was right. Openness fed weakness. The Americans were too trusting. And for that, Master Lavrenty thought, they would pay dearly.

Huge tarpaulins—lashed down with heavy rope and chains—hid the vehicle's cargo from view. Even so, the long cylindrical outline was visible beneath the dirty tarps.

Lavrenty and the others stayed to the shadows. On cautious, gliding feet they approached the truck.

The street was empty. Other than the rattling of the tarpaulins, the only sound came from a tiny scrap of paper that flapped in the wind under the windshield wiper of the truck's flat-nosed cab.

Lavrenty wore his goggles and white mask. He

pulled them off now as he crept up the side of the truck. Cold wind stirred his short hair.

Unlike the rest, Lavrenty carried no gun. With one bare knuckle, he tapped twice on the driver's-side door.

A startled grunt came from inside. Fingers fumbled the lock and the door popped open.

The face that appeared looked ill.

Ivan Kerbabaev's head was wrapped in bandages. A big wad of blood-soaked gauze was plastered to the spot where his nose should have been. Lavrenty noted that there was no bump beneath. The bandages ran below Ivan's eyes, tied sloppily at the back of his head.

Ivan hitched the cotton dressing up around his right ear as he climbed down to the cold street.

"Are all your men here?" Zhirinsky's aide mumbled.

Speaking obviously caused him pain. When Ivan winced, the twitching caused his bloody bandages to bunch.

"My men are all around you," Skachkov said, uninterested in Ivan's discomfort.

A wave of his hand brought the other commandos out of hiding. They had been lurking along the shadowed walls of the nearby buildings. At his signal, they faded up out of the darkness on either side of the road, stepping into the cold amber light cast by the streetlamps.

"What about the bissing ben?" Ivan said, struggling with the words.

"Not yet," Lavrenty said. "And those sent after Comrade Zhirinsky's...*souvenirs* have not reported in yet, either. However, I am not concerned. No doubt it is a communications problem. They understand the plan and where they need to be. They will arrive before the night is over."

"Berry well," Ivan said. He seemed more concerned with his own pain than with the missing men. "The rest of our men will be arriving from Russia soon. You will be coordinating with dem when dey land."

Lavrenty's spine stiffened. "Do not call them 'our' men," he said. "My men are here. Whatever else may come, they are inferior to us."

Ivan seemed not interested in the least in the white-haired man's disdainful words. He was shifting his bandages at his ears once more. He squinted at the fresh pain.

Lavrenty exhaled impatience at the pathetic little man.

"Is the warhead armed?" he spit.

Ivan's shaking hand scurried to his face. He cast a frightened eye back along the length of the truck. The tarpaulins continued to rattle in the wind.

"Yes," he said uncertainly. "I will contact the media as soon as your positions are secure."

As he spoke, a fresh gust of wind grabbed the scrap of paper under the truck's wiper, slapping it angrily against the glass. Lavrenty's face puckered in annoyance.

"What is that?" he asked. Reaching up, he plucked the paper free.

"A parking ticket," Ivan replied. "Comrade Zhirinsky did not give me any change for the meter."

At their leader's name, Ivan winced once more.

Offering a fresh look of disgust, Lavrenty wadded up the ticket, throwing it to the street. The wind took it, sweeping it off down the road, away from the trailer and its radioactive cargo.

26

Anna Chutesov's helicopter whipped over plains of snow. With whining purpose it screamed toward Fairbanks. In the back Remo's expression was dark.

"Who's watching your nuclear secrets over there, Bill Richardson?" he snapped at Anna. "With all you've got invested in that bum-twaddle program of yours, you'd think you'd at least lock your bombs in a KGB closet somewhere like you did with Hitler's brain."

"Crime is rampant in Russia," Anna explained, her own face grave. "Anything can be had for a price."

"You've got a lot to learn about selective control of criminals," Remo grumbled. "The trick is to cave to them on all the small stuff. That way the medium stuff looks big and they stay away completely from the really big stuff. That's the American way."

Anna's expression grew bland. "Thank you, but Russia will handle Russia's crime problems," she said dryly.

"Whizbang job so far, Anna," Remo said. "And at least when our Mafia talks kilos, you know they're measuring cocaine, not tons."

"There is no record of a warhead being stolen from any of our bases."

"Yeah, and the black market's just so good about filling out all the proper forms," he said sarcastically. "And maybe they didn't need to take a whole one. The way things are going over there, maybe they built one from spare parts."

Anna frowned. "There *is* some record of Boris Feyodov's group being interested in certain technical items. Some could have been used to construct a bomb."

"Could have been?" Remo said. "Anna, Feyodov was the guy who smuggled a Russian particle-beam weapon into California piece by piece, remember?"

She ignored his acid tone. "As I told you, they had been working together."

"Perfect," Remo said. "We're probably flying smack-dab into ground zero."

He glanced at the Master of Sinanju. "We can set down anytime, Little Father," he said. "No sense both of us getting fried."

The old man shook his head. "It is your destiny to face the renegade Master," he intoned solemnly. "Knowing you, you would become distracted by his night tigers and allow him to get away. Or worse. I cannot allow five thousand years of Sinanju history to end because of your flitting mind."

In spite of the words, they both knew the truth. Chiun was worried for Remo. Remo turned back to Anna.

"By the sounds of it, our work's cut out for us,"

he said. "According to Smith, they took over all the public buildings during the night. Once they took the city hall, their mouthpiece let everyone know about the loose nuke. Smitty had the Army base evacuated out beyond the city limits when they threatened to set it off."

"He would not explode the boom if he wishes to keep this city as a prize," Chiun observed.

"I'm thinking that the nice man who eats people's faces might not be that easy to predict," Remo said. "And we've got a city full of people to worry about up there."

"Not long ago you were willing to sacrifice another city," Chiun suggested. He was looking out the window.

"Those people weren't mine," Remo said, his voice low.

Anna frowned. "I thought your people were in Sinanju."

"They *are,*" Chiun insisted.

"Look, the fact is, I've got people there, people here. I've even got some stashed away on an Indian reservation. I'm up to my armpits in people. Right now I'm an American, and it's my job to protect the people in Fairbanks."

The Master of Sinanju's gaze was still directed out the side window. His hazel eyes narrowed.

"Tell me, Remo, for I have lost track," Chiun said. "Of all the many groups of people it is your duty to protect, which are the ones who are about to shoot us from the sky?"

As the old Korean spoke, there came a frantic shout from Anna's pilot. She darted to the cockpit even as Remo crowded the window beside the Master of Sinanju.

Two Navy F-14 fighters had appeared off the port side of the helicopter. Glancing over his shoulder, he saw two more through the opposite window. Their distance made them almost seem to match the Kamov's slower speed.

"Since they haven't figured out in Sinanju how to bang two rocks together to make fire, I'd say it's my American people," Remo said aridly. "I'd better go talk to them. One earful of Anna's accent and we'll be riding the rest of the way to town on the nose of a Sidewinder missile."

WHILE THE TOMCATS didn't shoot them down, they did force the Kamov to land a dozen miles outside of Fairbanks.

When Remo, Chiun and Anna climbed down to the snow, a hundred M-16 barrels were there to greet them.

A sea of U.S. Army soldiers surrounded the helicopter. The entire population of Fort Wainwright was bivouacked along the sides of Route 3.

"Why isn't anyone ever happy to see us?" Remo groused.

Digging in his pocket, he waved his bogus CIA ID over his head like a lit road flare until it attracted the attention of an Army Colonel. The man was in his early fifties, with a sour disposition and a face bitten raw with cold. The name Hawkins was stitched to his heavy coat.

"What were you doing in a Russian helicopter?" Colonel Hawkins demanded as he inspected Remo's ID.

"Mostly I was being irritated," Remo replied. "But until you guys showed up, it was pretty much just at the Russian limit-one-weapon-of-mass-destruction-per-crazy-man policy. Now, would you be a dear and let us take off? I've got World War III to stop."

"The Russians and Americans at war is the least of our worries," Chiun insisted. "Do not forget the curse of Wang."

"Sorry, sir," Colonel Hawkins said to Remo even as he eyed the old Korean. "There's a no-fly zone around Fairbanks. Orders from above. If you're not sanctioned by them to land, you won't get in in one piece."

"They have air support?" Anna asked.

Eyes widening, the Colonel took a step back. "She's a Russkie," he said. His hand dropped to his side arm.

"She's with us," Remo explained, uninterested. To Chiun he said, "And don't call it the curse of Wang. Makes it sound like we're out Viagra shopping."

The Colonel looked from Remo to Anna to the wrinkled face of the Master of Sinanju. When he looked back to Remo, he was shaking his head.

"You guys can't be for real," Hawkins said.

Remo was no longer paying attention to him. "We need transportation," he said to the others.

"That vehicle will do," Anna announced, pointing to a nearby Land Rover. It was parked amid a sea of Army trucks and jeeps on the snow-lined highway.

As the three of them hurried over to the truck, the Colonel jogged to keep up.

"That's mine," Colonel Hawkins said. "And just where exactly do you think you're going?"

Remo ignored the question. "Keys," he said, sticking out his hand.

"What?" the Colonel said. "No way. CIA or not, you're gonna need some kind of authorization for this."

"Chiun, you want to show the nice man our authorization?" Remo asked.

Colonel Hawkins saw a flash of movement in the direction of the old Asian. At least he thought he saw something. In the next moment the Colonel suddenly gave less concern to what he might have seen than to what he actually felt.

A bony hand clamped on to his ankle. Before Hawkins knew what was happening, he was being lifted off the road and the world was spinning up on end.

Holding the soldier upside down, the Master of Sinanju shook him until the Land Rover's keys slipped out of the man's pocket. They landed with a jangle in the powdery snow. Along with his wallet, comb, dog tags and automatic.

As Remo fished the keys from the snow, Chiun stuck Hawkins deep into a snowdrift until only his frantically kicking legs were visible.

"We'll try not to scratch it," Remo promised the Colonel's boots as the three of them piled in.

As soldiers began to dig out the Colonel, the Land Rover's engine roared to life. Squealing tires threw a stream of dirty snow back across the struggling men as the vehicle pulled away from the shoulder.

Flying away from the tent city, the Land Rover tore off up the lonely stretch of highway toward Fairbanks.

VLADIMIR ZHIRINSKY WAITED in ankle-deep snow. Through the wispy white blanket peeked the hard-packed, blue-tinged surface of a glacier. Frozen wind churned the choppy black surface of the Bering Strait. Whitecaps raged against the towering glacier wall.

Zhirinsky's destiny waited three miles away.

The ultranationalist was unbothered by the cold. Proud, bare Russian face mocked the desolate howling wind.

"Comrade?"

Zhirinsky glanced to the voice.

A soldier stood at his elbow, greatcoat collar drawn up tightly around his neck. Mucous dribbled from his nostrils, freezing on his chapped upper lip.

Zhirinsky stared hungrily at the man's runny nose.

The soldier pushed up one shoulder so that his nose was hidden behind his collar. "It is Comrade Kerba-baev," he said, his voice muffled. He handed over the portable radio he was carrying before retreating to a safe distance.

"Speak," the ultranationalist commanded.

Ivan's every word sounded as if it were causing him excruciating pain.

"Skachkov and his men have secured the city," the scratchy voice said over the radio. "I have also shown their city leaders the nuclear device. The Army is staying away. They have agreed to an air corridor to allow you entry to the city. You may come over anytime."

Zhirinsky's black eyes glinted.

"Before I reclaim Russia's property, I want the infestation removed," he said, his voice a low growl.

"Comrade?" Ivan asked, confused.

"The Americans. I want them gone," Zhirinsky said, the fire of long-smoldering rage swelling within him. "They are a disease. A poison. They pollute the world with their notions of freedom. They have corrupted Russia, corroding the will of a once mighty nation. I do not want to see a single American face when I set foot in Zhirinskygrad."

A pause on the line during which the only sound was that of the wind.

"Do you want them dead?" Ivan asked.

Beneath his great mustache, Zhirinsky's thick lips thinned. "All in good time. Once the Soviet Union has retaken its rightful position as superpower, we will deal with all of America. For now, expel them from my city."

Ivan tried to strike up a reasonable tone. "We did not expel the Poles or the Czechs or the Romanians," he said. "And with the American population gone, our position here will be weakened."

Zhirinsky's voice grew cold. "Do not make me

question your loyalty, Comrade Kerbabaev," he growled.

The threat hung heavy in the cold air.

"No, sir, comrade sir," Ivan whimpered. "I will tell Skachkov to begin an evacuation."

Zhirinsky snapped off the radio, tossing it back to the runny-nosed soldier.

"Start the engines!" Zhirinsky commanded.

Across the plain, men scrambled aboard two dozen waiting Hind gunship helicopters. As the engines coughed to life, Zhirinsky strode off toward them, eager to finally rendezvous with history.

THEY MET the first evacuees six miles out from Fairbanks. To Remo the trudging line of men and women was a vision out of some war-torn European country.

The people were wrapped in multiple layers of clothing. Some dragged duffel bags, suitcases—whatever they could carry. Farther down the road some luggage had already been abandoned. Weeping children cried freezing tears.

Remo pulled his borrowed Land Rover to a stop near a Fairbanks police department deputy. The haggard man was helping to shepherd the people along.

"What the hell's this?" Remo demanded, flashing his ID.

"We've been ordered to empty the town," the officer said.

Remo pulled his head back in the window. "How *Fiddler on the Roof* can you get?" he asked Anna and Chiun.

Powering up the window, he tapped the gas.

Mobs choked the road for miles into town. For much of the way the Land Rover had to crawl. It was only when they were a mile from town that the last stragglers slipped behind and the road opened up once more. Almost at once they spotted the roadblock. Soldiers in white patrolled a barricade of stolen cars.

"More friends of yours," Remo said to Anna.

In the back of the truck, Anna studied the men as Remo sped toward them.

"Their masks," she said. "They've changed their masks." As she spoke she fumbled in the pocket of her parka, pulling out a pair of small binoculars.

Instead of the ski masks the other commandos had worn, these men wore simple white hoods, their faces exposed. Their light, centered stances telegraphed basic Sinanju.

"Are there any more than the four I see?" Anna demanded.

"Don't know," Remo said. "Depends on which four you see."

"That is all of them," Chiun answered thinly.

"Good," Anna said, pocketing her binoculars. "You are safe, for none of them is Skachkov."

Chiun's prophecy and Anna's obsession over this one commando were finally getting to Remo.

"How good *is* this guy?" he muttered.

"Just be careful, Remo," Anna stressed.

When he glanced in the rearview mirror, he saw a look of genuine concern on Anna's pale face.

"Whatever," he grumbled. "Just stay in the car. Chiun and I will take care of these guys."

The soldiers didn't seem very concerned about a lone vehicle approaching their conquered town. One had been talking on a stolen cell phone as Remo's truck approached. He continued his conversation as the Land Rover stopped, a blandly arrogant eye directed toward the intruders.

Only when Remo and Chiun emerged did the soldier with the phone suddenly grow interested. As the other three commandos raised their weapons, the fourth man spoke in rushed, almost reverent tones into his phone.

"What gives?" Remo asked as he swung his door shut.

As he and his pupil walked over to the men at the barricade, the Master of Sinanju cocked an ear.

"He says he recognizes you," Chiun replied. The instant he said it, the old Asian's face registered surprise.

"What?" Remo asked, noting his teacher's expression.

"He claims to know me, as well."

"Just like the one in the camp," Remo mused. "And one of the guys in that village called me Master just before I pulled his plug. Gotta be Purcell. He told them about us."

"He did not tell them everything," Chiun intoned ominously. "For he obviously did not warn them of the penalty for stealing from the House of Sinanju."

Shoving in front of his pupil, he flounced over to

the commandos. "Attention, thieves!" he proclaimed. "Being Russian and, thus, used to having everything of value stripped from you all your wretched lives, including gold, dignity and sobriety, you no doubt knew that this day of atonement would come the moment you first chose to steal from Sinanju. Now, although you deserve no mercy, mercy shall be granted nonetheless. I promise you, your deaths will be swift. The line forms here. No shoving."

He folded his arms imperiously over his narrow chest.

Before him, the four Russians didn't know what to make of the strange little man. The soldier on the phone was whispering into the mouthpiece when he spotted something beyond Remo and Chiun. His eyes widened.

Hissing a few final words, he stuffed the phone away.

Remo had sensed Anna exiting the truck. Before he could tell her to get back inside, the men had raised their guns to her. A single shot cracked the cold air.

The bullet fired from Anna's automatic caught the soldier with the cell phone in the chest. He flopped back onto the hood of a Dodge that was part of their barricade.

As the first fell, the rest opened fire.

"Dammit, Anna, can't you keep it in your pants?" Remo growled. He was already moving on the men.

With the flat of his palm, Remo met the blazing barrel of a Kalashnikov in the infinitesimal sliver of time between fired bullets. A nudge sent the weapon launching back, severing the arm of the soldier at the shoulder. Both arm and gun flew backward, the itching finger still firing. Unfortunately for the commando, something had come between the gun and its original target.

Bullets fired from his own gun by his own traitorous arm popped the soldier's head like a ripe August melon.

"That woman is a menace," Chiun fumed, swirling in beside his pupil. A flying foot separated a head from its neck. "She has brought chaos to an orderly surrender. I don't know what you ever saw in her."

"Then you're not looking hard enough," Remo said.

There was only one soldier left. He twisted his gun between Remo and Chiun, unsure what had just happened.

"Gimme that, dummy," Remo said.

Tugging the rifle from the man's grasping fingers, he bopped the soldier on the head. The stunned commando dropped to his bottom on the cold road.

Even as the last man was falling, Anna was scurrying out from behind the Land Rover and hurrying to the barricade. Her gun was still clutched in her hand.

"We are in trouble," Anna said.

"Why? Did you run out of people to shoot?" Remo asked.

Ignoring his sarcasm, she waved her gun at the sky. Both Remo and Chiun had already heard the rumbling coming from the west. It had been soft at first, carried on the cold wind. But it was growing louder.

The black dots of a fleet of Hind gunships speckled the gray sky. A sound like distant thunder rumbled closer. Passing the road a mile to the north, the attack helicopters swept into Fairbanks.

"Zhirinsky," Anna hissed.

Remo glanced at her. "You sure?"

She nodded. "He purchased several dozen Hinds from General Feyodov's black market cell. And this grand entry is just like him. The conquering hero of the Soviet Union."

"There's something I've been meaning to ask," Remo said with a scowl. "If you people know everyone who's in the damn black market, why the hell don't you arrest them?"

She smiled sadly. "Russia is now ruled by a handful of wealthy black marketers, called oligarchs," she explained. "And there is a saying now—how many oligarchs does it take to rule Russia?" When she saw Remo's blank expression, her smile only grew sadder. "All of them," she said quietly, in answer to her own question.

On the ground the dazed soldier stirred. His eyes strayed to Anna. When he saw her, something that almost seemed like guilt surfaced on his wind-burned face.

"Guess we don't need to save one anymore," Remo sighed.

"No," Anna said. "We do not."

Before another word could be spoken, Anna raised

her automatic and fired point-blank into the soldier's face.

"When did they start paying you by the bullet?" Remo snarled, hopping back from the splatter.

But Anna was already turning away. Pocketing her gun, she headed back for their truck. Chiun padded in her wake.

Remo glanced down at the last soldier. When he looked back, Anna was climbing into the Land Rover.

"Hmm," Remo said softly to himself.

With a thoughtful frown, he trailed the others back to the waiting truck.

27

His years as director of CURE and as head of Folcroft Sanitarium had given Dr. Harold W. Smith a unique perspective into the mind of madness. As he and Mark Howard scanned the reports on Smith's monitor, experience would not allow the older man to share his young assistant's amazement.

"Unbelievable," Howard said. "Is this for real?"

"So it would seem," Smith replied. "The population of Fairbanks has been released. The first civilians reached Fort Wainwright's bivouacked Sixth Light Infantry Division ten minutes ago."

"Why let them go?" Mark asked, confusion filling his wide face. "Aren't they bargaining chips?"

"Not any longer," Smith said. "And if you are to survive in this job, it is vitally important for you to realize that madmen are not always as predictable as many textbooks and behavioral scientists would have you believe."

"Madmen? So you think Zhirinsky did this himself?"

Smith nodded. "This latest news came after Zhirinsky's incursion force of twelve Mil Mi-24 gunships were given free clearance across the Kuskokwim

Mountains. They've reached Fairbanks by now. I believe Zhirinsky was on one of them."

The assistant CURE director stood beside Smith's old leather chair. As he studied the computer screen, Howard's knuckles rested beyond the edge of the capacitor keyboard.

"I've been checking to see if the Russian government is involved," Mark said. "Their president's holed up in the Kremlin. And the last two presidents have disappeared. No one knows where they are."

Smith shook his head. "I just got off the White House phone twenty minutes ago. When news of the nuclear bomb in Fairbanks broke, our President received a call from his counterpart in Russia pledging support. The Russian president has even offered troops."

"Maybe he wants to get more men on the ground," Howard suggested.

"Mark, it is important not to read too much into situations. Your instincts are good, and it is sometimes necessary to extrapolate when enough information is not available. But it is possible to be too clever by half. Zhirinsky is a renegade, unpopular with the rulers of Russia. If they were to concoct such a scheme, they would not give it over to someone as unstable as him." Smith nodded firmly. "No, Zhirinsky alone is behind this."

Howard accepted his words with a thoughtful frown. "So Zhirinsky's alone in Fairbanks with a handful of troops," he mused. "What do you think his next move'll be?"

"More important, what is *our* next move?"

When Mark glanced down, he saw that the CURE director was staring up at him, a look of pinched expectation on his gaunt face. It was apparent that Smith knew something that needed to be done and was quizzing Mark to see if he knew, too.

Howard considered. "First thing we have to do is give Remo and Chiun room to work. We have to keep the Army out. I'd call the President and have him issue an order."

Smith nodded satisfaction. Like a first-grade teacher who had finally taught a troublesome student to raise his hand for permission to use the rest room. "Correct," he said. "Although there is no need to involve the President."

With nimble fingers he accessed the Pentagon's computer system. It took less than a minute to surreptitiously issue the orders that would keep the Army out.

"There," he said once he was through. "Now, as a safeguard to prevent the order from being overruled, I will phone the President."

Mark had to take a step back to allow him access to the bottom drawer and the red phone.

"You know, Dr. Smith," Howard said seriously as Smith waited for America's chief executive to pick up, "if Zhirinsky's as psycho as everyone says, he could set off the bomb the minute he hears Remo and Chiun are there."

"That thought had occurred to me," the CURE director replied with clinical detachment.

"Hello, Mr. President," Smith announced into the phone.

Whatever more was said, Mark Howard didn't hear. He had turned from the desk and its canted monitor. With one tired shoulder, he leaned against the big picture window frame.

Long Island Sound was cold and black.

"Are all your weeks like this one?" he said softly to himself. Behind him the CURE director continued to speak to the President of the United States in measured nasal tones.

As Smith spoke, Howard watched the waves roll into shore.

28

Ivan Kerbabaev waited on the cold tarmac to greet the future premier of the new Soviet Union. Behind him was a lone limousine liberated from a Fairbanks car rental service.

Sheets of snow swirled all around as the twelve Hinds settled like roosting birds to the freezing ground.

With pain in his eyes, Ivan blinked away the snow. A dull, throbbing ache came from beneath the many bandages plastered to his face.

At least it wasn't as bad now as it had been. Ivan had found an empty dentist's office near the parked nuclear device in downtown Fairbanks. He had hoped that when Vladimir Zhirinsky arrived, the novocaine he'd shot himself full of would dull all the pain. But it seemed proximity to the ultranationalist caused his raw nerve endings to spark.

Zhirinsky hadn't even landed when the aching started anew. It only got worse when that demented face with its bushy mustache appeared on the steps of the Hind.

The Russian hard-liner had changed into a surplus Red Army general's uniform. The medals and ribbons and pins and badges that festooned the chest and shoulders of the outfit made him resemble an ambulatory Soviet Christmas tree.

"Welcome to Zhirinskygrad," Ivan announced.

Zhirinsky shoved past him. He cast an awed gaze across the frigid landscape. With great puffs of rancid breath, he climbed down to his knees. Chapped lips sought asphalt.

He kissed the ground slowly and passionately. A little *too* passionately. Standing to one side, Ivan Kerbabaev swore Vladimir Zhirinsky was slipping Alaska the tongue.

As Zhirinsky lapped the asphalt, his small army piled out of the helicopters. They spread out across the airport.

Zhirinsky pushed up to his knees. "It is good to be home!" he boomed as Ivan helped him to his feet.

His smile only grew wider when he spied the man climbing out of the nearby limousine.

Lavrenty Skachkov didn't so much walk as glide over to the ultranationalist. Seeing the deadly serious face the young commando wore, Zhirinsky's smile faded.

"What is wrong?" he asked, shooting a glare at Ivan.

Ivan slapped both hands over his face.

"I have just received word that Anna Chutesov is here," Lavrenty said, stopping before Zhirinsky.

An angry cloud crossed Zhirinsky's face. "The whores in the Kremlin have sent her to stop me," he hissed.

"She is not alone," Skachkov pressed. "There are two men with her. Men trained as I am."

Zhirinsky waved a hand. "You said that the handful who remained loyal to this Chutesov female and stayed in Russia were nothing. Let her bring her traitors to the cause, and we will have them all for supper."

"They are not from the Institute," Skachkov said. "These two are Masters of my discipline. The discipline for which I know no name."

"Two men?" Zhirinsky mocked. "Have your teams find them and kill them."

Lavrenty shook his white head. "To become *Mactep*—to truly earn the title that has been bestowed on me—I must face these two alone. It is my destiny."

With that, he turned on his heel and slid silently away.

Zhirinsky looked from the departing young man to Ivan Kerbabaev. Ivan shrank from the sudden attention.

"He may have his destiny," the ultranationalist growled. "For I have mine and it is greater than any other man's."

Brushing aside his aide, Zhirinsky marched for his limo.

REMO HAD EXPECTED the streets of Fairbanks to be swarming with Russian soldiers. Instead, the roads they drove on were eerily empty.

"I thought you said there'd be a bunch more soldiers on those helicopters," he said. "Where are all the black boots and empty Stolichnaya bottles?"

"The normal capacity for a Mil is only twelve," Anna replied from the passenger seat. "That includes pilots and gunners. Even if he managed to squeeze a few extra on each of the twelve we saw, that is still only a handful of troops to occupy the city."

A thought occurred to Anna. Reaching over, she switched on the radio. Scanning the AM dial, she soon found what she was after. A Russian announcer was speaking excitedly.

From the back seat the Master of Sinanju listened to the radio along with Anna.

"Sounds like someone's got a full nelson on his nuts," Remo commented after listening to only a few seconds. "What's he so worked up about?"

"I was right," Anna said. "Zhirinsky is here."

As she listened intently to the announcer's words, Chiun sniffed contemptuously.

"I have heard these false claims before," the old man said, wrinkled face puckered with disdain. "He dares invoke the name of Czar Ivan."

"The terrible?" Remo asked. "What's he saying about him?"

"Some nonsense about an upstart who fancies himself to be the new Russian czar," Chiun answered. "Don't you believe it. These modern Russians are always full of promises about enslaving the people this, or ruling with an iron fist that, but it always ends up the same. With an empty throne. This is just a new excuse to peek though people's cupboards and take their last ingot of gold. It is just like that thing they used to try. What was it called again?"

"Communism?" Remo suggested flatly.

"Yes, that's the thing," Chiun said with a shiver.

Anna was still listening to the radio. "The announcer says that Zhirinsky will be making a speech shortly."

"He a typical Commie when it comes to hearing the sound of his own voice?" Remo asked. "If so, we just bought ourselves about nine hours of blabber time."

Anna was deep in thought. "We do not know where the bomb is," she said. "Until we do, we cannot dismantle the greatest danger."

Remo raised a finger. "Hello? Sinanju prophecy? Line of Wang ending, me having to fight some renegade Master. Could be bigger than a garden-variety Russian nuke." When Anna gave him a withering look, he shrugged. "I'm just saying, that's all."

"I do not like this program," Chiun complained from the back seat. "Try another station." He reached between them and began poking at the radio with the tip of one long nail.

Anna ignored them both, pressing ahead. "Since the people are gone, there is no longer a threat to the civilian population. We should cut off Zhirinsky's means of escape."

Remo nodded. "I gotcha," he sighed. "He's less likely to set off the bomb when he's stranded in the blast zone."

Anna shook her head. "Not at all," she said seriously. "In fact, he is unhinged enough that he might relish the notion of playing the martyr. If he feels threatened in the least—the *very* least—he could set off the bomb."

"In that case we should go after him first," Remo said.

"We do not know what sort of failsafes he has devised," Anna said. "To go after him could trigger the bomb."

"Perfect," Remo grumbled. "Damned if you do, nuked if you don't. Could anything make this day any worse?"

Chiun suddenly found a station that was playing a Wylander Jugg song. With a delighted squeal, the old man settled back into his seat.

"Ask a stupid rhetorical question," Remo muttered to himself. Hunching over the steering wheel, he headed off in the direction of the airport and the fleet of Hinds.

FOUR MEN in shabby Red Army uniforms marched proudly before the steps of Fairbanks city hall. Gloved hands chopped air with each accompanying sharp kick from highly polished boots.

When he stepped from his limo to the sidewalk, Vladimir Zhirinsky wept for joy at the sight of the men.

"Is everything ready for my address?" he sniffled as he brought a handkerchief to his great Russian nose.

Ivan Kerbabaev had stepped from the limo behind him.

Ivan was nauseous. The pain in his face was worse. He was in desperate need of another injection and didn't need his mad employer flaunting his own nose in front of him.

"Yes, comrade," Ivan said weakly. "There was a problem at first. The global satellite system suffered a great deal of damage earlier in the week due to an interstellar dust cloud. But we have found one to carry our signal."

Ivan dared not tell the lunatic that he had bought time on an American commercial satellite. He could only imagine what his employer would do if he found out his great call to arms to the Russian population to retake the nation for the people was being broadcast on an ABC-Disney-owned satellite.

Zhirinsky nodded satisfaction. Honking loudly, he stuffed his handkerchief in the pocket of his uniform coat and began mounting the stairs. Two steps up, he froze. He spun to Ivan, face twisted furiously.

"What is *that* still doing there!" he roared.

He pointed to the flagpole beside the steps. High above their heads, the American flag fluttered in the wind.

"I thought you would want to be here for this," Ivan said fearfully. He clapped his hands sharply.

The soldiers hurried to the pole. Hand over hand, they brought the flag down, dumping it unceremoniously into a metal trash barrel. As bare rope clanged against the hollow pole, another soldier marched forward carrying a bundle of tightly folded red cloth. The new flag was hooked and hoisted high into the air.

At the top of the pole, the wind took the flag and unfurled it wide. The golden hammer and sickle stretched proudly across the sky.

Vladimir Zhirinsky gasped.

"How proud this day," the ultranationalist intoned. "We will not soon forget it."

Dabbing at his eyes, he hurried up the steps.

"I gnow I won't," Ivan said glumly, gingerly touching his bloody bandages. Desperate for another novocaine fix, he trudged morosely up the stairs.

THEY SKIRTED the south bank of the winding Chena River, stopping at the top of a hill near the tall wire fence that surrounded Fairbanks Airport. Below, the twelve silent Hinds lined the main runway. Some of the soldiers who had flown over from Russia milled about between the idle craft.

Remo, Chiun and Anna stood near the fence. From their vantage point they could see almost the entire airfield. While some men worked around the Hinds, others stood sentry between the big gunships. Counting white camo suits, there were only a few Sinanju-trained soldiers at the airport.

"You sure Zhirinsky's not down there?" Remo asked.

"According to the radio, he plans to make his address from the city hall," Anna said.

"It's days like this that make me happy I forgot what little Russian I knew," Remo grumbled.

He grabbed hold of the fence, wrenching it apart. Links popped and brackets split. Peeling back a section, he and Anna slipped through.

Behind him Chiun clucked disapproval. Stepping up to his own section of undamaged fence, the Master of Sinanju pulled his hands from his sleeves as if unsheathing ten sharp blades. With sure downward strokes, he attacked the fence. The links split like soft butter, forming a perfect five-foot outline of his body, through which Chiun stepped.

The old man's face was deadly serious.

"You cannot always stomp and tear your way through life, Remo," the Master of Sinanju warned. "If you are not using me as a set of walking bolt cutters, you are attacking with your own clumsy mitts. While I know you stubbornly refuse to grow your nails to their proper length, be on guard. For the false Master of legend might."

Remo sighed. "Let's see about that," he said with tired determination. He turned to Anna. "Does this soldier of yours have long fingernails or short?"

It was one of the few times in his life he could remember seeing Anna Chutesov react with surprise. The moment her face fell, he knew he was right.

Anna quickly regained her composure.

"Just because he is Russian does not make him my responsibility," she said.

"No, him being your responsibility makes him your responsibility," Remo replied. He shook his head, annoyed. "You think I'm blind, deaf and dumb, Anna? I remember what that crazy Russian general said back

in California just before he died. He said you'd stolen
something from us. And you kept trying to shoot him
before he could talk, just like the guys you've been
shooting left and right here. It's that dumbass Mactep
program you told us about. The one where the Russian
government tried to blackmail us into going to work
for them. When that failed, they put their best agent
on the case. You. And the first thing you did was track
down that nutbar Purcell in order to train your unholy
army of the night. That's why you're here. To try to
put the toothpaste back in the tube and keep us from
finding out in the process. You double-crossed us,
Anna. And don't lie, because in spite of what you,
Chiun and the whole damn world might think, I'm not
stupid."

As he spoke, Anna appeared to grow very small and
cold. The weight of more than ten years of betrayal
seemed to suddenly fall like lead onto her shoulders,
her body sagging beneath its great burden.

"It is not what you think, Remo," she said softly.
"The decision to do this was taken out of my hands
long ago."

Beside Remo, Chiun's face grew shocked. "Do my
ears hear true?" the old man gasped. "It is *you* who
has stolen food from the mouths of the children of
Sinanju?"

Anna's shoulders sank lower. She raised her head,
defiant eyes of blue now filled with shame. "Yes,"
she said.

The wizened Korean's eyes saucered. "Perfidy!"
he whispered. "Jezebel! Viper in our very midst! I

knew you were harboring a secret, woman, but *this?*"
He spun on Remo. "If you value the sanctity of our
traditions, you will slay this treacherous female at
once," he commanded.

Remo's head was bowed. He was very quiet as he
considered his teacher's words. The world around him
seemed to still. The airport below, the men, the helicopters—all were background noise. A chorus of
nothing.

When he at last raised his head, his eyes were filled
with some unreadable emotion.

"This is bad, Anna," he said in a voice soft and
cold.

She winced at his words.

"Bad?" Chiun scoffed. "It is an outrage. If you
will not slay her, I will." When he took a step toward
Anna, he found Remo's outstretched arm blocking his
way. "You cannot protect her, Remo," he warned.
"Not with what she has done. Tradition in this matter
is clear."

Remo was trying to think. "I know," he snapped.
"Dammit, I know." When he looked back to Anna,
he shook his head. "This is bad, Anna," he repeated,
in a voice more frightening given the quiet conviction
with which the words were delivered.

And that was all. He turned from her and headed
down the hill.

Chiun shot her an evil look. With a shake of his
head that snapped the flaps of his winter hat, he followed his pupil down to the airport.

At the top of the hill near the torn-apart fence, Anna

stood alone. For a long moment she seemed to be trying to gather strength.

It had happened. After so many years of skulking and guilt, her worst fear had become a reality. And in the keenly analytical mind of Anna Chutesov, the outcome—at least for her—was now inevitable.

She finally moved, trudging down the hill on feet of lead. In the corners of her ice-blue eyes were frozen tears.

29

Piles of plowed snow lined the runway. Low-lying buildings offered cover for their approach. They made it down to the tarmac's edge undetected, stopping behind a pile of dirty snow.

"How many guys were trained, *exactly?*" Remo asked Anna once she'd caught up to them.

"One hundred and sixty-two," Anna admitted.

Both Masters of Sinanju knew she was telling the truth.

"Are they all in Alaska?"

"No. Eighteen remain in Moscow. Six are with the three Russian presidents who oversaw Mactep. Twelve more are recent trainees. They are at a safehouse near the Institute. I had not introduced them yet to the others in the program."

"How many have we knocked off so far, Little Father?" Remo asked Chiun.

"Thirty-two," the Master of Sinanju replied.

Remo started to add the numbers in his head. Seeing that they could be there all night, Chiun exhaled annoyance.

"That leaves 130," the old man hissed. "From that

we take away the eighteen she claims are not here. Assuming she is not lying about that, too.''

''I'm not,'' Anna promised, shamefaced.

''Okay, that's 114 here.''

Chiun gave him a withering look. ''And what was your excuse for skipping your math lessons?'' he asked thinly.

''Didn't skip. Slept. Why, that's not right?''

''It is 112,'' Chiun snapped.

Remo turned back to Anna. ''This guy who's supposed to be such hot stuff. He included with them?''

She had only been half listening. Head swimming, she was seeing the world now from the end of a long, dark tunnel.

''Skachkov is one of them,'' she nodded.

''Fine,'' Remo said. ''We take out the choppers and hopefully keep your guys contained. With any luck we can get rid of all the ones here before they skip town.''

He didn't even look at Anna.

The two Masters of Sinanju ducked around the dirty snow pile. Anna followed. Unzipping her parka pocket, she pulled out her automatic and headed out onto the tarmac.

Beyond the runway's edge, the three of them split up. Remo and Chiun left the nearest gunship to Anna. The two Masters of Sinanju glided toward the next helicopters, veering apart after a few yards.

Remo's Hind had no guard. Unseen, he ducked under the belly of the helicopter. There was a panel under the tail assembly. When he popped it, he found a greasy cable.

Remo grabbed the thick cable in both hands, snapping it in two. Running up the back of the compartment was a plastic hose. When he ripped it out, a river of oily black fluid splattered to the ground. Two more panels surrendered handfuls of multicolored wires.

"I might not know what makes it work, but I know what makes it not," Remo muttered to himself.

Dropping the wires to the frozen ground, he slipped out from beneath the Hind. On swift, silent feet, he struck off toward the next in line.

ACROSS THE WINDSWEPT runway, the Master of Sinanju slid unseen past a pair of armed soldiers. Once he was out of their line of sight, he moved under his helicopter's tail.

Coming up on the far side, the old Korean bounded up onto the wing. Not stopping long enough for the skirts of his kimono to settle, he jumped to the roof.

Sure feet found the outer fuselage.

Ducking below the main rotor, Chiun raced down the narrowing length of the tail. At the far end, one bony hand took hold of the crooked swept fin as the other found the thick bolt of the stabilizing rotor. With the scoring edge of his index nail he made two neat swipes across the bolt.

That was all. Finished with his task, he floated back to the ground. He hit at a sprint. Hands and feet pumping in perfect rhythm, the Master of Sinanju moved like a great flapping butterfly to the next helicopter.

THE HIND'S INTERIOR was cold and dark.

No one had seen her climb aboard. Anna Chutesov made sure no one was watching as she slid the cabin door closed. She latched it tightly.

She made her careful way up through the main cabin to the cockpit.

The extreme nose was empty. Gunner and navigator were not aboard. Above, the pilot was gone, as well. Sitting alone in the chilly upper level, the copilot was securing a small instrument panel, his back to Anna. With fumbling fingers he dropped a small screw to the floor.

When it rolled from sight, he swore softly to himself. They were the last words he ever spoke.

Anna raised her automatic and fired a single round.

The bullet struck the man in the back of the head, and the copilot fell across his chair.

Anna dumped the body out of the way. Pocketing her gun, she slid into the pilot's seat. With swift, experienced hands she began the start-up routine.

All around, the Hind seemed to shiver as the helicopter's engine coughed to life. As the rotors began to slowly turn, Anna watched them slice overhead. Shadows of a guillotine that seemed to drop lower and lower toward the doomed head of Anna Chutesov.

REMO WAS TEARING the guts from his third gunship when he heard Anna's helicopter splutter awake. When he turned, he saw the Russian agent through the cockpit bubble. She was fussing with the control panel.

"What the hell?" Remo asked.

The Master of Sinanju was just flouncing up beside him. The old man's lips thinned when he spied Anna.

"What's she think she's doing?" Remo demanded.

"Betraying us," Chiun said, his tone matter-of-fact. He shot a look over his shoulder.

The instant the tiny Korean looked away, Remo felt the pressure waves of a rifle barrel aiming his way. With it came a few shouted voices. He glanced back just as the lead Russian in an advancing squad of soldiers opened fire.

Dodging bullets, Remo frowned at his teacher.

"Care to explain yourself?" he asked as more Russians joined the first. Pockmarks peppered the nearby Hind.

"Only the moon can hide the sun," Chiun replied, swirling like a gaily colored pinwheel around a hail of lead.

"That a highfalutin way of saying you were spotted?"

The old man raised a haughty brow. "If I was, it was probably due to the distraction of having to worry about how you plan to deal with your treacherous harlot."

For this, Remo had no response. As bullets trailed him, he ducked under the Hind. Chiun followed.

They had no sooner reached the far side than the shooting stopped. At the same time, they heard the distinct sound of more gunships spluttering to life.

"And once more, Remo, your misplaced trust begets more betrayal," Chiun sniffed.

"Lay off," Remo said. His senses had suddenly tripped alert. "We've got company."

Chiun had felt it, too. The displaced air of advancing troops. Except unlike regular men, there were no accompanying footfalls or straining muscles.

When the first cautious face peered out from under the belly of the Hind, Remo grabbed a fistful of hood and steered the Russian's head into the helicopter's side. Flesh met metal with a crunching clang.

Several more men scurried into view, all dressed in the familiar uniforms of Anna Chutesov's Institute soldiers.

"Their breathing is pitiful," Chiun remarked. To underscore that point, eight sharp talons pierced a chest between ribs. They reappeared dragging dangling lungs in their wake like inside-out pockets.

"I'm thinking they're not even as good as ninjas," Remo said as he took out two more. "See? Simple thrusts at half-speed. Chuck Norris on a bad-wig day would've dodged that."

Chiun sent a heel into a brittle sternum. "Yes," he agreed. "They lack the finesse of even the lowly Japanese. If the Dutchman is responsible for them, he is a better adversary than he is a teacher."

Ten of the Institute men had been left to guard the airport. They flashed through the last few in no time.

Remo twisted the head of the final Russian. With a blinding snap, it completed two full circles on a rubbery neck column.

"And that's the end of that chapter," he said, clapping imaginary dust from his hands.

More shouts in Russian. Remo wasn't sure if he should be relieved they weren't directed at either him or Chiun.

"What now?" he complained.

When he and the Master of Sinanju raced back to the main runway, they found the soldiers who had flown in with Vladimir Zhirinsky from Russia had taken an interest in Anna's helicopter. Some were moving to surround it.

Inside the Hind, Anna had climbed down into the gunner's cockpit.

"What's she think she's doing?" Remo asked.

His question was answered in the next instant.

Like a blaze of hellfire, a Swatter missile erupted from the outboard pylon of Anna's Hind. Hopping the launch rail, the laser-guided missile screamed across the runway, impacting with the side of another helicopter.

The Hind exploded in a cloud of brilliant yellow.

No sooner had she fired the first missile than she let a second fly. Another idling Hind was engulfed in flame. The airport shook as smoking debris rained all around.

Anna's missiles had sent the Russian army scattering. Many raced for cover in a nearby hangar. Those who remained outside ran smack-dab into Remo and Chiun.

The first soldier in line tried to shoot Remo. Remo prevented him from doing so. He did this by separating from the rest of his body that part of the soldier's anatomy that was responsible for telling said rest of his body to do such nasty things as shoot people or swear or think unkind thoughts.

When they saw Remo lop off the soldier's head, the rest of the army froze. When he held the head aloft for them to examine, they gulped.

"Okay, here's the deal," Remo announced, waggling the head. "No surrendski mean no headski, *capisce?*"

Although the language was foreign, some things were universal. Forty rifles clattered to the ground, and eighty hands shot into the air.

"While we've got their attention, ask them where the nuke is," Remo said to the Master of Sinanju.

There were a lot of shrugs from the crowd. A few men replied in Russian, waving vaguely in the same direction.

"They think it is in the center of town," Chiun said. "But they do not know where exactly."

"Big help," Remo sighed. "Now we need a POW camp."

At the coaxing of the two Masters of Sinanju, the soldiers were quickly herded into the hangar where the rest had sought cover. Remo was dragging the door shut when he heard the sound of a helicopter lifting off. When he wheeled around, he saw that it was one of the first that had been in line when he and Chiun came onto the airport.

"Dammit, Chiun, that was yours," he griped.

He made a move to intercept the still-hovering Hind but the Master of Sinanju took him by the wrist, holding fast.

"Ye of little faith," the old man said calmly.

The instant he spoke, Remo's hypersensitive ears heard a gentle ping within the roar of the gunship's engine. Sharp eyes followed the sound. Only then did Remo see the faint marks where Chiun's hardened fingernails had scored the tail-rotor bolt.

As he watched, the metal pulled apart like taffy. It grew brittle all at once, snapping in two.

The three-bladed tail rotor shrieked as it skipped off the swept fin, striking the ground in a spray of sparks. Chewing up frozen asphalt, it bounced across the runway, burying itself deep in the side of a stationary helicopter.

Without its stabilizing rotor, the tail of the Hind began to spin. It completed a half circle before the tip struck pavement, drawing the spinning rotors of the listing helicopter inexorably toward the ground.

As the guiding edges of the blades were kissing the pavement, Remo and Chiun were ducking around the side of the hangar to avoid the chunks of flying shrapnel.

They found the soldiers they'd locked inside the hangar trying to sneak out a side door. When Remo took off another head, the remaining men hightailed it back inside.

"Don't make me come in there," he warned, slapping the door shut. As he banged it closed, an explosion sounded out on the runway.

When Remo and Chiun emerged into the open, the flames from the crashed Hind fed a thick black cloud that rose into the frosty white sky. And through the smoke flew three more Hinds.

Remo immediately spied Anna in the trailing helicopter. For a moment he thought she was going to fire on the other two. But as he watched, the nose of her Hind spun away. With a scream of engines, the helicopter tore off in the opposite direction. Away from the other two Hinds, away from Fairbanks. Away from Remo.

His face darkened as he watched her make good her escape. "So much for the old team effort," he grunted.

Before them, one of the gunships had swirled to face the hangar. The four-barrel guns in the remote-control turret under the nose screamed to life, chewing the ground at Remo and Chiun's feet. Frightened shouts issued from within the hangar as bullets pierced the flimsy walls.

With an angry scowl Remo stooped, snapping up a chunk of smoking rotor blade. His body automatically compensated for the heat of the metal by producing a protective sheen of sweat on his palm. Hefting the metal fragment over one shoulder, Remo dropped his arm. With an audible snap the metal left his fingers.

Whistling all the way, the blade segment zoomed through the air, impacting with the nose of the firing Hind. The metal tore up through the cockpit at an angle, striking the gunner square in the face. Continuing up in a deadly spiral, it made it as far as the main cockpit before coming to a final, fatal stop in the chin of the pilot.

With a lurch the helicopter plopped back to the runway.

By this time the second airborne Hind had gotten its bearings. Nose tilted, its weapons were aimed squarely at Remo and Chiun.

Remo grabbed another chunk of broken rotor blade. The Master of Sinanju quickly tugged it from his hands.

"You already had your turn," the old man clucked.

Remo eyed the helicopter warily. It had not yet fired its guns, yet the gunner could still be seen through the frontal dome fussing around his instruments.

"No fooling, Chiun," Remo warned. "I think he's going for the rockets this time."

The Master of Sinanju held his ground. "Wait," he commanded.

Narrowed eyes grew tighter until they became slits of wrinkled parchment as the old man studied the movements of the gunner. When the Russian finally lunged for the panel, Chiun made his move.

The broken rotor section was up and around in a slivered heartbeat. Kimono sleeves snapping, the metal left his bony hand like a jet-propelled spear.

Across the runway two Swatters were detaching from rails on opposite sides of the Hind. One left on a plume of fire, soaring from the wing toward Remo and Chiun. The second was stopped in midlaunch by Chiun's metal fragment.

The blade impacted with the nose of the rocket before it cleared the pylon. The ensuing explosion ripped the pylon, flinging it up into the swirling rotors even as the flames from the blast were engulfing the Hind. The gunship burst apart like shattered glass.

Remo and Chiun weren't there to witness the blast.

As the second loosed missile screamed across the runway, the two Masters of Sinanju were running full-out away from its path. By the time it struck the hangar where they'd been standing, they were half a mile away and still going.

Only when the flames and the heat had subsided did the two of them double back.

They found the hangar in ruins. Fire licked the two walls that were still upright. Charred bodies of the Russian soldiers they'd herded inside were scattered all around.

"This has gotta be against the Geneva Convention," Remo said as he eyed the bodies.

Chiun surveyed the damage, his expression bland.

"They tried to get Master Hwa to sign that silly white agreement. He chained their emissaries to the Horns of Welcome and let the seagulls feast on their carcasses."

Turning on his heel, he marched off through the smoke.

Remo's eye strayed from the old man's retreating back. With a thoughtful frown he watched the sallow sky in the direction Anna had flown.

He finally turned away. Face grim, he trailed the Master of Sinanju across the battle-scarred runway.

30

Word of what was happening in Alaska had seeped into the outside world. In Russia many greeted the news of the takeover of Fairbanks with nationalistic optimism. For the first time in years, some saw hope for a nation in despair to recapture the pride of days long past. Men and women who ten years before had demonstrated in the hope of what free elections would bring, only to be held captive by poverty and corruption at the highest levels of government, had begun to take to the streets. It was beginning to look like 1917 all over again. And with a new threat from Vladimir Zhirinsky to address the nation on a pirate radio frequency, civilian and military authorities had been placed on high alert.

Director Pavel Zatsyrko of the SVR had been summoned to the Kremlin before events had become known to the greater Russian populace. For the past two days of the escalating crisis, he had been directing the operations of his agency from the Grand Palace itself. He was reviewing the latest data on leaders of the hard-line movement currently residing in Moscow when the door of his temporary office burst open.

A deputy raced in without knocking, his youthful

face pale. "He is on the phone!" the young man blurted.

When he saw that the agent wasn't carrying a gun, the SVR leader hid his great relief. With the gangs now marauding through Moscow's streets, he had feared that the rebels had pierced the defenses of the Kremlin itself.

"You are to knock before you enter this room," Zatsyrko said with forced bluster.

"But he is on the phone *now*," the young man cried, breathless. "He called the switchboard. He wishes to speak with the president."

"Who is on the phone?" Pavel Zatsyrko asked unhappily.

When he learned who it was that had made his young deputy risk his career by abandoning agency protocol, all color drained from the face of the SVR director.

Barking an order to wait five minutes before putting the caller through on the special line, Zatsyrko raced from the room. He flew through the corridors of the Kremlin. Veering from the main polished floors, he ran into an unused wing off one of the less ostentatious buildings. In a dusty corridor well off the beaten path, he exploded into a small room.

The president of Russia sat at a tiny table in a cramped kitchen. Four men sat on a bench across the room. When Zatsyrko flew into the room, they looked up in unison.

The furnishings in the room were almost a century old. The only sop to the times were a banker's lamp that sat in the middle of the table and a clumsy yellow telephone that rested at the president's elbow.

The phone had just begun to ring as Zatsyrko burst into the room. "It is him!" he panted. Wheezing to catch his breath, he stabbed a finger at the phone. "Zhirinsky."

The president had been reaching for the ringing phone. When he learned who was on the other end of the line, he hesitated. His small hand hovered an inch above the phone for a moment before he gained the courage to lift the receiver to his ear.

"Zhirinsky, what is this madness?" the president of Russia demanded without preamble.

"Oh, you are there," Vladimir Zhirinsky said with bland surprise. "I assumed when you took so long to answer that you had fled Russia. I should have known. After all, you are the fool who not only publicly arrests those who should be shipped in silence to gulags, but you also remain on vacation as submarines full of sailors suffocate on the ocean floor. I gave you credit for having too much sense."

"Sense?" the president blurted. "Zhirinsky, you are a menace. I will see to it that you are forced to live on rats and muddy water in the deepest, dankest cell in Lubyanka Prison for the rest of your lunatic life."

"I do not think so," Zhirinsky said with oily superiority. "Do you think I don't know what is happening in Mother Russia? The match is lit. The people have heard the cry of revolution and have taken to the streets. Moscow is mine, and you do not even know it. You are a prisoner in your own palace, *Mr. President.*'' The words dripped contempt. "When I make my address at midnight tonight, the days of lapping the boots of the capitalists will be over.''

The president's grip tightened on the phone.

It was true after all. He had hoped that the rumor was false. The crazy man Zhirinsky intended to address the Russian population. And with the current national mood, the madman could actually become a figure of revolution.

The great purges under Stalin and Lenin, the nightmares of the gulags, the persecution of any dissenting thought, the decades of the evil terror of the KGB— all would be as nothing compared to what would become of Russia if Vladimir Zhirinsky were to take the reins of power.

"I will stop you," the president vowed darkly.

"You cannot," Zhirinsky replied. "You have not the capability to disrupt my signal. If you were a wise man, you would land a helicopter within the Kremlin's walls and fly out this evening. You have been a dutiful lapdog. The Americans would no doubt let you hide behind their skirts.''

"I have spoken to their President," the Russian leader said. "I have offered military assistance to remove you.''

He could almost see the smile bloom beneath Zhirinsky's bushy mustache.

"Send your soldiers. When was the last time any of them were paid? Every true Russian will turn to my cause. Not only that, but you know it to be true, for I smell your fear. If I were you, I would begin packing. And if you are still there when I arrive in Moscow in triumph..."

There came a delighted sound of clicking teeth on the other end of the line. With that, the phone went dead in the president's ear.

With wooden movements he replaced the big yellow receiver. His fingers felt fat and clumsy.

Pavel Zatsyrko still stood near the plain wooden door, an anxious expression on his face.

"Is it true?" the SVR man asked the president. "Did you offer troops to the American President?"

At his wobbly table, the president looked up. Dark bags rimmed his pale eyes. "He refused," he said. "According to him, they have their best already in Alaska." The Russian glanced back at the four men seated against the wall. "But I do not see how two men could go up against an army," he muttered under his breath.

"Only two men?" Zatsyrko asked, amazed.

The president shook his head. "He did not tell me that. I heard this from our agent in Alaska. She is on her way back here even as we speak. She has assured me that they are more capable than any army."

Pavel Zatsyrko did not ask who this mysterious woman was. Apparently she was very highly placed, for she did not come under his jurisdiction at the SVR.

"Let us hope so," Zatsyrko said seriously. "For if Zhirinsky truly does have a nuclear bomb and uses it within the United States, the anarchists who roam

Russia's streets will become the least of our problems."

The president didn't seem to hear. Tiny fingers drummed the wooden table.

"The two former presidents are still here in the Kremlin?" he asked suddenly.

"They could not leave if they wanted to," Zatsyrko said. "Their cars would not be able to get past the mobs."

"Bring them here," the president insisted. "And have them bring their bodyguards with them." His voice grew soft, his gaze distant. "If she is correct, the worst for me may come if the American agents somehow manage to succeed."

BEHIND HIS DESK in the Fairbanks city hall, Vladimir Zhirinsky took his hand from the phone.

Framed in the window at his back was the fluttering hammer and sickle of the *Sovyetskii Soyuz.* The flag waved proudly over Zhirinskygrad's cold night streets.

The ultranationalist smiled into the camera.

"And…cut," Zhirinsky ordered.

Across the room, an aide lowered the video camera he'd taken from the home of a Fairbanks real-estate agent.

"We must record every moment of this," Zhirinsky insisted. He smoothed out his mustache with two quick strokes of his index finger.

With fussing hands he picked up the pen from his desk and began to make grand sweeps across the clean, top sheet of a yellow legal pad.

"Um, Comrade Skachkov phoned a few minutes ago," the aide said nervously. He held the camera protectively to his chest. "He is still looking for the American spies."

Zhirinsky noted the quaver in the man's voice. His pen froze in place as he raised his dark eyes. "Is there something wrong?" he asked suspiciously.

The man with the camera thought of what Skachkov had told him. About all the dead soldiers at the airport and the fact that every one of their helicopters had been destroyed. He also thought of what Zhirinsky had done to Ivan Kerbabaev.

The nervous young man worked only part-time two days a week in the ultranationalist's Moscow office. And if his boss was willing to bite the nose off a full-timer, he dared not imagine what Zhirinsky might do to him.

"No, no," he said, smiling sickly. "Nothing more. But perhaps you should deliver your speech now instead of waiting until midnight. By all accounts, the people are ready. You have inspired them with your actions here. There is no reason why the revolution needs to wait any longer. We can leave for Russia as soon as you are done."

"Nonsense," Zhirinsky said. "We have all the time in the world." He tapped his pen to his chin as he licked the bristles of his bushy mustache. "What rhymes with 'invade Afghanistan'? Ah, yes."

Sticking his chin deep into his uppermost medals that adorned his jangling chest, he got back to work.

With a feeling of deep dread, the man with the camera backed quietly from the room.

31

Ivan Kerbabaev's eyes were clamped tightly shut. With one hand he clasped the door handle. With the other he gripped firmly on to the front of the rear seat.

"Hurry," Ivan begged.

"I will try not to cause any pain."

"I am already in pain," Ivan said, his voice quavering.

Ivan sucked in a gust of injured air at the sudden tearing at his face. Opening his eyes, he saw nothing between them but a tiny nub of white bone. The spot where his nose should have been felt wet and open.

Ivan made a few pitiful sobbing moans.

On the back seat next to him, the Russian soldier who had just removed the bandages winced.

Blood bubbles percolated out of exposed nasal cavities. A strand of cartilage hung from the tip of the triangular bone. The discolored flesh around the wound was curling inward. Teeth marks were visible on the skin.

The soldier forced an encouraging smile. "It does not look so bad," he said.

Ivan had just caught a glimpse of his deformed face in the rearview mirror.

"Oh, *God*," Zhirinsky's aide wailed pathetically.

"Maybe you should see a doctor," the soldier suggested.

"There are no doctors," Ivan moaned. "That bristle-faced lunatic has banished them all from town."

The soldier stiffened. Comrade Kerbabaev's words were troubling. They would need to be reported.

Careful to remain without expression, the young soldier rolled down the window. He threw the bloody bandages out into the street. A cold wind grabbed the gauze, blowing it away. Rolling up the window, he reached to the floor of the car where he began fussing with a small case Ivan had liberated from the downtown dentist's office.

"Aren't you ready yet?" Ivan begged after what seemed like an eternity. "I am in agony."

"I am all set. Do not move."

Ivan opened his eyes just a crack. He saw the needle closing in. With a groan he squeezed his eyes shut.

The soldier held him by the side of the head with one hand while he slipped the needle in. Ivan felt a tiny prick near the bone of what had been his nose. When the needle came back out a moment later, Ivan's shoulders sagged.

It would take a moment for the novocaine to take effect. Ivan kept his eyes closed as the soldier applied fresh gauze.

"When the new revolution comes, Russia will once more have the best doctors in the world," the soldier said as he bit off a strip of masking tape he'd stolen from the health-and-beauty-aids section of the local Sam's Club. "They will fix you up."

"Russia never had good doctors," Ivan moaned. "My father went to a clinic to have an ingrown toenail removed and they cut off his foot. He died of gangrene. The only doctors that might have been able to do anything at all for me were chased away by the crazy man in whose belly my nose now rots."

The soldier's eyes grew flat at the treasonous words.

"State doctors are the best," he insisted dully.

"There is no state," Ivan spit. "There is a small city in the middle of nowhere. No matter what the madman thinks, the Americans will not wait forever." He leaned back against the seat. "My only hope is that they take pity on me for what the crazy man has done to me."

The soldier applied a final piece of tape, stowing the dispenser in the case with the novocaine and needles.

"If that is your attitude, why did you participate in this glorious crusade?" he sniffed.

Ivan opened his eyes. He could see by his body language that the soldier was displeased. Good. Maybe he'd report him. At this point Ivan didn't even care.

"I am scared to death of that lunatic, that is why," Ivan said morosely, shutting his eyes once more. The novocaine was blessedly starting to take effect. "When I answered his newspaper ad, I did not know better. I had heard the stories about him, but I didn't believe them. After that it was too late. Did you ever try quitting a job when your boss is certifiably insane? Every day I tried to, and every day I saw visions of him slamming my head in the filing cabinet or pushing me down the elevator shaft. I *knew* I should have taken that job as second-shift manager at the Moscow McDonald's.''

For a brief instant Ivan felt a shiver of cold. He assumed the soldier who had driven him here had rolled the window down to throw something else out into the street. Opening his eyes lazily, he was met with a fresh shock.

When he saw that the face looking back at him was no longer that of the young soldier, Ivan jumped so hard he banged his head against the roof.

"Kto dyela?" he winced, dropping back to his seat.

"Speakie the English," demanded Remo Williams.

Remo now sat in the back seat across from the Russian. Looking around, Ivan saw no sign of the soldier who had been tending to his wound.

Ignoring the swelling bruise on his head, Ivan instinctively covered his bandaged face. "Who are you?" he repeated in English. His voice was pained and nasal.

"The spirit of America," Remo replied evenly. "I'm hiding out in Alaska these days, 'cause it's as far as I can get by Studebaker from the Washington, New York, Boston axis. Now how about being a good invader and tell the spirit how to pull the plug on this nuke of yours?"

Ivan's eyes grew sick. "What is nuke?" he asked weakly.

"The spirit has had his fill of Russians lying to him today," Remo said darkly.

Grabbing Ivan by the throat, Remo dragged him from the rear of the parked car.

On the street Ivan saw the young soldier who had bandaged his face. He was lying in the road, his limbs twisted at impossible angles. Above him stood a wizened figure whose weathered face and imperious stance reminded Ivan of one of the Inuit totem poles he had seen around town.

Beyond the Master of Sinanju was the tarpaulin-covered flatbed trailer on which sat the Russian nuclear device.

"Get disarming," Remo ordered, flinging Ivan at the back of the truck.

"I told you it was the boom," Chiun insisted.

"It looked like a logging truck," Remo said. "When they said bomb, I thought bomb, not missile." He turned to Ivan. "What are you doing dragging an ICBM around on this Smokey and the Bandit thing? Can't you just unscrew the nose?"

"Comrade Zhirinsky liked better the idea of an entire intact missile rather than just a bomb," Ivan explained.

"Doesn't take Sigmund Freud to figure out his problem," Remo grumbled. "Okay, let's go."

He dragged Ivan down the length of the trailer.

Both Masters of Sinanju could feel the contaminating radiation. It didn't seem high enough to cause damage with short-term exposure.

At the back, Remo tossed Ivan up under the tarpaulin. He and Chiun hopped up after him. The crinkling tarp rattled above their heads as they ducked alongside the missile. They hurried past the rocket, up the shaft to the warhead.

When they stopped, Ivan turned his gauze-wrapped face to the two men, unsure what to do.

"Disarm it," Remo ordered.

Ivan hesitated. "It is difficult," he said.

"That so? Let me make it easy."

The Russian offered too tempting a target. Shelving the more intricate Sinanju methods of persuasion, Remo did something a little more direct. He socked Ivan in the face.

Remo's balled fist struck hard in the middle of Ivan Kerbabaev's bunched-up bandages. Blood spurted anew, streaming down from beneath tape and gauze.

Ivan screeched in pain.

"I did not say I would not do it!" the Russian cried, grabbing at his aching nose bone.

"Good," Remo said. "Then get cracking."

Ivan's eyes were pleading. "I do not *have* to," he explained desperately.

"No? I've got five reasons why you do," Remo said. He punched the back of Ivan's hand, knocking it into his face.

Ivan shrieked, falling back against the shiny silver warhead. "Please!" he begged. Both hands now cradled his bleeding face. "You do not understand!"

Remo's brow dropped low. "What don't I understand?"

"Limit your response to this device," Chiun suggested. "For a complete inventory of things Remo does not understand would maroon us forever in this wasteland."

Ivan's mouth was stained red. He gulped, swallowing watery blood. "The bomb does not work," he insisted.

Remo blinked. "Come again?"

"It does not work," Ivan explained. "The bomb is defective. Broken."

Remo looked at the metal casing. Radiation continued to seep from the device. He looked back at Ivan, suspicious.

"It's radioactive," he warned.

"Residual radiation," Ivan promised. "It was disarmed in Ukraine years ago. The plutonium was removed before it was shipped back to Russia. It is worthless."

Remo drew back his fist. "Are you pulling my leg?"

Ivan recoiled. "Please, it is truth!"

It was plain to them both that the Russian wasn't lying.

"Why would this man have a boom device that does not work?" Chiun asked.

"Zhirinsky wanted a missile. Any missile," Ivan explained, teary eyed. "I would give the *grymza usraty* whatever he desired, whether it worked or not."

"Zhirinsky doesn't know it's broken?" Remo asked.

"*Nyet,*" Ivan insisted, shaking his head fervently.

"Lemme get this straight. You got this dud for him

and you never bothered to tell him before he invaded Alaska that it doesn't work? What kind of crummy henchman are you?''

''I am not henchman, I am prisoner,'' Ivan moaned. ''He *likes* me and the *govnyuk* still bit off my nose. What do you think he would have done to me if I told him his missile was broken? Yes, I arranged for it to be bought from the black market, but even I could not bring myself to purchase the plutonium it needed.'' His black-rimmed eyes begged understanding above his thick wad of gauze.

Remo absorbed his words. ''Just to tie up all the loose ends, this black market twit who sold it to you was Boris Flavoricc, wasn't it?''

Ivan nodded. ''Boris Feyodov, yes,'' he said. ''He is powerful figure in Russian Mafia.''

''Tell that to the hundred tons of rock that made his head go squish,'' Remo said dryly. He turned to Chiun. ''His nuke and army are gone. That leaves us with the big nut himself, about a hundred Sinanju-trained guys and a Wang prophecy to deal with. The day's starting to look up.''

''We will dispose of the armies of death first,'' Chiun intoned. ''He of legend will find us when the time comes.''

Spinning, the old man marched down the missile's length.

When Remo turned back to Ivan, the Russian cowered.

''You know where his men are?'' Remo asked.

Ivan nodded. ''Yes,'' he said.

"Good. You just got promoted to tour guide."

As he was grabbing Ivan by the jacket collar, the terrified man looked up at Remo, sad hope in his watery eyes.

"As typical body-conscious American, you would not happen to have number of good plastic surgeon?" he asked.

As he spoke, another piece of tape popped loose.

32

"So did Anna ever work with Zhirinsky?" Remo asked as they sped down the street.

Ivan Kerbabaev was sandwiched between the two Masters of Sinanju in the front seat of the Land Rover.

"Anna?" Ivan asked, confused. The light dawned. "Ah, Anna Chutesov. As far as I know, they have never even met. Zhirinsky first mentioned her to me this week. She is apparently director of a secret organization in Russia. A man by the name of Lavrenty Skachkov contacted Zhirinsky months ago. He and the other specially trained soldiers worked for this Chutesov woman until they decided to defect to Zhirinsky's cause a few days ago. Apparently, they were dissatisfied with the restrictions she placed on them."

"Why?" Remo asked. "She only let them kill every other Saturday?"

Ivan shook his head. "From what I understand she never let them out. That was the problem."

Remo shot a glance at the Master of Sinanju. "Sounds like Anna kept a tight lid on Mactep," he said, a hint of uncertainty in his voice.

"That does not matter," the old man sniffed.

"Maybe it should," Remo said softly.

Between them, Ivan looked from one man to the other. "Mactep?" he asked as he stuck loose bandage tape back down. "That is what the others call Skach-kov."

Remo scowled. "Yeah?" he said. "Well, Master Scratchpost is about to find out who the real Master is."

A blinding flash. Like something sparking in his brain.

Remo's eyes blurred, and he felt the wheel go mushy in his hands. When he snapped back around an instant later, the shoulder of the road was racing toward them. He fumbled for the steering wheel, but a bony hand was already there.

With a squeal of tires, Chiun steered them straight.

"Wow," Remo said, his hands fumbling to take control once more. "Another head rush."

His mind was clearing. As it did, a thought that had almost formed scampered back into the back of his brain. And as it fled, his earlier frustration returned.

"Still sure you don't want to tell me what it is I'm missing?" he asked the Master of Sinanju.

The old man shook his head. "You must find your own path."

"Great," Remo muttered.

Ivan wasn't sure what had just happened. "You are not from the Institute," the Russian said evenly.

"We're from better than the Institute," Remo replied.

Ivan looked first at the ancient Korean sitting on one side of him, then to the younger man in the light windbreaker who had just had some kind of seizure that had almost driven them off the road.

"Skachkov is very, very good," he warned.

"I'm sick of people saying that," Remo snapped. "Now, unless you want an elbow to that nose-nub of yours, you'll pipe down and tell us where to go."

Ivan did as he was told.

With Zhirinsky's aide offering directions as they went, Remo eventually stopped near a medical building around the corner from Fairbanks Hospital. It was a plain two-story structure. A few trucks were parked out front.

From the car Ivan pointed up at the brick building. "The Brezhnev Brigade is in there."

"Wait here," Remo instructed as he and Chiun popped their doors and slid out.

As Ivan ducked behind the dashboard, the two Sinanju Masters met at the front of the car.

"Stealthy or straightforward?" Remo asked.

Chiun's neck craned like an angry bird from the brocade collar of his kimono.

"Prepare to pay in blood for your thievery, Russian dogs!" the Master of Sinanju cried up at the first-story windows. Fists knots of righteous anger, he whirled up the front staircase.

"Settles that," Remo said to himself. Hands thrust deep in his pockets, he strolled up the stairs after Chiun.

The two men disappeared inside the building.

Alone in the car, Ivan waited. He jumped when, a

minute after the two men had disappeared inside, there came a few muffled shots from the building.

That was it. They were dead.

Maybe he could convince Vladimir Zhirinsky that he had led these two into a trap. Who knew? The delusional lunatic was probably so far gone by now he'd believe anything. Not that it really mattered to Ivan any longer.

He was about to start the engine when the driver's door sprang open. Remo shoved Ivan from behind the wheel.

"For future reference, I don't like my seat kept warm," Remo said as he got in next to Ivan. "That goes double for Russian asses."

Ivan felt a stinging swat on his right knee. When he spun to its source, he found Chiun sitting calmly next to him.

"Stay on your side," cautioned the Korean.

"What's this bring us down to, Little Father?"

"Eighty-six," the old Asian replied.

"Wish there was a faster way to thin this herd," Remo frowned. He started the engine and pulled from the curb.

Craning his neck, Ivan looked back at the building, amazement blossoming on the visible parts of his face.

"There were sixteen men in there," he said.

"I know," Remo said, peeved. "It's a pain running all over the place like this. At least he had all those other troops at the airport. Lot more convenient for us that way."

"Yes, they are there for now," Ivan said. "But he

plans to disperse them to fortified positions after his speech.''

"He'll need a set of barbecue tongs," Remo said. "And you should work on your tenses, schnozzy. I said 'had.' I meant by putting all the Russian eggs in one basket it was easier for us to handle. Bizz-bang-boom, we were done."

Ivan seemed to finally realize what Remo was saying.

"You mean you eliminated all of his troops at the airport?" he asked, inching up to a sitting position. A tiny spark of hope swelled in the pit of his cold stomach.

"*I* eliminated most of them," Chiun interjected.

"Technically, they mostly eliminated each other, Little Father," Remo pointed out.

Ivan watched them both. "Do you intend to kill Zhirinsky?" the Russian asked, eagerness in his soft voice.

"Now that we know he can't melt the polar ice-caps," Remo replied.

Ivan's eyes grew cunning. "Let me help. I offer my services as a double agent."

"What do you think you're doing right now, genius?"

The cunning changed to a look of cold vengeance. "Kill me, then. I no longer care. But before you do, allow me to tear off the lunatic's nose."

"Sorry. Got dibs on that," Remo said darkly.

Ivan slumped back in the seat like a pouting child.

A wet moan of disappointment rose from beneath his mound of bloody bandages.

Remo rolled his eyes. "Look, tell us where the next batch of Institute guys are and you can have an ear."

A grin sprang so abruptly to Ivan's face, another piece of tape popped free. "Take the next left," Ivan Kerbabaev instructed giddily. With joyous, nimble fingers he pressed the tape back to his mangled face.

Ivan quickly turned from reluctant tour guide to eager collaborator. The next stop was the Fairbanks chamber of commerce. As an afterthought as they were getting out of the car, Remo tapped three fingers to the Russian's forehead. Ivan was frightened when Remo came at him, but when his captor's hand withdrew, a look of great relief washed over the Russian's face. His facial pain had disappeared.

As Remo and Chiun walked away from the car, the look of love Ivan gave Remo was the sort generally reserved to dogs for their owners.

"You do not need to spoil him," Chiun complained.

Remo's face was flat. "His whimpering was getting to me. Besides, I need him for something once we're done here."

They mounted the steps to the chamber of commerce.

"Only five inside," Remo said, tuning his senses to the interior of the building. "Sounds like they're asleep."

Chiun nodded sharp agreement. "We will send the thieves to eternal slumber," he intoned.

A sharp slap opened the door. Chiun swirled inside.

Remo followed the wizened figure up the darkened main hallway. They found the five soldiers curled in sleeping bags on a first-story office floor.

"Think we should wake them up?" Remo whispered. "Hardly seems sporting not to give them a fighting chance."

The old man gave him a baleful look before turning away.

Kimono hems whirling around his bony ankles, Chiun bounded from the door. One sandaled heel found the crunching skull of a slumbering man. Springing from head to head as if seeking stones in raging rapids, Chiun quickly finished off the five. Giving his heel a grinding crunch to the final skull, the Master of Sinanju padded back to Remo.

"Leave chance to sport," the old man said blandly. "I am a professional."

They were about to leave when Remo spied something on the floor next to one of the dead soldiers.

"Wait a sec," he said. "I have an idea."

He headed for the body.

At the door Chiun paused impatiently. "I have warned you to inform me beforehand when that one special day in each decade comes around," the old man droned, "that I might arrange to be out of town."

"Don't knock my ideas," Remo warned as he snatched up the soldier's portable radio. "I'm sick of running all over this icebox. Besides, you're gonna love this one."

VLADIMIR ZHIRINSKY STARED at the radio in his aide's hand with a look of dumb shock.

The man had run into his office a few seconds ago. The future premier of the reborn Soviet Union couldn't believe what he was hearing.

"Calling all Commies, calling all Commies. Sitting-duck American spies spotted in vicinity of chamber of commerce building. This is not a trap. Over."

The radio crackled with static.

Sitting at his desk, mounds of wadded paper all around, Zhirinsky glared up at his aide.

"Whoever he is, he began broadcasting a few minutes ago," the young man offered worriedly.

Zhirinsky licked his mustache. "Who is stationed at the chamber of commerce building?" he asked.

"The Trotsky Brigade," his aide said. "I have tried to raise them, but I cannot."

The American voice broke in again.

"Okay, so it *is* a trap. But there's only two of us. What's the matter, you chicken or something?"

Zhirinsky frowned as the radio speaker began to emit clucking sounds. "What is 'chicken'?" he asked his aide.

The young man shrugged nervously.

Zhirinsky's brow grew heavy. "It sounds like he is *mocking* me," he said with low menace.

The voice on the radio stopped clucking. "Hey, Chiun, how do you say stupid in Russian?"

Another voice chimed in from the background. *"Tupitsa."*

"Zhirinsky's a *tupitsa*-ass," taunted the first man.

In his office the ultranationalist's eyes nearly launched from their sockets. "He *is* mocking me," he gasped.

A raspberry issued from the speaker.

Ropy knots of rage tightened in Zhirinsky's neck.

"Send all of the Institute men to their location! Whoever they are, I want them dead. Where is Skachkov? Where is that spineless assistant of mine, Kerbabaev?" Spittle flew from his spluttering lips.

"I will check," his aide said, scurrying from the room.

On the radio the voice had begun singing the "Star Spangled Banner."

Eyes furious, Zhirinsky snatched up the microphone. Blue veins bulged on his pale forehead.

"Who are you?" he bellowed.

"The spirit of America," replied the hateful voice, "here to tell you that the only good xenophobe is an American xenophobe. Now, you wanna hurry up and kill us already? I've got a prophecy to hammer out and some overdue videos to bring back to the Juneau Blockbuster."

With a sharp crackle the radio went dead.

Zhirinsky's address to the Russian people was forgotten. His ascension to power, the new Soviet Union, the turmoil back home—all faded into a chorus of nothing. His focus was now aimed entirely at this detestable American who would dare mock Vladimir Zhirinsky.

"I will show you who is poultry!" the ultranationalist raged. Grabbing the radio, he heaved it against the wall. Like Zhirinsky's sanity, it shattered into a hundred pieces.

33

The first truck slowed to a stop on the cold Fairbanks street at 10:17 p.m.

From a darkened second-story window in the chamber of commerce building, Remo watched eight Russians with rifles disembark. Each wore a white face mask and goggles.

"They must only own one party dress," Remo commented.

Chiun sat in a lotus position on the floor, his hands resting lightly on his knees. "If I know my Russians, their government took their spare kimonos to give to those who didn't have kimonos and then traded them to Iraq for oil," he said dully. "Do any of them look like the false Master?"

"Tough to say," Remo replied as he watched the men outside. "With those masks I can't see if they fit the description Anna gave. So far they look like the same klutzes we've already met."

A yellow school bus pulled up. From the front and rear doors, thirty more soldiers climbed stealthily down to the dark street. Behind the bus, a few more large trucks unloaded even more men.

"Looks like the last of them," Remo said as the men grouped in the street.

The Master of Sinanju rose silently from the office floor, sliding in beside Remo at the window. Slender nails split the miniblinds wider.

The Russians were fanning out around the building. Some had already slipped around back. They kept to the shadows, joining with the darkness.

To Remo and Chiun's keen eyes, they might as well have had a hundred searchlights trained on each of them.

"This really burns me, Little Father," Remo said softly. "They don't deserve Sinanju. Not even a hint of it."

Chiun's weathered face was hard. "So it was with the others who stole from the House through the years," he intoned. "They are all dancers and board breakers who have appropriated but a reflected ray of the Sun Source. Unlike the other times in our history, we have an opportunity here to eliminate every practitioner of this illegitimate art."

"Hmm," Remo said absently.

The soldiers approached from all around. On the street they moved toward the front. Those around back had to be closing in by now. A creak came from above, followed by soft footfalls.

"Looks like the gang's all here," Remo said, turning from the window. "You wanna go front, back or roof?"

Chiun's keen ears filtered the many thudding heartbeats that were converging on the three-story building. Only a few came from above.

"The roof," he said firmly, his hand snaking from the blinds. The metal slats closed soundlessly.

Side by side, the two men ducked out the door. Dark specters, they slid through the elongated shadows of the hallway. The stairwell brought them up to the roof-access door. At the steel door Remo paused.

Eight heartbeats came from beyond. Two were just outside the closed door.

As Remo waited, he felt a fingernail press his lower back.

"Go," Chiun breathed impatiently.

Remo held up a staying hand.

On the other side of the door, the handle rattled. A scuffed foot sounded on the roof.

Remo made a disgusted face. "Purcell's gotta be the crappiest teacher in town," he whispered. In punctuation he slapped the flat of his palm against the door's surface.

The steel door sprang open, sweeping into the two men who stood just beyond it and carrying them around to the wall. With a horrid crunch of bone, the two startled Russians were crushed between door and wall.

The remaining six men who were creeping across the roof saw barely a flash of movement from the door before Remo and Chiun exploded through the opening.

Remo took the ones on the left, Chiun the three to the right.

The Master of Sinanju's flashing nails formed gills of spurting blood in the throats of his three commandos. As they fell to their knees, clutching necks, three pulverizing heel strikes to the forehead launched Russian bone shards deep into Russian brains.

Beside the old man Remo grabbed a commando head in each hand. He snapped them together, the head of the third soldier in between. Skulls cracked and commandos dropped.

All six soldiers formed a tangled pile of limbs on the dark roof.

"Count?" Remo asked, spinning to Chiun.

"Seventy-three," the old man replied.

He tipped his head, reconsidering.

Whirling, the Master of Sinanju's outstretched toe caught the chin of a commando just peeking over the roof's edge. The man's head came loose in precisely the way heads weren't supposed to. The head bounced to the neighboring roof, rolling to a stop near an air vent. The body plummeted to the dark alley below.

The wizened Korean turned a bland eye to his pupil.

"Seventy-two," he amended.

Remo heard the headless body thud to earth. Hushed voices called urgently to one another far below.

"Say, Chiun, I've got a game for you," Remo said. "Ever play lawn darts?"

Chiun stroked his thin beard. "I do not believe I am familiar with it."

"You're gonna love it," Remo assured him. "It's right up your alley. Or down, as the case may be."

Remo quickly gathered the eight rifles that had been dropped by the Russians. Bringing them to the edge of the roof, he leaned seven on the ledge, keeping one in his hand.

"The object is to use a dart," Remo said, holding out a gun, "to hit your target. Permit me to demonstrate."

Raising the rifle like a spear, he leaned over the edge of the roof. With a crack the gun rocketed from his fingers, disappearing down into the dark alley.

Leaning on the ledge, both men watched the rifle scream into the head of an Institute soldier who was standing among the group that encircled the decapitated body.

The flying barrel buried deep into skull and torso. By the time it stopped burrowing, the soldier looked as if he'd sprouted a gun-butt dorsal fin.

"See?" Remo said, smiling at Chiun as the other commandos began firing in a blind panic up at the roof. "Lawn darts is more of a suburbs thing. I had stickball and kick-the-can growing up. But there's really nothing to it."

Chiun appeared to agree. "Move, amateur," he commanded. Muscling past Remo, he grabbed a gun in each hand.

The frantic firing of a moment before had begun to slow, but as soon as Chiun's bald head peeked over the roof's edge, the shooting began in earnest once more. Bullets whizzed around the flaps of the old man's hat. Frowning, Chiun ducked back, the guns still clutched in his hands.

"Am I given extra points for distractions?"

Remo shook his head firmly. "Part of the challenge."

Chiun nodded. "I accept your rules," he said. As he tilted forward, fingers like sticks of bone hurled the guns down.

The soldiers in the alley barely had time to register the blurry black apparition high above before two more rifles howled into their midst. Two upraised faces snagged the guns in midgoggle. The barrels exploded out the backs of skulls, burying deep in asphalt. Like insects in a science project, the men were pinned to the alley floor.

The shooting intensified, even more frantic than before.

Chiun dodged the bullets, clapping his hands delightedly.

"Bull's-eyes!" he sang happily as he slipped back to the safety of the roof.

Bullets continued to zing through vacant air.

"Not bad," Remo said. "But I wouldn't make room in the trophy case yet. We've still got sixty-nine more to go."

Reaching over, he grabbed another makeshift dart.

THEY LOST CONTACT with the Khrushchev Brigade at 10:30 p.m. When they called the Molotov Brigade, the Institute commando in charge failed to answer his radio.

When the first sounds of gunfire pierced the night,

Vladimir Zhirinsky jumped. Afterward the silence seemed all the more deafening, all the more menacing.

The voices that did come over the radio were panicked and undisciplined.

It was the Institute training. The men were former athletes and dancers. They weren't soldiers. They had encountered something unexpected and were reacting to it like a bunch of frightened gymnasts and ballerinas.

"This is not happening," Zhirinsky said, his voice a barely audible rumble.

The walls of his office were very close. The world had closed in. Tighter than the room, smaller even than the space in which Vladimir Zhirinsky existed. He felt the crush of his collapsing universe behind his bleary eyes.

Around his ankles was a pile of crumpled paper. His great speech to Mother Russia. Worthless now.

After the American voice had taunted him, he had decided to take his aide's advice and move up his address to the Russian people. Not only did he learn that the satellite on which the signal was to be broadcast belonged to Mickey Mouse, but he also found out that he had been dumped off the feed. The people would not hear his carefully crafted call to arms.

He snapped. In a moment of rage he decided to set off his precious nuclear bomb and ride the mushroom cloud into oblivion along with his unknown American tormentors. But when the men he sent to detonate the device attempted to do so, it flared to life, launching off the flatbed trailer before coming to a spluttering stop in the drive-through arch of a downtown bank. It failed to explode.

When he vowed to visit vengeance upon the incompetent head of the man to whom he had entrusted both the satellite and the missile, he learned Ivan Kerbabaev had disappeared.

And so Vladimir Zhirinsky sat. Dark lids failed to blink over bloodshot eyes.

More weak gunfire popped somewhere across town.

Zhirinsky climbed to his feet, clutching his stomach. Sick eyes looked out the window.

Beyond the frosty pane the Soviet flag waved mockingly at him. Zhirinsky pressed a palm against the glass, his sagging face filled with longing.

When his part-time aide hurried into the room, Zhirinsky didn't even acknowledge his presence.

"Comrade, we must leave," the young man announced.

Zhirinsky continued to stare out the window.

The dream was gone. The Americans had sent in some sort of commando force. Greater even than the men from the Institute. The Soviet Union was gone. Vanished into the mists of time like all great empires. It would never return.

"Comrade," the voice behind him pressed.

Zhirinsky turned from the window.

His aide's face was pleading. "If we are to escape with our lives, we must go *now*," he begged.

The distant gunfire intensified, then ceased.

Zhirinsky considered his words. He tried to think,

tried to force some small, rational part of his mind to understand the wisdom of the words.

"We have failed," Zhirinsky admitted softly. "Listen. The gunfire has stopped. The men do not report that they are victorious, therefore they have failed."

"Which makes it all the more urgent that we go now."

"Go how?" Zhirinsky asked. "You have told me that our helicopters have been destroyed. We cannot take another plane from the airport, for our pilots are dead and I put into exile any Americans who could fly. I am trapped."

The aide shook his head urgently. "The vehicles that brought the commandos here are still parked at the edge of town. Comrade Skachkov told me where they are. We can escape into the wilderness. There are provisions for a hundred men hidden at the camps the men were using. When they stop looking for you, we can flee back to Russia."

Zhirinsky absorbed the man's words.

"Skachkov," he said quietly. "You have spoken to him?"

"He called a few minutes ago. His radio malfunctioned, so he did not know that the others were sent to the chamber of commerce building. He is on his way there now."

A spark lit in Zhirinsky's coal-black eyes.

"The tables have just turned," he intoned.

He was thinking of that day he had met Lavrenty Skachkov in Gorky Park all those months ago. Zhirinsky had never seen his like—not even among the other Institute men. Whoever these Americans were, they could not be equal to Skachkov.

"The dogs think they have beaten us back this day," Zhirinsky said ominously. "But we will be victorious. In case Skachkov is late arriving, I will fall back for now. Once he is successful in wiping out these capitalist spies, we will hasten back to Russia while the mood of the people is still with me. This revolution will be fought like the first. From house to house and in the streets."

The words were spoken with proud certainty.

Grinning like a conqueror, Vladimir Zhirinsky pushed past his aide and marched quickly from the small office.

FLASHES POPPED like minifireworks from the alley floor. As Russian commandos laid down cover fire, nearly two dozen more mounted the fire escape.

Remo and Chiun had exhausted their supply of makeshift darts, eliminating six more Institute soldiers. As bullets whizzed through air, they hunkered down behind the brick upper ledge of the Fairbanks chamber of commerce building.

A bony hand slithered out, clasping on to the uppermost metal rail of the fire escape. Chiun tuned himself to the vibrations of the men climbing the stairs. When the first commando was nearly in striking distance, the Master of Sinanju nodded sharply.

"Now," he hissed.

Remo took the cue. Like a shot he flipped up and over. Shoulders didn't have time to brush the ledge before he was out in open air. He dropped like a stone, his legs curled tightly up to his trunk. Three stories down, his legs unbuckled, absorbing the fall like coiled springs.

He fell so fast the men in the alley hadn't seen him. Goggles aimed skyward, they continued to shoot blindly into the air even as Remo spun to the fire escape.

Remo slapped the metal twice. Flying hands cracked the heavy brackets that fastened the criss-crossing ladder to the rear wall. Three stories up, the Master of Sinanju shattered the upper bolts. Vibrations raced up and down the zigzagging structure, meeting with explosive force dead center.

A sound like that of church bells striking a sour note rang out in the cold night.

The Russians in the alley stopped shooting. On the fire escape the rest of the men froze.

In the ensuing silence, all ears heard the first gentle creak. It was followed by a groan.

And like a great metal dinosaur surrendering its last, the fire escape began to pull slowly away from the wall. By the time bolts started shooting like bullets into the side of the adjacent building, the men were already panicking.

Russians on the ground tried to run. Those high up on the escape scrambled desperately for the top. Men jumped and screamed as, with a shriek of angry frozen metal, the fire escape buckled and dropped. Weighted down with its cargo of twenty-three Russian soldiers, it crashed in a mangled heap on top of eleven more in the alley below.

As clouds of snow rose into the night, seven men who had avoided the crash attempted to flee the alley. Remo fell in among them.

Hands and feet cut through them like a thresher's blade. He finished off any who had survived the crash just as quickly. Leaving the dead behind, Remo raced around the front of the building, ducking through the main entrance.

Two men lurked inside the door. As he flew past, Remo launched an elbow into each skull.

Another group of four commandos stood in the ground-floor hallway, backs braced against the wall, guns at the ready. They peered up into the dark depths of the staircase from which shots could be heard.

Remo flew past the men, a flattened palm snapping out as he passed each in turn. Heads buckled plaster in a cascade of dust as Remo bounded into the stairwell.

On the first flight of stairs he met another six. Screams and severed limbs fell in his wake.

At the roof door he nearly plowed into the Master of Sinanju. The old Asian was springing into the landing.

Chiun's weathered face was tight with concern.

"How many?" the old man demanded.

"We got a total of forty-one with the fire escape and in the alley. I got twelve more inside. What about you?"

"Ten came through the roof door."

"No kidding?" Remo said with a deep frown. "Then that's it for the ones here. Anna said the rest were in Russia. So much for the great Master from Sinanju who isn't from Sinanju. He must have been one of these guys." He waved a thick-wristed hand out toward the open roof door.

Chiun shook his head firmly. "No," he insisted. "There is one more."

"You sure? My count makes it—"

He stopped dead.

The two men still stood inside the open door. Chiun's back was to the roof. As Remo spoke, he spotted movement over the old man's shoulder.

A dark figure had just scurried over the ledge. It landed on the roof on two certain feet. Slivered eyes sought out Remo and Chiun.

Lavrenty Skachkov no longer wore the off-white uniform of the other Institute soldiers. He was dressed entirely in black. A stiff wind touched his close-cropped white hair.

Chiun sensed the movement behind him. He followed Remo's gaze, turning back to the roof. When he saw Skachkov, his face turned to stone.

"Guess you were right with your adding," Remo said. He started out the door, but a touch to his elbow stopped him.

"Beware the false Master, Remo," Chiun cautioned. "For although the scrolls record Wang's prophecy, they do not foretoken the victor."

Remo glanced out at Lavrenty Skachkov. The

young man stood a few feet in from the edge of the roof. Waiting.

He seemed flawlessly balanced, spine in perfect alignment to the rest of his body. The Russian's hands were free at his sides as he watched Remo.

"You've got a lot to learn about pep talks," Remo said.

When Remo turned and walked back out the door, the Master of Sinanju came and stood just outside the door, a pinch of worry on his weathered face.

On cautious, gliding feet Remo crossed over to where Skachkov waited. He stopped six feet shy of the Russian.

For a cold moment, neither man spoke. They seemed to be sizing each other up. As the wind whirled around them, biting at their backs, Remo studied the Russian's lips.

A cold hiss of air escaped as thin white steam into the breeze.

"So what do we do now?" Remo asked when the silence had gone on too long. "Stare at each other until we both turn into ice sculptures?"

Skachkov slowly shook his head. "Those who called me Master are dead," he said in heavily accented English. "To avenge them and truly earn the title, I must defeat you. *Both* of you," he called over to the Master of Sinanju.

Chiun still stood over near the entrance to the stairwell. His frozen expression did not change.

Before Skachkov, Remo's face was also impassive.

''Gotta get through me first, sweetheart,'' he said coldly.

Something like the beginning of a superior smile touched the corners of Lavrenty Skachkov's lips. It did not have time to form completely before the Russian lashed out.

In a wink he was up and out, his hand cutting air.

All the hours of training, all the pain he had endured, everything he had learned was focused in that single moment of perfection. And to the Russian's delight, his target seemed oblivious to the crushing blow that was steering a deadly course to his wide-open, exposed throat.

34

Skachkov's flashing hand got far enough to compress air to a microsliver before Remo's Adam's apple. At the last instant Remo tipped to one side.

The Russian's face grew shocked. Forward momentum unstoppable in the stroke, Skachkov flew forward. Bones cracked and muscles tore. His arm popped audibly from its socket as he landed face first on the roof. Scraping skin from chin and neck, he slid to a painful, protracted stop, finally coming to a rest at the toes of a pair of plain wooden sandals. He spit bloody gravel from his mouth.

"That's it?" Remo complained. "*That's* Wang's big bad prophecy? You got me all worked up for some huge Godzilla vs. Megalon showdown. I could see him breathing, for crying out loud." Stepping over, he toed Skachkov onto his back.

The Russian groaned in agony.

The force of the unspent blow had cracked loose several ribs. A fracture split his sternum just over his heart.

"Prophecies are not always clear," Chiun said, puzzlement evident in his own voice. He poked Lavrenty in the chest with his toe. The Russian screamed. "Still, most are better than this," he added, stroking his beard.

Remo sighed. "Maybe we shouldn't gripe. For once we got off easy." He turned his attention to Skachkov. "Okay, twinkle toes, Anna told us there were only 144 of you guys here. That right?" To insure a truthful answer, he kicked the Russian in his dislocated shoulder.

"*Yes!*" Skachkov cried.

"That's all of them, then, Little Father. Except for the ones Anna said are still in Russia, the armies of death have taken a powder." He motioned to the prone Lavrenty Skachkov. "You want to do the honors?"

"Wait," Chiun said. "There is one more question to ask." He turned his penetrating gaze down to the Russian. "How did you and these others come to possess your limited skills?" he demanded.

Remo assumed he already knew the answer the white-haired commando would give. He was therefore surprised when the man did not instantly blurt out Jeremiah Purcell's name, the only other man on the planet possessed of Sinanju abilities. Remo was even more shocked by the Russian's eventual answer.

Flat on his back, stabs of white-hot agony coursing through his body, the pain on Lavrenty Skachkov's face flickered to a brief moment of confusion. He looked from Chiun to Remo and back again, at last shaking his head.

"*You* taught me," admitted Mactep Lavrenty Skachkov.

And the puzzlement in his voice was reflected full on the faces of both Masters of Sinanju.

35

The limousine bearing Vladimir Zhirinsky zoomed around the corner. Stomping hard on the gas, the ultranationalist's aide steered the big car away from the chamber of commerce and the silence that had followed the raging battle there.

He had memorized their escape route hours ago. With any luck the highway would take them safely out of town.

"When it comes, it will be all the more glorious for the shock it will give them all," Zhirinsky growled in the back seat. Dark eyes watched the scenery flash by. "Perhaps it is even better this way. They believe they have beaten me, but all they have done is force the cobra in a box. When we return to Russia, I will strike out at the hand that dares to cage me. Me, the beating heart of the Soviet Union."

His aide was too busy concentrating on driving to respond. As they sped along, his eyes strayed to the mirror.

"Oh, no," the young man said, his voice thick.

"What is it?" Zhirinsky asked. Following his driver's gaze, he turned in his seat, looking out the back window.

A truck was following them.

Zhirinsky frowned. "Is that Ivan?" he demanded. "Stop the car at once. I will take the cost of that malfunctioning missile out of his worthless hide." His brow lowered as he peered out the window. "Who is that he is with?"

The trailing truck drew close. Despite Zhirinsky's order, his driver did not slow. Eyes still on the mirror, he pressed harder on the accelerator.

"What are they doing?" Zhirinsky growled.

As he spoke, the trailing Land Rover's doors sprang open. The vehicle swerved for a moment as Ivan lunged for the wheel. In the moment he took control, two shapes hopped out either side of the speeding truck.

Zhirinsky was amazed when the men didn't fall and break their necks. Amazement turned to horror when he realized that, not only did they not stumble, the running men were actually gaining on his own car.

"How is this possible?" he gasped.

His driver didn't answer. Hands tight on the steering wheel, he checked the speedometer. The limousine was racing just over seventy miles per hour. He stomped harder on the pedal, but it was already down to the floor.

Sickly eyes found the rearview mirror.

The men were gone.

Even as his hopeful brain was registering the disappearance of the men, his peripheral vision caught a blur of movement to his right. When he looked over, his stomach clenched in watery fear.

A cruel face was looking at him through the window.

"License and registration!" Remo called through the tinted glass even as he slammed his fist through it.

In the back seat Vladimir Zhirinsky saw a thick-wristed hand reach through the shattering window, grabbing his driver's collar. In a flash his young aide's shoes were disappearing out the opening.

The hand appeared again, jerking the steering wheel sharply. With a smoking shriek of tires, the limo bounced and spun a perfect 180 degrees.

Somehow it didn't flip over. As Zhirinsky was flung around the rear seat, the car flew back in the direction from whence it had come.

Ivan's Land Rover was racing up the road directly at the out-of-control limousine. Horror-struck, Zhirinsky jumped up, scrambling over the rear seat. Belly stuck to the back of the driver's seat, he clamped on to the steering wheel.

"Get out of the way, idiot!" Zhirinsky screamed as he jerked the wheel.

Ivan spun the other way. The Land Rover missed the limo by a hair, slamming into a mound of dirty snow.

The limousine soared past.

Still balanced precariously over the seat, Zhirinsky saw something had been jammed onto the gas pedal. It looked very much like the short white hair that had capped Lavrenty Skachkov's head. The rest of the Institute commando's body was nowhere to be seen.

As the dull shock of realization sank in, strong hands grabbed him from behind. Sweaty palms slipping from the steering wheel, Zhirinsky dropped roughly back to his seat.

Remo Williams sat calmly beside him. "This the bus to Vladivostok?" he asked coldly.

Zhirinsky fell away from the intruder. "Who are you?" the ultranationalist demanded, his voice flirting with fear.

"I'm a Yankee Doodle Dandy."

Another voice broke in on the other side.

"I am a Korean Doodle Dandier."

When Zhirinsky twisted the other way, he found another man sharing his seat. A mask of wrinkles regarded the Russian with deep distaste.

"This thing considers itself a czar?" Chiun sniffed to Remo. "He is not fit to mend Ivan the Good's *lapots*."

Zhirinsky was stuck between their verbal Ping-Pong. When he spun to see what the young stranger would say in reply, he found that Remo was now gone. Whirling, he saw the Master of Sinanju was missing, as well.

The rear doors were now open.

All at once, he remembered he was in a runaway car with no driver. Zhirinsky lunged for the steering wheel.

Too late.

The city hall building was flying back toward him.

It was too late to turn. Too late to jump. Too late for anything.

By the time the inevitable registered dumbly in the mind of Vladimir Zhirinsky, the limo was already crashing into the line of cars parked in the street before the big building.

The nose snagged and the long car flipped up and over a Ford Explorer, landing in a crumpled heap near the front staircase. Even after the car had slid to a painful, grinding stop, the engine continued to idle softly. One tire spun lazy circles in the chill air.

Inside, Vladimir Zhirinsky blinked away a wash of red.

Something big and soft was all around him. Holding him. Protecting him.

Of course he could not die. The world would not allow it.

Zhirinsky battled back the air bag. On all fours, he crawled through the shattered windshield of the upended limo. He made it out to the sidewalk.

Blood ran from a gash in his forehead. He wiped it from his eyes, smearing it on his thighs. When he looked back up, he saw something even redder than his own blood. It was floating toward him, dancing in the breeze.

For one brief moment Zhirinsky caught the stark gold outlines of the hammer and sickle. And then the brilliant red tightened around his neck.

"America—love it, or leave it the hell alone," a voice whispered very close to his ear.

The old Soviet flag was pulled tight. For a tortured moment the world of Vladimir Zhirinsky grew very red.

And then it grew very, very black indeed.

36

Remo called Smith from the Fairbanks city hall.

"Report," the CURE director ordered, his voice taut.

"The Russians are going, the Russians are going," Remo announced. "And on a personal note, it's about damn time."

"Explain."

"The short of it is that we pulled the plug on the commandos here and that big bomb was a big dud. I think there might be a few loose fuzz-hats running around up here, but Chiun and I got all the Sinanju ones, so the rest won't be any problem."

"Several have already surrendered to the Army a few miles outside of Fairbanks," Smith told him. "What of Zhirinsky?"

Remo glanced out the window. The body of Vladimir Zhirinsky dangled halfway up the city hall flagpole, its neck firmly entangled in the flag of the Soviet Union. Glassy dead eyes stared out at the night.

Far above Zhirinsky, the American flag flew once more, illuminated by floodlights from the ground.

"He's gonna be hanging around up here for a while, Smitty," Remo replied.

Across the room sulked Ivan Kerbabaev. The Russian stood near a tall window, a frown creasing his mass of crusted bandages. Ever since Remo had dug him from his snowbank, he had been complaining about the fact that he wasn't going to be allowed to rip off one of Zhirinsky's ears as promised.

On the phone Smith could tell by Remo's tone that it wasn't necessary to press further about Zhirinsky.

"It is safe, then, to send in the Army," the CURE director said. "I will issue the proper commands. You and Chiun may report back to Folcroft."

"No can do, Smitty," Remo said. "We've still got a couple of loose ends we have to tie up."

Smith grew puzzled. "I thought you said everything in Alaska was secure."

"In Alaska," Remo agreed. Voice trailing off, he dropped the receiver back into its cradle.

A CONTINENT AWAY Harold W. Smith frowned at the dead air issuing from his phone.

Across the desk from the CURE director, Mark Howard sat on his usual hard-backed chair. His jacket was draped over the back of the battered couch near the door.

"Is something else wrong?" Mark asked when he saw the look on his employer's face.

Smith was still holding the blue contact phone. He looked up at Howard. "No," he said tightly.

As the CURE director replaced the phone, Mark stood.

"So they came through?"

"Yes. Apparently, Zhirinsky's bomb did not work. They have eliminated the special troops. The crisis is over."

"You didn't tell him about the satellite," Mark said.

It was Smith who had learned of Zhirinsky's plan to broadcast a call to arms to the Russian people. He had used CURE's resources to deny Zhirinsky access to the satellite.

"It wasn't necessary," Smith said absently. "Our work here is to identify crises and, when necessary, to support the efforts of our field operatives. They do not need to know all the details."

Booting up his computer, Smith began ordering the troops from Fort Wainwright to return to Fairbanks.

Mark went to retrieve his jacket. As he was pulling it on, he glanced back at Smith.

Ghostly shadows thrown up from his hidden monitor gave the old man the appearance of an ambulatory cadaver.

"Are you—" Mark hesitated. "Are you going to tell them about me?" he asked all at once.

Smith peered up over his glasses. The gray line of his brow was shadowed in black. "I told you," the CURE director said. "They do not need to know every detail."

He turned his attention back to his computer.

Across the room Mark gave a tired smile.

With a nod of silent relief, Mark Howard slipped from the office, leaving the gray-shrouded man to his life's work.

37

Remo and Chiun spoke little on their flight from the United States. At Moscow's Sheremetevo II Airport, they parted company. The Master of Sinanju took one taxi while Remo climbed into another with Ivan Kerbabaev.

"Kitai Gorod," Ivan instructed through his gnarled knot of loosening bandages.

Crowds of people wandered Moscow's streets. From what Remo could see, no one looked very happy.

The two cabs rode together for a short time. Near the Kremlin, Chiun's veered away. Remo and Ivan continued deeper into the city.

They followed a tangle of crisscrossing streets and narrow lanes. More feckless crowds clogged the roadway.

Whenever the cab stopped, Ivan acted as interpreter. Remo quickly learned the Russian for "I don't know" was *Ya ne znayu*. It took some time, but they at last found someone who was able to direct them where they wanted to go.

An hour after leaving the airport, the cab pulled to a stop in front of a pair of somber gates. Looming above was a menacing building with bricked-up windows.

Remo stepped out onto the sidewalk.

The Institute building was of typical Soviet design. Big, blockish and ugly.

After taking only a few steps, Remo paused. Doubling back, he leaned in the cab.

"Beat it," he said to Ivan Kerbabaev.

Much of the masking tape sprang free. "Truly?" Ivan asked, pushing the bandages back in place.

"Don't tempt me," Remo warned. "And leave the cab."

Ivan hastily instructed the driver to remain at the curb. He quickly climbed out of the small car. Holding a hand to his flapping bandages, he ran down the cold Moscow street. He was gone from sight even before Remo had slipped through the heavy Institute gates.

ANNA HEARD the muffled gunfire through the thick walls.

There were only twelve of them here. They were the latest trainees to come to the Institute. Now they would be the last. She had left them out beyond. Left them to their inevitable fate. The same fate that would be hers.

It wouldn't be long now.

When the gunfire stopped, her fingers clenched reflexively around the object in her hand.

She didn't hear the footsteps as they came up the hall. Not that she expected to. She only knew he had found her when the iron door began to groan inward.

The door surrendered in a crunch of metal and exploding concrete. Buckling, it crashed into the office.

Remo found Anna Chutesov sitting alone behind her desk. Across the room a television flickered. As he stepped inside, he noted the image on the TV screen.

The picture quality wasn't great, but it was good enough. He watched the videotaped image of himself and the Master of Sinanju walking through a crowded concourse.

Anna watched him watch the TV. "You do not seem surprised," she said without inflection.

He pulled his eyes from the screen. "Your boy Skitch Henderkov, or whatever the hell his name was, told us. By the way, you didn't have to be so worried about him. He was about as tough as college-football math class."

Anna's smile was weak. "I'm glad," she said. "His abilities far surpassed the others. I did not want you and Chiun put at risk because of me." She raised her chin to the TV. "You remember when this was?"

Remo glanced at the television. On it, the Master of Sinanju seemed to suddenly vanish. The Remo on the screen followed suit. When the camera caught up to him, he was talking to a man in a bear suit. Armed men stood all around. And as the tape rolled, the men abruptly began dying.

"Last time we met," Remo said, turning from the TV. "Just before you faked your death at that amusement park."

"Yes. After I fled, I happened upon the park security shed. Your enemy had made extensive video surveillance tapes of you. I took them back to Russia with me.''

''Why, Anna?'' Remo asked. There seemed something almost close to pleading in his dark eyes.

They both understood the predicament this presented for Remo. As Apprentice Reigning Master of Sinanju and future head of the village, he was duty bound to seek vengeance against any who would steal from the House.

She shook her head. Short blond hair did a lazy twist around her long neck.

''I honestly do not know,'' she admitted. ''That life was over for me. Maybe I took them as a memento, maybe to find a weakness in your techniques. I was not thinking clearly at the time. By the time I returned to Moscow, I had made up my mind to destroy them. But then some fool KGB functionary at the airport chose that trip to search my luggage. The tapes found their way to the president of Russia. It was after his attempt to blackmail your President into making you come to work for Russia. Even though you had made him forget the events of that incident, the Mactep program was still active. When the tapes were discovered, General Feyodov was relieved of his position here, and I was installed in his place.''

''To train an army in Sinanju,'' Remo said.

Her shame was evident. ''I did not wish to do so,'' she stated. ''But it was made clear to me that someone would have this posting. If it was not me, it would have been Feyodov. And I do not know if he or any other man would have been able to keep the Mactep troops from ever being used. I kept them under lock and key for more than ten years. If not for that idiot Skachkov and the lunatic Zhirinsky, the men would have remained warehoused here forever.''

"I don't get it," Remo said. "These tapes aren't anything. You can't even see the stuff that matters. How'd you use them to teach these guys anything?''

"We made copies from tape to film," Anna explained. "The films were enhanced by computer and the speed of your actions was cut down considerably. The men were hooked into a system that monitored their movements. They were then instructed to mirror you in every detail, with punishments given if they failed. As the men progressed in training, the speed of the films was increased.''

Remo nodded. "That's why they did that wrist thing Chiun says I do," he said. "They were copying everything they saw." His eyes narrowed suspiciously. "And this sounds like something I saw on TV once. They were getting baseball players to adjust their swings by hooking them up to computers to correct their stances.''

"It has been used with great success in sports," she agreed. "The technique used here was essentially the same.''

Sighing, Remo looked around the small office. "I guess you thought of everything," he said. "This is some setup. Although I noticed on the way in here that you cut corners on furniture. The place seemed pretty empty.''

"I had it emptied out after the men escaped," Anna said. "The barracks and the training facilities have been dismantled. The technicians used to operate the equipment were rotated in and out frequently and never knew what exactly was going on here. All computer data on you and Chiun has been purged. My government has no record of your existence other than the knowledge possessed by the past three presidents of the federation. I destroyed the films made from the tapes. All that remains are the originals." She nodded to the open safe in the corner of the room. Inside, a dozen plastic tape cases were lined up on a shelf.

"Looks like you've erased all traces," Remo said.

"All but one," she admitted quietly.

Slender fingers tightened once more around the object on her desk.

Remo had noted the gun lying under her hand as soon as he'd entered the office. He had assumed she planned to use it against him. But when she lifted it from the desk blotter, Anna didn't aim the gun at him. Jaw firmly set, she brought the barrel to her own temple.

He was across the room in a heartbeat. She was starting to pull the trigger even as he ripped the gun from her hand.

"Are you nuts!" he snapped angrily.

Her calm blue eyes never wavered. "It is the only way," she insisted calmly. "I am to blame for these events. And Sinanju precepts certainly must demand retribution. I know you too well, Remo. Were you to do this thing, you would be haunted by it. We both know that there is only one way out for me, and it would be unfair to have you do the deed.''

Despite the forced strength in her voice, hot tears burned the corners of her eyes.

Beside the desk, Remo clenched the gun. He didn't even look at her. He was staring at the wall, lost in thought.

At her desk Anna sniffled.

"It is ironic, Remo," she said softly. "Years ago you refused Smith's order to kill me in the name of America's security. Now when you finally come to carry out his order, you do it for the security of Sinanju."

Remo scowled at her. "No one's killing anyone, okay?" he snapped. He had reached a decision.

Anna shook her head. "There is no other way, Remo," she insisted logically.

Remo reached for her. With the edge of his thumb he brushed away a single tear.

"That's the problem with people in your business, Anna," he replied. His voice was soft in a way she had not heard in years. "All logic, no imagination."

The thrill of his touch and the warmth in his tone lasted only as long as it took Remo to stab his finger into a knot of nerves at her jawline just behind her ear. But for Anna Chutesov, it was enough to feed an eternity of longing for something neither of them could ever have.

And then the lights went out, and she collapsed into the arms of the only man she'd ever loved.

38

The president of the Commonwealth of Independent States felt the wet spot on his pillow when he rolled over in his sleep. When he opened his tired eyes, he found that he was face-to-face with one of his Institute bodyguards.

Although the man's head shared the Russian president's pillow, the rest of his body was nowhere to be seen.

Screaming, the president threw himself out of bed. The jostled head of the Institute man rolled out behind him, thudding to the bare wood floor.

"Murderers!" the Russian president yelled. "Pavel, I need help! Anyone!"

"You are beyond help," said a squeaky singsong voice.

Still seated on the floor, the president wheeled around.

A tiny figure in a brocade kimono stood near the door of the small Kremlin apartment.

"Russia has been beyond help ever since it abandoned its czar and entrusted its future to a gaggle of troublemakers with pitchforks," the old Korean concluded.

The two previous presidents of Russia stood with

Chiun, one on either side. The more recent one seemed oblivious to what was going on. Dazed from drink, he stood reeling in his nightshirt. The other former president no longer wore his hat. For the first time, the present president of Russia saw the hateful expression that had been tattooed over the bald man's birthmark and around his head.

In the Master of Sinanju's slender fingers were five lumpy bundles.

Somehow in death the eyes of his Institute protectors seemed to stare disapprovingly at the president of Russia. Their condemnation was reflected in the hazel eyes of the wizened Asian.

Chiun dropped the heads.

"How fitting that you should hide here," the Master of Sinanju sniffed as he looked unhappily around the drab room. "The cheapskate who once lived here tried to hire my father. It does not look like they have painted it since then."

"These are Lenin's quarters," the president insisted, still trying to come to grips with what was happening.

"That was his name," Chiun nodded. "Another Russian who didn't want to pay the House."

The old man took a step toward the president. Pushing up, the president fell back from the terrible apparition. His hand dropped into the blood puddle on his pillow.

"What do you want?" he asked, his voice quavering.

Chiun's eyes became penetrating hazel lasers.

"I am going to make you an offer you cannot refuse," the Master of Sinanju said coldly.

39

Remo caught up to Chiun at the boarding gate of the Moscow airport.

"If this is the last time I have to smell Russia for ten years, I'll die a happy man," Remo said, falling in beside the wizened Asian. "So how'd it go with their president?"

"He has listened to reason," Chiun said simply.

"How costly is reason, dead-body-wise these days?"

"The last six Sinanju thieves are no more," Chiun replied. "There were also a few Kremlin guards along the way. Not very many—I know you and Smith do not like that. Oh, and one of their presidents. Retribution demanded it."

"Current one or stain-head?"

"Neither. It was the rum-soaked one in between."

Remo tipped his head, considering. "That's probably okay," he said. "Smitty wouldn't want us to ice the one they've got now, and I invested too much time in tattooing chrome dome's head."

Chiun fussed with the hem of his sleeve. "Not that I will receive any credit," he sniffed. "Knowing the Russians, they will say he died of a cold or heart failure. I suppose I will have to take comfort in the tribute they agreed to pay for their stolen lessons.''

Remo was hardly listening. ''What are they paying you in, rubles or turnips? 'Cause if it was up to me, I'd take the turnips.''

The old Korean noted his pupil's distracted tone. He raised a thin eyebrow as he looked up at Remo. ''What about the woman?'' he asked. There was a hint of paternal concern in his hazel eyes.

Even though Remo knew the question would come, he still dreaded having to answer.

''I didn't kill her, Little Father,'' he admitted. ''By the sounds of it, Anna was bamboozled into all this by the pinheads who run this dump of a country. And, I don't know, this could have been partly my fault for the way I left it with her at the end years ago. So I just gave her the Sinanju amnesia thing. I ditched the bodies of the guys I killed at the place she works, and I trashed the tapes of us and threw them in the river. When she wakes up, she goes back to being an adviser to the president with no memory of us. And who knows, maybe someday she'll come in handy for us in a pinch.

''And before you carp at me for defying a billion years of Sinanju tradition, don't forget I'm gonna be Master someday, and I've got this big prophesied future as the herald of some new golden age for the House, so maybe this is part of it. Maybe I'm supposed to be the guy who starts a kinder, gentler House of Sinanju. So there, that's it. You can start yelling at me now.''

Chiun remained silent, allowing Remo to blurt out everything he needed to say. When his pupil finally stopped talking, the old man frowned skeptically.

"A kinder, gentler Sinanju?" he asked blandly.

"Yeah," Remo replied. "Well, maybe not. Guess we'll just have to wait and see."

"I pray I have passed into the Void long before I have to witness such a time," Chiun said. Hands sought opposing wrists within his kimono sleeves.

Remo was glad when he didn't press the point further. He stuffed his hands deep in his pockets. The line began moving toward the gate.

"None of this is easy like it used to be, Little Father," he said. "Everything's complicated these days."

"Your life is changing," Chiun said. "Perhaps what you need now is an island of stability in the storm of your life." His hands reappeared from his sleeves. The old man began reading one of his real-estate pamphlets.

Remo shook his head firmly. "No house in Maine," he insisted.

Chiun shrugged. "In that case you figure out where to put the treasure I extorted from these godless, thieving Russians. We are running out of room back home."

Nose deep in his brochure, he passed through the gate.

Standing in line behind the old Korean, Remo didn't know whether he should laugh or cry.

Epilogue

She was called Sonmi.

No one in the village knew much about her. She was from one of the older families. But since none had moved into the village in many generations, they were all members of the older families by now.

Her mother had died giving birth to her more than seventy years ago. Her father had died only recently.

Some said the old man was a powerful shaman. All in the village stayed away from him and his daughter. When he died, only Sonmi wept.

On this day, as the cold sun peeked above the eastern horizon, old Sonmi picked her careful way down the rocky shore. A small fishing boat of fine Egyptian cedar was tied to a wood post. Sonmi unhooked the rope and climbed aboard.

It took a long time to row. Her withered arms were sore by the time she made it far enough out into the bay.

From a pouch on the belt of her coarse dress she produced some blessed herbs. She scattered them upon the black water, reciting the mystical chants passed down to her from her father and his father before him.

Once she was done, she stood at the edge of the wobbling boat and jumped overboard. The cold waters of the West Korean Bay accepted her body with barely a splash.

Beyond the empty boat, across the bay and up the rocky shore, the village of Sinanju where the dead woman Sonmi had lived all her life, stirred awake.

James Axler

OUTLANDERS®

SARGASSO PLUNDER

An enforcer turned renegade, Kane and his group
learn of a mother lode of tech hidden deep within
the ocean of the western territories, a place once
known as Seattle. The booty is luring tech traders and
gangs, but Kane and Grant dare to infiltrate the
salvage operation, knowing that getting in is a life-
and-death risk....

*In the Outlands, the shocking truth
is humanity's last hope.*

**Readers won't want to miss this exciting
new title of the SuperBolan® series!**

DON PENDLETON's

MACK BOLAN®

Power of the Lance

**THE
TYRANNY
FILES**

BOOK II

The Temple of the Nordic Covenant has the weapons, connections
and skinhead shock troops to fulfill their mad vision of a Reich
reborn. Bolan teams up with a Mossad agent in Germany in a race
to halt the slaughter of German Jews in a next-generation
Kristallnacht. Steuben and his fanatics are also planning an
assassination that will rock Europe—and set the stage for a rebirth
of the Nazi reign of terror.

Available in July 2001 at your favorite retail outlet.

Or order your copy now by sending your name, address, zip or postal code, along with
a check or money order (please do not send cash) for $5.99 for each book ordered
($6.99 in Canada), plus 75¢ postage and handling ($1.00 in Canada), payable to Gold
Eagle Books, to:

In the U.S.	In Canada
Gold Eagle Books	Gold Eagle Books
3010 Walden Avenue	P.O. Box 636
P.O. Box 9077	Fort Erie, Ontario
Buffalo, NY 14269-9077	L2A 5X3

Please specify book title with your order.
Canadian residents add applicable federal and provincial taxes.

GSB79

When all is lost, there's always the future...

JAMES AXLER

DEATH LANDS ®

THE SKYDARK CHRONICLES Book III

Shadow Fortress

The Marshall Islands are now the kingdom of the grotesque Lord Baron Kinnison. Here in this world of slavery and brutality, the companions have fought a fierce war for survival, on land and sea—yet the crafty baron still conspires to destroy these interlopers. They cunningly escape to the neighboring pirate-ruled Forbidden Island, with the baron's sec men in hot pursuit...and become trapped in a war for total supremacy of this water world.

Available in September 2001 at your favorite retail outlet.